IT MIGHT
HAVE HAPPENED
ANY TIME . . .

It could have happened any night, any day, any hour since the hot June night when Jack Manders had been killed. But it happened then.

Because Myra was carrying her coat, because she caught her heel in a dragging fold of it, because she fell backward and flung up her hand and caught at the newel post, hard, pushing backward and up with all her weight in order to save herself from falling, she found the gun.

The Gun. The gun that had never been found. Richard's gun.

Mignon G. Eberhart
ANOTHER WOMAN'S HOUSE

POPULAR LIBRARY • NEW YORK

Dedication:

*To Harry and Edna Maule
with deepest affection and
gratitude*

All the persons and events in this book are entirely imaginary. Nothing in it derives from anything that ever happened.

CHAPTER 1 ■

It was still another woman's house. Nothing in the house had changed; nothing perhaps could change. Alice with her beauty, her grace, her unerring taste for beauty might have put a spell upon the house and everything within it.

The room itself, a library, beautiful, gracious, was so completely a product of Alice's skill and taste that it suggested her almost as provocatively and as tantalizingly as did her wide bedroom upstairs, with its windows overlooking the Sound, and the scent of lilac sachet. Myra had entered the room one day, not knowing it was Alice's, seeking a loosened and banging shutter, and everything was as if its former occupant were expected any day, any minute. The perfume bottles glittered, the light pink cover was folded neatly on the satin-covered chaise longue; a bit of frothy lace was caught in one of the doors to the mirrored dress closets, the scent of lilac was everywhere, summoning up the lovely image of Alice so poignantly that Myra felt she might speak. She had gone quickly away.

No one, Myra had thought, ever entered that room; but obviously she was wrong; obviously someone entered and aired and dusted it regularly.

The door to Richard's room, adjoining, was closed and bolted. And there was a tacit agreement, Myra knew, that Alice's room was a guest room; actually house guests were now rare.

The library with its wide French windows opening upon

the terrace, with its fireplace and old rugs and old books, had been a favorite room of Alice's. She had selected the mellow dull blue of the paneling between bookshelves, the bowl for the yellow daffodils, the ruby-red cushions of the chair in which Myra sat. Near Myra against the wall stood a tall secretary, its old mahogany glowing; behind a glass section of the doors a Capo di Monte cupid, which Alice's hands had placed in exactly that position, looked smugly and blandly at Myra. As if he knew a secret.

As indeed, in a very horrible way, he did know a secret. An ugly little question caught at Myra. What would he say if he could speak?

The fire crackled. The little French clock on the mantel ticked in as lively and sprightly a way as if time had no importance. As if this were not in all probability the last time that Myra would sit in that room, waiting for Richard. It was, of course, too early to expect him. So much the better, for it gave her time to rehearse again the reasons she was going to give for her decision.

And so much the better because for the last time she could sit there in the ruby-red chair, intensely aware of the room, of its beauty and warmth and—which, as a matter of fact, was rather odd—of its present tranquillity. She would remember it all, later; she looked around again striving to impress every detail upon her memory and yet knowing that there was nothing she could ever forget.

It was going to be very difficult to tell Miss Cornelia. It was going to be difficult to tell Richard.

She got up and went to the tall yellow daffodils and rearranged them needlessly with nervous fingers. And glanced again at the little gold French clock; the small, gaily enameled pendulum glittered within its glass walls as it moved quickly back and forth, marking the seconds, marking the moments, inevitably and finally.

Four o'clock. Richard could not possibly arrive before five, even if he happened to come out early from town.

A daffodil fell and she bent to pick it up. As she did so there was a sound of voices from the terrace. The door was open and Myra straightened, the yellow daffodil in her hand, in time to see Miss Cornelia's wheel chair come into view, then Miss Cornelia, limping defiantly beside it, with her thin, veined old hand upon the back of it to steady herself, and then Barton, pushing the chair. Myra went quickly to meet the small cavalcade and hold the door wider for its entrance. "She would walk, Miss Myra," said Barton, puffing slightly. "I couldn't do anything with her ladyship. She walked all the way from the garden."

"It's an easy walk," said Miss Cornelia and slid her hand through Myra's arm. Her bright eyes sparkled; she crooked a rather mischeivous eyebrow, still slim and dark in spite of her snow-white hair, toward the elderly butler. "As we get older, Barton, we should eat less starch."

Barton had got his breath. Ignoring the reflection cast on his very substantial figure, he said patiently, "Do you wish me to help you upstairs now, Madam?"

"No, thank you. I'll stay down for a bit. You can put the wheel chair away, Barton. You and Mr. Richard can carry me up later."

"Very well, Madam." He glanced at the clock, cast a rather fishy but efficient eye around the room as if mentally checking on the orderliness of its details, gave his extremely well-filled waistcoat a tug downward and addressed himself again to the wheel chair.

"That one," said Miss Cornelia, steering Myra toward Richard's deep arm chair before the fire. "Thank you, my dear." Her small old hand relaxed as Myra helped her down into the chair and she looked up and sighed.

Miss Cornelia—who had been Lady Carmichael for fifty of her seventy years and, except for occasional slips which Barton permitted himself, was yet, in that house, called Miss Cornelia—was still an attractive and distinguished-looking woman. She was small and slight and a little stooped with age; but her snow-white hair was beautifully done, her wrinkled skin still soft and fragrant looking, her delicate veined hands had slender fingernails, defiantly varnished in scarlet. Her dark-gray eyes were bright and vivacious and altogether too observant at times. She had been a beauty and there was still an occasional coquettishness about her which suggested her age and generation, but she had actually a civilized and tolerant turn of mind, active and vigorous common sense, and a great fund of generosity and loyalty. She wore now a beige tweed skirt and jacket, shabby, since it had outlived the war, but faultlessly tailored, a white silk blouse knotted at her throat, pearls in her ears, sapphires on her hands and an expression of exasperation.

"I broke that damned hip nearly two years ago, two years

in June, exactly," she said. "Shouldn't you think I could walk more easily by now?"

"You are really much better, darling. It takes time."

Miss Cornelia sniffed. "Time," she said rather grimly, "is something I am not well supplied with." She sighed and leaned back and reached in her pocket for a gold cigarette case and an ivory holder. "Cigarette?"

"Not now." Myra went to the table for a match, and returned to hold it for the older woman. Her jeweled hands with their scarlet tips were delicate and sure with the cigarette, her face as still and carved as the ivory holder; she leaned forward a little toward the small flame. "Richard back yet?" she asked, looking up at Myra.

"No."

"Well, it's not time, of course. Is Tim coming out this week-end?"

"I don't know. I phoned him yesterday at the office, but the girl said he was out of town for the day."

"Some errand for the firm, I suppose."

"I suppose so. The girl didn't say. I'll try his apartment to-night." Myra reached for an ash tray and put it on the arm of Miss Cornelia's chair, and then went back to the bowl of daffodils. Now, of course, was as good a time as any to tell Aunt Cornelia the thing she must tell her; and Tim's name was an opening. But she procrastinated, dreading it. Slowly and carefully she thrust the thin, tall green stalk of the daffodil she held among the others in the great vase. It was even more difficult than she had anticipated.

Perhaps she wouldn't have said it then; perhaps she would never have said it actually; but while she hesitated, dreading it, summoning her courage to speak, Miss Cornelia herself began it. "Myra, what's wrong?"

The stalk caught on the long, spiky leaf of another. Miss Cornelia added gently, "You're worried about something. I've noticed it for several days. What is it? Tim?"

It is not really easy to lie to anybody; to lie to Miss Cornelia was next to impossible. Myra disengaged the daffodil and turned slowly to face the older woman and still could not find the words she had to speak. Miss Cornelia, smoking and giving her quick bright little glances, said, "Because I really think, my dear, that there's nothing to worry about. Tim has an aptitude for architecture. It's true he's not trained but he learns quickly. He's been rather—well, morose lately, moody. Not like himself exactly. But that's the effect of the war. He'll be all right; you'll see."

The lovely golden cups beside Myra sent up a clean, spicy odor. The fire crackled softly. Miss Cornelia went on quietly, "You've always taken your responsibility to Tim rather heavily, my dear. Simply because he's your younger brother. I was never sure that it was right of me to separate you and Tim, as I did, but it seemed right at the time." She looked into the fire and said rather doubtfully, as if wishing to reassure herself, "Tim had to be in school anyway and I wanted him to go to an American school, not an English school, and it seemed best to take you back to London with me." She sighed again, thoughtfully and wistfully. "I didn't think the war would come as it did and keep us there so long."

The doubt and touch of uncertainty in her manner was to Myra poignantly moving. She cried, refuting it, "Everything you did was right! Neither of us can ever thank you enough. You've been like a mother . . ."

"Well," said Miss Cornelia, still looking into the fire thoughtfully but smiling, "say grandmother."

"You sent Tim to school; you took me home with you; you've done everything for me. . . ."

"No, that's where you are wrong, Myra. You've done everything for me."

It was like Aunt Cornelia. Myra laughed softly. "I was a child! I was sixteen! Tim was eleven! We owe you . . ."

"Nonsense," interrupted Miss Cornelia crisply. "If an aging and childless woman can't give herself the pleasure of taking care of the orphaned children of her dearest friend, what pleasure can she have?" She smoked and then sighed again thoughtfully. "I loved your grandmother; I loved your mother and, for all her life, she was a daughter and a dear and loved friend to me. You are very like her, Myra; I've told you that before. So let's have no nonsense about owing me anything. You've done far more for me, my dear, than I have for you. I'm an old woman and with this hip a semi-invalid. I've needed you. Especially since . . ." A shadow crossed her face and she said, ". . . especially during the last two years." She put her ivory cigarette holder to her lips, smoked for a thoughtful moment and said, "We've been through much together. A war and a broken hip and . . ." Her eyes did not travel around the room; her jeweled hands were quiet. She might as well have looked—at the terrace doors, the bookshelves, the narrow, important window above them; she might as well have pointed at the rug before the fire. Naturally, by no conceivable leap of the imagination could she have done either. She said quietly, ". . . and the situation here. But we've weathered it all. Tim is at home and wasn't wounded and has a job. The house in London was blitzed, but it was too big anyway. I don't care. And this house, since we came back last fall, has achieved a—" She hesitated, hunting for words—"a normal, sane everydayness," she said. "A recovery. As if it had been sick, like a person." The shadow returned and fixed itself upon her face.

"I could do little; you have done much to restore that—that normalness of feeling." She said simply, "I think Richard has been thankful to have you here."

Myra dropped the daffodil in her hand and stooped to pick it up. Miss Cornelia said, with an effort of briskness, "So let's have no more talk of gratitude, my dear! From you or Tim."

Myra stood. She said rather desperately, "That's what I'd meant to say. It's—about—about Tim."

Miss Cornelia's voice was suddenly alert and clear. "What do you mean?"

"You've done so much for us, money, everything. So now that Tim has a job . . ."

"Are you trying to tell me that you want to leave me?"

"Yes," said Myra, her hands unsteady on the flowers.

There was a long pause. Again the fire crackled softly while the room—Alice's room in Alice's house—listened.

"Stop fooling with those flowers," said Miss Cornelia at last. "You'll have them all on the floor. Look at me, Myra."

Reluctantly, yet relieved, too, because she had said the thing she had to say, Myra turned to meet Miss Cornelia's clear and bright gaze.

"You don't really want to leave me, do you?" she asked after a moment.

"No."

"I thought not. I know you, perhaps better than you know yourself. Well . . ."

She looked away from Myra. Her fine old face with its sharp, carved ivory lines was silhouetted against the mellow blue walls. Finally, she said very quietly, "I cannot leave Richard to face things alone. That's why I came back here to live. You realized that, of course. You came back with me, into

this house. Into . . ." Again she made no gesture, gave no
glance about her, and might as well have done so. ". . . into
this room. I've been sick and lame. It was you, Myra, who
restored its peace. When must you go?"

"Soon, I'm afraid."

Miss Cornelia, staring at the fire, nodded slowly. "I don't
know what to say. Age does not necessarily bring wisdom,
my dear. Only acceptance. I love you, my dear. If you feel
you must go, then you must go."

How much did she know? How much did she guess of the
truth?

"Come here, Myra," said Miss Cornelia suddenly and
gently.

So Myra went and knelt down before her; she put her head
against the old woman's knee. They remained for a moment
in silence. The beige wool skirt was warm against Myra's
cheek, the fire crackled softly. Cornelia Thorne, Lady Carmichael, had given her everything that had made life a happy
and gracious thing, and every moment now that Myra stayed
on in that house was a denial of a deep obligation.

How much did Aunt Cornelia know? she thought again.
How much did she guess?

Miss Cornelia sighed and put her fingers lightly on Myra's
head. "I've lived long enough," she said musingly, "to know
that there is never any end to the shift and change of human
relationships. There is only one certain factor in any human
relationship and that is its continuation. The stubbornness
and tenacity of its life. I don't think you understand now
what I mean; you will understand. Now then, my dear, we'll
not talk any more of this just now. Only . . ."

Myra lifted her head and Miss Cornelia's bright eyes were
very gentle and tender. She said, "Only remember I love you,
my dear. And that I've watched you grow up and that I know
you. And I'm very proud of you."

Barton in the doorway cleared his throat. Miss Cornelia,
without turning, said, "Yes, what is it, Barton? Is Mr.
Richard home?"

"Miss Wilkinson has called, Madam."

"Oh. Well, ask her to come in here."

Barton disappeared. Miss Cornelia gave Myra a gentle little
pat, sniffed once and said, with a briskness that did not quite
cover emotion, "I've never known Mildred Wilkinson to
come at a time when you really wanted her. A statement for

which I'd have roundly spanked you at any time when you were younger. Besides, Mildred has been very faithful to us. Loyal in spite of everything. Don't be sad, my dear; there's always a way out. Even if we can't at the moment see it. Now get up and go and fix your flowers. Let's not give Mildred anything to speculate about. She's a lonely, idle and frustrated woman in spite of her money, poor thing. Living alone in that barracks of a place with nothing to think of since her father died except herself and her imaginary ills and her neighbor's affairs. Well, well; get up, my dear."

But as Myra rose she caught her hand and pressed it lightly to her cheek.

Barton's returning footsteps were padding along the hall accompanied by the regular thud of Mildred's sensible country shoes. Myra bent and kissed Miss Cornelia's soft cheek swiftly and went back to the flowers. It would give her, as Aunt Cornelia had known, a moment to steady herself. She hoped Mildred would not stay until Richard came.

Mildred reached the doorway. "Good afternoon, Lady Carmichael."

"Come in, Mildred. How nice of you!"

"I brought you my first lilies of the valley. The moment I saw they had bloomed I thought those are for Lady Carmichael. I gathered them for you myself."

"Oh," said Miss Cornelia. "Thank you."

"I know how terribly difficult it is for you to get outdoors and enjoy the spring. So I brought it to you!"

"Well," said Miss Cornelia rather dryly. "I've just come from a walk in the garden. But it's very nice of you, Mildred."

"Aren't they lovely?"

"Beautiful," said Miss Cornelia. "Beautiful. Myra, dear, do you suppose you could find a vase?"

"Oh, hello, Myra," said Mildred. "I didn't see you."

Myra turned. "Hello, Mildred. How are you?"

Mildred Wilkinson, tall and drooping somehow in appearance, so that, in spite of inordinately expensive clothing, she always presented rather concave lines, stood beside Miss Cornelia, her long, freckled hands full of flowers. She was a woman in her mid-thirties or more, although even those who knew her best were not likely to know exactly Mildred Wilkinson's age. This was not, however, due entirely to vanity. Certainly Mildred spared no expense as to facials, per-

manents and clothing, but the Wilkinsons had always been
very rich, and, so far as their own affairs went, very close-
mouthed. Except, in Mildred's case, about her health; she
was in no sense a hypochondriac; her vague complaints, her
interest in pills and capsules were mainly and rather pathetically due to her lack of interest in other things. And
that, too, was rather pathetic. Never, perhaps, an attractive
or an energetic woman, she had lived since school days a
secluded and ingrown life, alone with her father, unsociable,
stiff-necked and extremely rich old Nelson Wilkinson. After
his death she had seemed unable to stir herself from the
lethargy of those years.

She said now, "Not too well. My headaches again and not
sleeping . . ." She sighed and then brightened. "Dr. Haven
always tells me to get out and get more exercise. See more
people. Really sometimes I think he's getting too old to practice. But father liked him." She thrust the lilies of the valley
into Myra's hands.

Miss Cornelia said, "Do sit down, Mildred. Did you walk
over?"

"Oh, no; I wasn't quite up to it!" She sat down in the ruby-
red chair. Her colorless light hair was tightly waved; a heavily marked line accentuated her mouth; she adjusted her
rather long brown tweed skirt and gave a bleak, shrinking
look around her. "You always use this room!" she said dis-
tastefully.

Miss Cornelia's lips tightened, but after a second or two
she replied quietly, "Certainly. Why not?"

She knew, of course; everyone knew why not. Mildred's
pale eyes returned to meet Miss Cornelia's direct gaze. She
did not reply. She said instead, "How are you now, dear
Lady Carmichael? How is Richard? How is . . . ?" She
cleared her throat and said distinctly, "How is Alice?"

CHAPTER 2 ■

The sweet fragrance of the lilies was as delicate and gentle as the image of Alice that Mildred's question evoked.

And the lilies gave Myra an excuse to get away. As she went toward the hall she heard Mildred say again, "How is Alice?"

People, as a rule, did not mention Alice; but then so few people came to the house. Certainly Mildred had been, as Aunt Cornelia had said, faithful and constant in her visits to a house a less faithful friend might wish to avoid; certainly she had been devoted to Alice. Alice, indeed, had been one of Mildred's few friends. Mildred was older than Alice, yet they had been in school together and, after Alice's marriage, they had been neighbors. She had every right to ask questions.

The great hall was empty. Myra walked back along it, across the stately dining room with its dim portraits and mirrors and sparkling chandelier, to the little room off the butler's pantry where Alice had so faultlessly arranged her flowers.

The small chromium sink glittered; the vases stood in orderly rows. She selected a low, pale-green bowl for the tiny fragrant stalks—pulled off unevenly, as if Mildred had jerked at them quickly and impatiently.

The first step had been taken; she had told Aunt Cornelia.

Now to tell Tim; to explain that she wanted to live with him; that they could take a tiny apartment; that she'd do the cooking and cleaning and see to him; that their expenses really wouldn't be much. Tim loved her in his own rather incalculable way; he might not understand her action but she could count on his affection. In any case, she'd get some sort of job.

How much had Aunt Cornelia seen and guessed? How much did she know of the truth?

Myra stood for a long time looking at the lilies.

She was indeed so lost in thought that when at last she roused herself it was with an abrupt sense of much time having passed. And when she took up the bowl and went back to the library, dreading Mildred and her inevitable talk of Alice, Mildred had gone.

And Richard had returned.

He was standing before the mantel, talking to his aunt, his hands thrust into his pockets. Both of them looked up as Myra entered. "Hello, Myra," said Richard.

He was a mediumly tall man with a compact, solid body. He did not at all resemble Miss Cornelia; he was too hard and masculine, but he had her forthright manner of speech and direct eyes.

"Mildred's gone," said Miss Cornelia. "She said she could only stay a minute; she had so much to do. I can't imagine what. Poor thing, she'd be happier if she did have something to do. The flowers look very nice, my dear."

The last time, thought Myra—the last time. Suddenly she hoped that Aunt Cornelia would remain in the room, stay downstairs to dinner; permit no moment for Myra to be alone with Richard.

She put the low green bowl down on a table near by. Barton came in with the tray of ice and glasses, soda water and decanters. He moved toward the ruby-red chair and lowered the tray to the table that stood beside it. "Anything else, sir?"

"That's all, thank you."

Barton moved a decanter a fractional inch, eyed it scrutinizingly and, satisfied, went to put on a fresh log. Miss Cornelia said wearily, "I think I'll go upstairs now, Richard. Barton . . ."

"Yes, Madam."

The two men made a linked cradle of their arms, and Miss Cornelia, leaning on Myra, slipped from the chair in it. She said, with a rather subdued twinkle, "I like all the attention I can get. Myra, if Tim phones tell him I insist on his coming."

"Comfortable?" said Richard, looking down at the face so near his shoulder.

"Oh, quite." She waved at Myra, and the butler and

Richard, walking slowly and carefully with their light burden, carried her out of the library.

Myra went to the French window and looked out across the terrace. It was late; the clear glow of the spring afternoon was leaving.

Perhaps it would be better not to talk to Richard at all.

But he came back almost at once, striding swiftly along the hall and into the room, and he already knew. He came directly toward her.

"What's all this about leaving, Myra?"

She met his eyes for an instant and looked quickly away, but it was curious how, even when she didn't look at him, when she wouldn't look at him, she could still see him so clearly, the hard, compact lines of his face, the expression of incredulity—and question—in his eyes. Her throat was tight; she put her hand up against it. He said, "You can't be serious! Aunt Cornelia needs you. This is her home and yours."

He was wrong; it was Alice's. Myra moved away, toward the ruby-red chair and the table with the glasses and decanter. "You've made me more than welcome, Richard," she said stiffly.

Richard made a swift, impatient gesture. "Good Lord! You and Aunt Cornelia—well, you ought to know, you must know what it's meant to me to have you both here."

"She wished to be with you, Richard."

"She came to stand beside me," he said bluntly. "She came as quickly as she could. She's like an army with banners, bless her. So are you, Myra."

It was going to be even more difficult than she had expected. She said slowly, "I love her, Richard. I needn't tell you that."

"But then why . . . ?" he broke off abruptly, stared at nothing for a moment, then came to pour drinks for both of them. He put a glass in her hand, and said, "Let's talk it over a bit. I don't see—well, sit down."

So she sat again in the ruby-red chair where she'd sat for, now, so many evenings. He rubbed one hand through his hair impatiently, and frowning, went to his own arm chair opposite.

"Look here," he said, and stared at the fire and drank slowly and repeated, "Look here. Why do you want to leave?"

Truth put itself into words: Because I discovered, only a

few days ago, that I love you. Because you are Alice's husband.

Myra did not, of course, speak the words which truth so swiftly chose. She said, "Aunt Cornelia is much better. I'm going to live with Tim."

Richard's face was in the shadow of the wing of his chair, but she knew that he glanced at her quickly and then looked back into the fire.

The house—Alice's house—was very quiet. By this time Aunt Cornelia was having her own sip or two of sherry and listening to the radio in the big, comfortable corner room upstairs; the room she had had as a child long ago. The radio would be drawn up close to her sofa, the door closed. Servants, quiet, deft, trained by Alice, were busy in the back of the house. Presently, as the twilight grew deeper, Barton would paddle back into the room to draw crimson curtains across the French windows, to offer the evening mail and papers on a silver waiter, to glance efficiently at the table before Myra in case the ice needed replenishing, or to put another log on the fire.

Her heart seemed to close against a sharp little stab of pain. How strange it was that in a few months one could grow to love a house and all its customs. Or a man! How did love begin and when? All at once, fully, with deep sudden tide, or little by little, small currents adding themselves together gently and so secretly that by the time it took on its real identity and was recognizable as love it was too late to do anything about it.

She knew exactly when she had recognized the thing that had happened; there was nothing, however, that was dramatic about it. It was, in fact, rather silly because she'd been brushing her teeth. Brushing and thinking of the day ahead of her and suddenly it occurred to her to wonder why an ordinary, pleasant but merely routine day should be in prospect so touched with an anticipatory excitement, something mysterious and gay and promising.

It's like Christmas morning, when I was a child, she thought. And then, instantly: I'm in love with Richard.

It had disclosed itself to her like that, absurdly, between one brush and the next. Why do I feel like this? Because I love him. She had stopped automatically, struck with it. An absurd figure, too, not romantic with her dark hair curled up from the shower and twisted in a tight knot on top of her head, and her face shiny from soap, toothpaste on her lips, and an enormous white bath towel wrapped tightly around her. It was a ridiculous Greek statue effect; she'd seen that, absently. And thought: it cannot be true, what am I thinking!

But it was true.

And if there had been no beginning, there had to be an end.

A useful old phrase stirred in her consciousness. It would have to be nipped in the bud. But it wasn't in the bud, unfortunately. It was in full bloom.

Richard had been silent for a moment or two. He said gently, "You are smiling."

Smiling? At herself, then; wryly, at her own expense. She said, avoiding a reply, "Another drink?"

"No—yes." He rose and came to her and poured it, standing tall and square before her, his solid body outlined against the glow of the fire. Again she would not look up into his face; she watched his hands on the glass decanter, the clear amber pouring into the glass. He added soda and ice and went back to his chair opposite her and sat forward, elbows on his knees, twirling the glass in his hands absently. He said abruptly, "Myra, please stay."

She had not expected that. She said, confused and also abrupt, "No, I can't."

"Why?"

"I told you. Tim needs me. Aunt Cornelia has given me already more than I can ever try to repay."

There was another deliberate second or two before he spoke. He said then, "Your reasons are mixed. Aunt Cornelia loves you. She needs you. And I . . ." he stopped and looked at the glass in his hand.

What had he been about to say? I want you? Suppose he had said that! Her imagination raced irresistibly on—suppose he'd said, "I need you—I want you—please stay. Not to take care of Aunt Cornelia; not to see to the household orders; not even to sit with me during this lonely, haunted hour before dinner, but because I want you."

She swirled the cold glass in her hand so the ice tinkled lightly. Richard did not complete his half-begun words. He said instead, "Of course Aunt Cornelia feels that you must be free to do what seems best to you. She said that when she told me, just now."

Myra leaned forward quickly. "She has done everything for me, Richard. You know that. And for Tim. It seems ungrateful, selfish, to leave her now. I realize it, Richard. But I . . ." She checked herself, dismayed. What had she been about to say? That she must go; there were reasons—a reason?

Richard said gravely and directly, "You and Aunt Cornelia are too close, you mean too much to each other for there to be any talk of obligations between you. If she's been like a mother to you, you've been a dearly loved daughter to her. But if you feel Tim needs you, you must go, of course. When were you planning to leave?"

So the short, small battle was over.

Suddenly, now that her purpose was accomplished, it seemed incredible that she had undertaken it; incredible that she had voluntarily given up all the things that were so deeply and so blindingly dear to her. How could she have made an irrevocable choice! How could she have said words that would remove her from that house, from Richard, from the satisfaction of being in the same house with him, eating at the same table, meeting him like this for an hour or so alone before dinner? In doing so she had prepared her own heartbreak.

But heartbreak for her was already prepared; it came with love for Richard. It was an inextricable part of it, and to love him was to accept it. It struck her briefly that it was strange to describe anything that had to do with Richard in melodramatic terms; melodrama did not go with Richard's saneness, and matter-of-factness.

Was it possible that now for the last time she sat with Richard during that quiet hour of dusk before a fire?

But her decision had been made. "Tomorrow, Richard," she said.

"Tomorrow! That's very sudden!" His eyes sharpened. "Tim hasn't got himself into any trouble, has he?"

"No, no."

"He seemed to me a little jumpy when he was out here last week-end. There's nothing on his mind, is there? Any—worry, I mean. Money or . . ."

"Oh, I don't think so, Richard. I'm sure he'd tell me." She thought soberly of Tim. Her preoccupation with her own problem had distracted her from the problem of helping Tim to settle quietly into civilian life. She realized, rather guiltily, that Tim had not seemed quite himself on the previous week-end, or, indeed, since he had returned from China. She said, "He does seem very quiet. Aunt Cornelia said morose. But I don't think there can be any special reason for it, except the aftermath of war. I think he'd tell me. And he likes his job. He particularly wants to do well at it, because you got it for him."

"He will," said Richard reassuringly. "Don't worry about the youngster, Myra."

She looked at him gratefully and then saw the closed, withdrawn look she now recognized settle over his face. Because of Tim, of course; he was remembering; the thing had happened during Tim's last leave before he went overseas. Timothy Lane had been, in fact, a witness.

Myra said quickly, to divert Richard's thought, "I'll be in New York, only forty-three minutes away, if you want me" —her tongue slipped there; her own private interpretation of the phrase made her momentarily shy and self-conscious; she went on hurriedly—"if anything goes wrong, I can come back. In any case, I'll come back often to see Aunt Cornelia."

"And me, I hope," said Richard, and leaned back in his chair.

There was an air of conclusion about it. So she had got what she wanted. Or rather not what she wanted; but what she must have. Naturally she didn't want it. How long did it take to get over loving anybody?

Already she knew regret. No longer to listen for Richard's car about dusk, for the excited bark of the Scotch terrier, for the sound of the door, for the murmur of words with Barton and then the quick, hard steps along the hall, back past the stairway, to the library where he'd find her and a fire and flowers with, now, the cool spring dusk outside the French windows.

Well, it was done; she couldn't change it. The glass felt cold in her hands, as if its chill could creep into her body and remain. The beauty of the room was dulled; the fire had lost its warmth and glow. She put down the glass and clasped her hand around the ruby silk of the chair, soft and smooth to her touch. And thought of Alice who had chosen it; Alice with her beauty, Alice with her fair skin and hair; her soft and fragile loveliness.

Richard said, from the shadow of the wing of the chair, "Is it the house, Myra? Is it—this room?"

Even though she had been thinking so strongly of Alice, for an instant she did not see the significance of his question. Then she sat upright quickly. "No!—Richard, no!"

"You and Aunt Cornelia have been here so long that I didn't think you minded. That is, not now. But I expect some people do rather—mind."

Had they too looked at the Capo di Monte cupid and wondered what it had seen and what it could tell and what worse it had heard? Particularly the words it had heard? No one had even known that.

And Richard had never in all those months spoken to her even obliquely of Alice.

She did not wish the silence to last. "It is a very beautiful room," she said quietly. "The whole house is beautiful."

Again he seemed to glance at her sharply from the short triangular shadow.

"That's not why I stayed here," he said and got up and went to stand before the fire, facing her. The lamps were not lighted. Barton would light them, going quickly from one to the other, when he came to pull the curtains. The thin soft April twilight lay now in the room; the sky was lemon and blue beyond the windows; the firelight behind Richard silhouetted his dark head and solid figure but his face again was slightly shadowed. He said, "I love the place. I've always known it was to be mine, naturally; I had no brother. I was trained to see to it; as I was trained in business, and the responsibility that goes with money. The house is too big; in these days nobody would build a place like this. But considering the vast houses that were built at about the same time this house was built, when there were no taxes and little regulation of business, this place isn't really bad; it could have been worse. It is still practicable to live in. But the point is, it is my home."

He paused and drank and went on thoughtfully. "My great-great-grandfather chose the site. My great-grandfather supervised the holly hedge; my grandmother laid out the rose garden. My mother tended the roses." He nodded toward the hall. "Aunt Cornelia came down that stairway fifty years ago in her mother's wedding gown, white satin and rosepoint. My father, then, was about ten, home from school for the occasion, slightly confused, he told me, because of champagne and because Cornelia was going to England with her new husband and her new title. The next time he came

home from school there was a Christmas party and he met
my mother. She came in from the snowy night and she was
wearing a little white fur hood and—he said once—the winter stars were in her eyes." His voice was very quiet; he
paused for a moment and said, "He was a nice guy, hard in
a way, and hard to know, quick to make decisions and all
hell wouldn't move him when they were made. Quick to anger, too, but just. Cold on the outside; loyal to the bone.
Generous. Stubborn."

"Like you," she said irresistibly, smiling.

He gave her a quick look and said, amused, "Am I stubborn? I wish then I had his certainty; he never doubted the
chosen course of his own life."

A sudden pulse leaped in her throat. What choice and
course of his own did Richard question? But then at once,
without explaining, he went on, "I think my mother was his
guiding star."

The swift pulse beat quieted as quickly; he hadn't meant
anything. She said, quickly, too, as if to cover an awkward-
ness which actually, since he had not meant anything, did not
exist, "Her portrait was one of the first things Aunt Cornelia
showed me when we arrived."

It hung in the formal ivory-and-gold drawing room—a
pretty, gentle-looking woman, in an evening gown of the
period with bare shoulders and pearls and her brown hair
done in a very high pompadour. Alice's portrait, too, still
hung in the same room—incredibly beautiful in her wedding
gown, the misty lace of her veil framing her face, pearls at
her white throat, her soft brown eyes luminous and young.
At first she had wondered why it was not removed. Pride
in his name on Richard's part? Then, as time went on, she
grew accustomed to it. She failed to see it. And, as a matter
of fact, the room in which it hung was almost never, now, in
use.

Richard said, "My mother's portrait used to hang here,
over the mantel. I used to come to this room when I'd be at
home from school. My father would summon me once during
each vacation, question me about school reports and life in
general in a very brisk and businesslike way, then, having
discharged his duties as a father, he'd pour me a small glass
of sherry and rub his mental hands together in a sort of satisfied way and sit down for a man-to-man visit. He was"—he

paused, and the fire crackled and Richard said again, half
smiling—"he was a nice guy."

He put his glass on a table near by, beside the great bowl
of yellow daffodils. He lighted a cigarette and went back to
stand before the fire.

"This room, of course, was different then. Ugly, I suppose,
great heavy cases of books with glass doors; furniture that
had drifted in from the rest of the house—stiff, old—a roll-
top desk was there, and a couch—black leather with a rolled
head. This fireplace had a dark fumed oak mantel. There
were no French doors, but a couple of narrow windows. The
terrace was there and, of course, the view. But it was very
different."

His voice was different too, no longer rather tender and
musing. It, like his face, seemed to change and close in upon
itself whenever some word or thought led to Alice. And, of
course, Alice had made the changes in the house. Alice who
had been a perfect wife. Alice with her perfect taste for
beauty, her perfect housekeeping. Alice who had been perfect at everything except in one instance.

Richard said suddenly, looking directly at Myra, "What I
started to say is that this is my home. Nothing can change
that. Not even"—he took a breath of smoke and said—"not
even murder."

Myra's hand was digging into the ruby-red arm of her
chair. The word was out, the word that all of them knew,
and could not escape, that had made itself an inextricable
part of the house, that had taken up its dreadful residence
within those walls, and yet that none of them ever spoke.
The one instance of Alice's imperfection.

She had been startlingly imperfect about murder.

Richard said, in a matter of fact way which was too terse
and too matter of fact, "People asked me if I intended to stay
here. Naturally there was nothing else to do. This is my
home. These are my friends. Why should I leave?"

Suddenly Myra remembered the day Alice was sentenced
—that final, terrible day. It was autumn by then, the trial had
dragged along for months. Aunt Cornelia had broken her
hip, ironically, the week before the murder, ironically, again,
she had emerged from blitzes in London only to slip on a
wet flagstone of her peaceful country garden in Devonshire.
It was months before she could be moved to a wheel chair,

months more before she was permitted by either doctors or priority needs to return to America and Richard. On the day of the final sentence she had been still in a nursing home in the country, waiting for a cable. Myra had brought it to her; Myra had had to read it: "Sentence life imprisonment. Thorne."

She had not known then that terrible and tragic though that message was, it would actually one day so drastically affect her own life.

She had sent Aunt Cornelia's reply, too. "I am coming as soon as I can. My love always. Cornelia Carmichael."

The silence had lengthened, as if the mention of Alice had imposed it, like a finger at their lips. Richard was frowning, looking at the lilies of the valley without, Myra thought, seeing them. His mouth was straight and uncommunicative. She felt suddenly very tired; her lips were dry. She must leave. She must leave the house the next day, and the library and the talk with Richard immediately, for she could not bear it a moment longer.

She rose, and Barton entered with the papers and the mail on a tray. Richard whirled around abruptly to toss his cigarette in the fire and said, "Come for a walk with me, Myra. There's an hour or so before dinner. Barton, will you get Miss Lane's coat?"

She didn't want to go. She had to escape, but she did not. She stood still, a slender, straight figure in her light-gray country suit and sweater. Her face was rather white, and her eyes, in the mirror over the fireplace, were dark blue and troubled, but she did not see her own reflection. Barton came back with her loose scarlet coat which Richard took and placed round her shoulders. He opened one of the French windows—perhaps the window which Jack Manders had opened on a night nearly two years ago, strolling from the cottage he shared with Webb Manders—the small, comfortable cottage, suitable to two middle-aged bachelors, living alone—around the point to the Thorne House. Through the warm, quiet night, to chat and borrow a book, Alice had always said.

They went out on the terrace.

It had turned colder and the spring twilight was clear and chill. The dogwoods and lilacs were in bud but their bare branches still made a fine brown tracing against the pale sky. There was a golden haze around the forsythia. The air was cool and moist with a light smell of the sea and a bright star hung low on the horizon. The whistles of the peepers in the woods between the house and the road made a delicate, fluting fabric of sound through the tranquil dusk.

Richard closed the door behind them and they crossed the damp flagstones of the terrace toward the wide steps and thus did not hear the telephone which rang several times, loudly, at the extension in the hall. Barton, in the pantry, finally answered it.

CHAPTER 3

As the path curved toward the pines, there was a view of the house, clear against the evening sky.

It stood on a point above the Sound.

It had no name, really, but it had always been called Thorne House. It had changed very little from the time old Phineas Thorne, having built the Thorne fortune, looked around for a site and built the Thorne House upon it. It was solidly and well built because Phineas would have been content with no other way of building; that it was also beautiful was due to the chance of securing a fine architect who, besides a knowledge of balance and proportion, had the wisdom to yield to Phineas' own innate sense of simplicity and grace.

The result was a happy one. The house was of no particular period; it escaped the cramped rooms and narrow halls of the typical New England house by borrowing the generous height of ceiling and spaciousness of the great Southern houses of the time. The Thornes were of English and Scottish descent. From England, perhaps, came the plan for the wide central hall, the numerous chimneys, the thickness of walls and the solid, but gracious lines of the house.

Also from England, perhaps, came much of the feeling for

substantial materials, wood and stone that would last for generations. Phineas Thorne had felt that he was building a family as he had built a fortune. The house itself was brick, especially ordered, especially kilned; a mellow, pinkish brick, weathering through the years to the softness of a well-ripened peach; wistaria with trunks as thick as a man's wrist, and deep, dark-green ivy, brought from England, clung to the old bricks, the luxuriant growth clipped back from windows and doorways. The window frames themselves were cypress and, inside the house, the floors were teakwood, the stairways cypress, too, the balustrades mahogany, worn satin-smooth by the pressure of many hands.

Walls surrounded the estate on three sides, shutting out the world, enclosing the house with the sea. Even the walls evidenced Phineas Thorne's sturdy feeling for the substantial and the permanent; they were made of rough-hewn New England rocks which were now weathered with age, moss-grown and lined with great banks of laurel and hemlock and old whispering pines.

Somehow Thorne House had escaped rebuilding during the extravagant, halcyon days of the eighties and nineties when there was no stopping the tide of money flowing into the Thorne coffers. The Thorne shipping line boomed into popular favor; its ships, built as well and solidly as Thorne House, went all over the world; the Thorne banks waxed fat and bursting with prosperity and Northern capital.

But the period that saw monstrosities built all along the New England coast, a period that founded the fabulous and ridiculous houses of Newport and along Fifth Avenue, saw Thorne House already built and invulnerable. A wing was added in 1889, but it kept to the original dignified and generous line of the house; hothouses were built in 1893, but they glittered gently from beyond well-matured gardens and hedges which had been laid out at the time the house was built.

Inside, of course, there were changes. It was Alice who had finally weeded out the ugliness and had restored and collected damaged or hidden beauties. She was efficient; she had time for everything. Even the gardens had improved under her painstaking care, so now the whole place, inside and out, measured up to the standard of beauty set originally by Phineas Thorne.

A belt of woods lay inside the walls, between Thorne House and the public road; through it wound what had once been a narrow carriage drive, bordered with glossy banks of laurels. It was now wider and neatly graveled and emerged from the woods upon a sweep of green lawn, as smooth as the English turf old Phineas had admired.

The gardens with their velvety turf paths, their dense clipped hedges of privet and box, lay along the south and east. In summer there were masses of bloom, a succession of color marching through the balmy days of early June with white lilies and blue campanula and slender spikes of pink and purple lupin and foxglove, and, later, great festoons of crimson roses, on into the brilliant orange and red of the August annuals. Now, in early spring, there were blue and white hyacinths and yellow daffodils and the pungent, bitter odor of the dark box.

The terrace overlooked the Sound, which lay like a silver band below a slope of grassy lawn, more pines and then a sudden strip of rocky wilderness which descended sharply to the sand along the water's edge. Paths wound downward here and there; there was a small sandy bathing beach and a new and modern boathouse; there Richard Thorne kept his sailing boat, the small and now rarely used yacht which had belonged to his father, and one or two motor boats, slow and utilitarian and, as with the yacht, rarely used. During the war yacht and motor boats had been loaned to the Coast Guard; since the war no one in the household had cared to use any of the boats. Perhaps they had grown accustomed to their absence; perhaps nothing about the place had quite resumed its former tempo since the war and since the June night during the war when Alice Thorne, the law later said, had taken a revolver in her beautiful hands and shot a man to death.

Certainly there was something different. The routine, the gracious little forms and customs went on as smoothly and as carefully as if Alice herself was still there to supervise their performance with that astonishing efficiency of hers. The floors and the silver were as brightly polished, the linen closets as delicately scented with lavender, the flowers as beautifully arranged, the turf paths as green and closely clipped, the menus as neatly written out in Miss Cornelia's small, old-fashioned handwriting as when Alice had typed them, swiftly and precisely on the small machine in her bedroom.

But the house was different. It was as if all the strength and sturdiness of old Phineas' building had not yet summoned the power to resist the memory of murder—and of Alice.

But that was comprehensible. Again Myra thought, it is still Alice's house.

She had not spoken to Richard, nor he to her. There was only the sound of their feet along the path, the shrill, far-away whistles of the peepers, the regular hum of an airplane distant in the evening sky.

They entered the pines.

"Mind the branch. I'll hold it back," said Richard, and held the fragrant green boughs aside so she could enter the path. The house vanished. The soft dusk below the pine trees closed around them. The path was narrow. Myra walked ahead of Richard, along the slippery brown pine needles, intensely aware of the man who followed her, the scent of the cigarette he carried and the sound of his footsteps. The pine needles gave way to sand and they came out beside the rocks, rough and white. The water lay directly below, soft and clear, reflecting a pink glow from the lingering band of pink in the sky. They crossed the sandy strip of beach and stopped. The boathouse lay at the right; it was so quiet they could hear the water lapping evenly at the piles, and its soft slap and murmur against the boats.

The distant shore of Long Island was gray; nearer were several small islands, faintly yellow with willows, but veiled, too, in the soft spring twilight. Far away the hum of the airplane diminished.

"We could be a thousand miles from New York," said Richard suddenly, his hands in his pockets. "We could be on a different planet. Except it would have to have the same stars and the same moon and the same smell of spring and sea."

Tomorrow she would be in what was equivalent to a different planet. Actually, New York was scarcely an hour's time distant, yet it might as well be in another world. She would visit Thorne house again; she would chat with Aunt Cornelia over the telephone. She would never live in Thorne House again; she would never again see Richard on the terms of the past months, daily, with the easy, friendly accustomed-ness of habit. There had been a warm domesticity about it—false, of course, but kind.

It had been dangerous, too, but she had not perceived its danger. Well, this was the last time. When she left Thorne

House the next day she left Richard Thorne too, forever. Even if he wished to he could not see her—not often,
that is, not unselfconsciously. She could hear the little com-
ments: "I saw Dick Thorne in town the other night. He was
with that girl of Miss Cornelia's—secretary, ward, whatever
she is. Tim Lane's sister."

Everyone knew Tim, of course. He'd spent most of his vacations at Thorne Hall all the time he was in school. It had
been like a home to him, thanks to Richard (and Alice—she
reminded herself—and Alice) then and later, while Myra and
Miss Cornelia were caught by the war in England and Tim
was in boot camp.

She could hear the replies, too. "Really! I wonder—but of
course Dick can't marry." "No. Too bad. But there's no way
out for him."

All of it kind, none of it malicious. But Richard would hear
it and avoid her. Actually, Richard knew as well as Myra that
if he dined with a woman in town too often or at all,
if he talked more than a few moments to the same woman at
a cocktail party—if in any possible way Dick Thorne showed
any woman marked attention, such comment was inevitable.
Up to then, so far as she knew, there had been no comment;
where Cornelia Carmichael went Myra went; everyone, she
thought, accepted that without question.

Once she left Aunt Cornelia, once she went to live with
Tim, it would be different.

There was a scurry and rush of feet along the sand and a
small Scotch terrier skidded to a stop at Richard's feet. His
red tongue showed, his black eyes glittered, his whole small
body waggled furiously. "Hello, Willie," said Richard, and
scooped up the dog who rolled his eyes in lavish disregard for
his usual taciturnity and strove to lick Richard's face.

"He's been hunting." Myra reached over to pull a burr
from his shaggy stomach. "Usually he's waiting and listening
for your car."

Richard gave the dog a pat and put him down on the sand
and took out cigarettes which he offered Myra. He said, holding his lighter for her, "I'm sorry you are going to leave."

Perhaps because in her heart she so wanted other words
said in a different way, it seemed flat and perfunctory. So her
own reply sounded as flat and as perfunctory. "I'm sorry,
too."

He waited a moment, almost as if he were waiting for her

to say more, then he turned. "Shall we walk?" he said, and picked up a piece of driftwood to throw for Willie.

Willie waited, bounding, quivering, his eyes fastened on the stick in Richard's hand. Richard said, "It's extraordinarily difficult to look at things—and people—objectively. I happened to see the Governor a month ago, in a restaurant. I left rather than run the risk of a chance meeting. He was only a public servant, performing his duty. To me he was the man who had risen to that office in a large degree because he had sent my wife to prison."

He threw the stick, harder and farther than he intended. Willie missed its flight, was bewildered, bounced, seeking it, this way and that. Richard said, looking straight ahead, "I heard somebody speak of Webb Manders one time this winter. To me he wasn't the Webb Manders I know, good-natured, friendly; he was Jack Manders' brother, the eye-witness. The man who stood there in the witness stand, giving the testimony that actually convicted Alice. I'm an adult. I realize the circumstances. Nevertheless . . ."

Willie came back, apologetic, panting, without the stick. Richard stooped to find another, and threw it, not so hard this time and Willie scrambled after it.

He had never talked of Alice and the thing that had happened in the gracious, charming room they had just left. Why, she thought with a dull sense of something like anti-climax, did he do so now? The portion of her life which like a thread had been caught and woven briefly into the pattern and fabric of the house that stood above her, pink and lovely against the twilight sky, had come to an end. Another life lay before her now and Richard was to be no part of that life.

Again an airplane came from the north and Myra could see it riding high. Its lights were like small meteors hurtling through the quiet evening sky. Richard said then, suddenly and harshly, "What I'm trying to say is that I'm discovering, only now, that there is no past. It is always here, in the present. We are never free." He tossed his cigarette toward the slowly breaking waves. "It is inescapable. It is a part of life. Forever."

Because he still loved Alice.

She had never thought of that. It was incredible that she had not, for she had thought of everything else. So how could she have been so stupid, so childish as not to realize that Richard, naturally, was still in love with Alice!

And why not? They had married; she knew little of that marriage except that they had both been very young, but he must have loved her then and he was not a man to change.

That, of course, was why the beautiful and gently smiling bride in her pearls and her lace veil, Alice's portrait, still hung in the gold-and-ivory drawing room! Richard still loved the bride, and the woman she had become.

And then the inevitable, logical corollary of that thought caught at her as if it had hands and it too was a question.

Was it possible that Richard believed Alice innocent?

She tried to marshall facts. He had been loyal to Alice all during the trial and appeals. He had never, so far as Myra knew, admitted her guilt, but he would be loyal, he would never have admitted Alice's guilt, whether he accepted it in his heart and mind or rejected it. No matter what he really believed he would do exactly as he had done. And would continue to do.

Yet Alice couldn't be innocent; she had been tried and convicted; she'd been seen in the very act of murder. How could Richard really believe her innocent?

She would not think of that; it lay in the pattern of life which she must leave, and must forget.

The last glow was leaving the sky; the water looked gray and cold and desolate. She pulled her coat up around her throat and Richard saw it and said quickly, "You're cold. We'll go back. I'm a selfish son of a gun. But the fact is . . ."

They had stopped. He was facing her and, without intending to, she met his eyes. He said, "I'll miss you, Myra."

A wave broke with a little soft whisper against the sand. Willie, digging somewhere, diverted, gave a sharp bark. Myra dug her hands into her coat pockets to stop their trembling. The airplane was almost overhead, its droning engine like the beating of a pulse that could not be denied.

Richard said, "Myra—I don't want you to go." And took her in his arms, all at once, strongly, holding her tight to him. She moved her head and his mouth came down warm and hard upon her own and the regular beat of the airplane engine became her own heart, his heart, all life beating around them.

Willie barked sharply. Richard let her go. He looked out across the gray water.

"I didn't mean to do that. I didn't mean to say that. Forget it—will you, Myra?"

"Forget . . ." Forget his arms, forget his mouth upon her own? Forget that in an instant's time so much had changed?

"Forgive me, Myra—I suppose we'd better go up to dinner." He went away from her. He made Willie a pretext and walked toward the dog who was still digging furiously in the sand. His compact, solid body, his dark head seemed to recede from her forever into the twilight.

Shadows were gathering now everywhere, turning the water darker, robbing it of its rosy light. The shore of Long Island was an indistinct dark line along the horizon. The sky was deeper blue; the evening star above his head was brighter but very cold, very distant. It was nothing you could touch, nothing you could reach up to and pull down into your embrace. Into your heart.

The airplane was passing on, the beat of the engine was already a distant drone and the havoc and tumult of the instant or two that had accompanied it was passing too. Up above them a light would shine from the house. Alice's house.

"Come on, Willie," said Richard in the distance. He bent again and scooped up the little dog who resisted, flailing his short, black legs, and came back toward her. "Well—you're shivering. We'd better go up to the house."

There were words that must be said, now. There was no time to debate whether or not it was better for them to be forever unspoken; there was only a strong compulsion to hurry, to get something that was very important said, something clear before it was too late. Before Richard himself put a seal upon words. She put both hands on his arm and Willie bent to put his chill little nose against them.

"Richard—Richard," she said, "you see why I must leave."

The throbbing sound of the airplane diminished altogether. There was only silence, and the gathering night and the man before her, looking down into her face.

He said at last, "You've known . . ."

"About myself. Yes, Richard."

"That's why you were leaving?"

"Yes."

Another long moment passed while they stood there, searching each other's eyes. Then Richard said, "Yes, I see. You're right, of course. There's nothing else for us to do."

She thought for an instant that he was going to take her in his arms again; she wanted him to do so with every vein in her body.

He didn't. He put his hand rather gently under her arm. They turned together and started along the sandy stretch toward the path through the rocks.

Dinner would be waiting. It was very nearly dark.

The sand seemed heavy and cold and clung to her pumps. The water was darker and a little menacing with sudden night. The rocks loomed up white and barren ahead of them. They could not from there see the lights of the house.

When they reached the path through the rocks Richard's hand tightened under her arm. He swung her around toward him.

"I'm going to divorce Alice."

CHAPTER 4 ▪

"Richard!" The last light of the evening was clear upon his face, and she could read nothing in it. He did not speak, he only stood there before her, holding the little black dog in the crook of his arm.

"You can't divorce Alice!" she said unevenly.

"Why not?"

So many reasons, all of them tragically valid. She cried, "Richard, it's impossible!"

"Nothing is impossible. I love you. I've known it for some time. I'm not going to talk like a boy about it. We both know what it means. Until tonight I was not willing or resigned to losing you, but I had yielded to the situation. Accepted it. But now, if you meant what you said—if that is really why you felt you must leave . . ."

"That is why, Richard."

"Well, then. Things are different. I'm going to divorce Alice."

How easy it would be to say yes! Only a breath, only an instant and the thing was settled. She didn't dare look into the vista one word, one gesture would open before her.

He said, "Listen, Myra. You know about Alice. You know the whole story."

Her heart was pounding in her throat. All at once the question of his belief in Alice's guilt or innocence was terribly important. If he believed her guilty then there was in a quite definite sense a measure of justification for their love, hers and Richard's. If he believed Alice an innocent and tragically wronged woman, that was different; everything was different. She said, "We read the papers you sent. We may have missed some—the mails were lost occasionally during that time. But I suppose I know what everybody else knows."

He waited a moment, his eyes still seeming to search her own. Then he turned to look out again toward the darkening water. "The main facts were in the papers. I was glad, really, that Aunt Cornelia couldn't come until it was all over. We've never talked of it. She never asked me and I didn't want to talk of it. In a way I've always rather felt it was my fault."

"Oh, no, Richard!"

"I mean—well, I was away. Alice was alone. If I'd been there it might not have happened. It was the servants' night out, too; there were only Barton and his wife and a maid, Francine, in the house. They'd all gone to a movie."

His profile was clear and white against the gathering night. He shifted the dog a little, and said, "I got home about midnight and the police were already there. Jack Manders' body was in the library, just before the fireplace. They'd covered it with a rug but hadn't taken it away yet. Alice had told them the story of what happened; she was in the dining room, sitting at the table, and somebody had fixed coffee for everybody. She was quite cool and collected and never deviated in any detail from what she told them then. I remember she had on a white dress, a thin, long white dress and there were small streaks of blood down the front of it. Where she'd knelt beside Jack. To see if she could help him, she said, after she'd heard the shots." Willie gave a wriggle and he set him down carefully on the path.

"And then, of course . . ." his voice was flat and weary. "Then, of course, the business of the gun came out—my gun. Alice stuck to her story, naturally. She was advised to do so even after she was convicted and sentenced. The point is that everything that we could do for her failed. There is no possible recourse. Alice is in prison for life."

But did he believe her guilty? Did he believe her innocent?

He turned. "Look at me, Myra. You must understand. There is nothing more that I can do for Alice."

"You can't divorce her."

"Why not?" he demanded again and repeated it almost angrily. "Why not? What's wrong about it? Who's to say anything against it? We have our lives ahead of us. I—want you, Myra."

"No . . ."

"I'll phone our lawyer. I'll let him tell her. I'll ask her to get the divorce. I'll phone Sam tonight."

"Richard . . ." The tears she kept from her eyes were in her voice. He stopped his headlong, defiant rush of words. "What is it? Myra, are you crying?"

"No, no. I—listen, Richard. You supported her all through the trial. You did everything for her. You would never admit her guilt. You were loyal . . ."

"She was my wife."

"But don't you see! It's you—it's your code—it's Richard. You could not desert her then. You cannot now . . ."

He stopped her, suddenly and sternly. "We've got to have things clear. I'll say what I've never said to anyone, not even to Sam. It's about—Alice."

Her heart tightened. Strangely, though, there was a matter-of-factness, a lack of barrier between them, so his look, his words, were all at once clear and unemotional.

"Actually, whether or not Alice is guilty of murder makes no difference to our situation, yours and mine. Nothing can change that; she has been convicted of murder and imprisoned and there is no further appeal. But in another way, it does make a difference between us. I do not mean as justification; there is nothing in my love for you that requires justification. I only feel that the truth, as I know it, must be known also to you." He paused. "Yet the trouble is, of course, I never really knew the truth—about Jack, I mean, and Alice. You knew, everyone knew, that if she killed him there was only one conceivable motive. That motive had to have its roots in some sort of more or less violent affair between them. Mere friendship does not give rise to murder. Only violence breeds violence. Yet if that was true"—he paused again and took a long breath—"I never knew it. And no one else knew it. In all the tangle of evidence and investigation there was never one shred brought forward which really supported that theory, except for his presence in the house while I was away and that could equally well have been, as Alice said it was, a completely innocent and insignificant happening. They saw each other often, but we saw a lot of people. It is true that he was a sort of special—oh, escort if I happened to be away; he could always fill in as extra man at dinner parties. But bachelor friends are likely to be popular in that way. If there was ever anything serious in his certainly constant but apparently perfectly open friendship with Alice, there were no special indications of it. So, if that motive existed I did not know it. If she killed him I do not know that either."

The lack of barriers, the new candor between them made it possible for her to ask the questions she must ask.

"What do you believe?"

But she had been wrong to ask it; the moment of close and clear understanding seemed to retreat. His eyes clouded. He replied promptly, but it was with a kind of effort, as if he wished to retain that closeness and frankness and yet could not. And he said, "The slugs that killed him were fired from my gun. They proved that. A man may have a gun all his life, practically, and never use it, but Sam and Tim and I had been target shooting, only a few weeks before the murder, down here on the beach, as a matter of fact. The slugs matched, all right. It was my gun that killed him. And then my gun disappeared. She was alone in the house with Jack. And Webb Manders saw her do it."

He had not really replied. But he would never reply to that question; he would never say "I believe she murdered him."

That was because he was Richard; and then she saw that the road they had traveled was a circle, that they had come back to the exact point at which they had entered it. Richard Thorne being Richard Thorne, he would never say, "I believe my wife committed murder." And he would never, as long as Alice lived, be able to withdraw in her terrible need the support of his name and his loyal relationship.

Perhaps she, Myra, could not let him do so.

She said, blindly choosing trite and inadequate words,

"You cannot change your own sense of loyalty, of your own creed and code. It's bred in your bone; it's part of your body."

He understood all the argument below it. He understood too that it was a fundamental argument in her own heart. His eyes deepened, searching her own. He said suddenly, "Myra, you *must* see this sensibly; you *must* be realistic and . . ."

"Oh, Richard, Richard!" She cried despairing, and put her head against his shoulder.

He would not yield. He would not take her in his arms. But she felt his acknowledgment, his gradual surrender. He said at last in a tired voice, "It's so silly, Myra. You and I—it isn't as if she were ill or an invalid. It isn't as if—really in our hearts we could ever hope for release. She's young and, in spite of her fragile look, she's extraordinarily healthy."

"Don't . . ."

"I don't want her to die. I didn't mean that! But it's so horribly unfair, Myra."

"We cannot change it."

He didn't move; still did not so much as touch her.

"I don't want to have an affair with you. I want you for my wife."

On the fringe of her thoughts she had considered that, desperately, perhaps, yet quite coolly and sensibly, too. It probably could be arranged; probably no one would know and, if they did know, nobody was likely to blame them too much. Even Aunt Cornelia who could not fail to see all those intangible things that link a man and a woman who are lovers, even she would not blame them.

No, it could be arranged. In a way they could share the life and the years that lay ahead of them. And it, too, was simply, flatly impossible. She knew it. Richard knew it.

She said, her head still against his shoulder, the quiet and stillness of the chill spring night all around them, "Is there no way, Richard? I mean—a new trial—an appeal . . . ?"

"Impossible. We always came up against the same three, cold, hard facts. I told you what those were a moment ago. She was alone in the house with him when he was shot and nobody could ever prove that anybody else was there. The slugs that killed him were fired by my gun and my gun was gone from the drawer of the table where it was kept and was never found. And, of course, the main, the clinching evidence was that Webb Manders said he saw her shoot him."

"What do you think happened to the gun, Richard? What *could* have happened to it?"

"I don't know. Nobody ever knew; God knows they looked for it—tore the house apart. But the disappearance of the gun was our big argument. It saved her life. Otherwise she'd have got the death sentence."

His voice was hard and dry. He'd lived with the thing, turning it over and over in his mind, twisting it around, seeking loopholes. He was silent for a moment. She knew his mind was groping back into that dark and ugly labyrinth of Alice's trial and conviction. He said at last, "I was right when I said there is no past. It's still here; it may hurt you sometimes. I'll try to prevent it. I may not always be able to. But there's the future, Myra. For you and me."

So easy, so easy to say yes! Two lives instead of one; she and Richard on one side of the balance—Alice, frail and delicate and lovely, on the other. Alice's life was a living waste, in any case. It had been so since the night she had killed Jack Manders. There was nothing that Richard or any of them could do about that; so why not take the happiness that offered itself for her, for Richard?

He put his arms around her, hard and tight again, defiantly really, and she clung to him, allowing herself one moment out of time.

But the defiance admitted the truth.

"No.

"Why not? There's no reason . . ."

"Because you are you, Richard. If you were not I couldn't love you so much."

" 'I could not love thee, dear, so much, loved I not honor more?' " quoted Richard and laughed abruptly. And quite suddenly sobered and said flatly, "Well, all right then. This is to be all, is it, Myra? For all our lives? I can't come to see you, you know."

"No."

"We can't even meet in town, drive, have dinner together."

A sense of recklessness caught her with swift argument. It was not possible, it was not right, to give up everything life promised. She cried, "We'll see each other. Sometimes . . ."

His arms tightened again around her. Over his shoulder she could see the evening star which was very bright now; a segment of sky was blue. In the far distance the peepers made a high shrill music. The scent of the spring night and of the sea lay all around them. She thought, this moment is mine. I can be sure of this.

Yet, it was farewell, too.

Richard lifted his head and looked at her slowly in the soft dusk and kissed her. The bright evening star and the tranquil darkening sky, the sound of the peepers and the scent of the spring night all drifted together and there was only the man who held her as if he would never let her go.

But he did let her go. And, as she stood there, holding to him, knowing that whatever he decided, whatever he said at that moment she would not have the will to resist, he said, "It's no good, Myra. I suppose I knew it from the beginning. There's not a chance for us. Where's the dog? Oh, yes, come on, Willie." He whistled and the little dog scrambled into sight. Richard said slowly, "If we can't marry, we can't see each other. You should have a rich and full life, everything. Not in any sense a half life, a surreptitious, shoddy kind of thing. It's not good enough for you. I think . . ." he paused, studying the sandy path at his feet. Finally he went on, "I think if I asked you to, now, you'd undertake that kind of life. You're so good, Myra, and so generous. I think you'd take the secret, hidden kind of thing that would enable us to meet—at little quiet restaurants, hoping nobody we know would see us, a drive together along the country roads, hoping we'd not meet somebody who knew my car, who might catch a glimpse of you. 'There's Thorne—the man whose wife is in prison for life. Who's the woman with him? Myra Lane!' Everywhere we went, everything we did would be suddenly an evil sort of thing, distorted, not as we want it to be. You're not a worldly person. I don't think you realize what it would mean to both of us, but mainly to you. I've seen more of the world and of men and women than you have. You can't have that sort of life. You're too good for it. And I love you."

"Do you mean I'm never to see you again?"

He said quietly, "Not like this. I ought not to have kept you down here so long. It's cold and it's late." He slipped his hand under her arm again and turned her toward the house.

"But Richard . . ."

"You were right; I was wrong."

They reached the path through the trees. How could this be the end of love? The end of Richard. The end of Myra.

Dried pine needles rustled under their feet along the path. A feathery branch touched her cheek like a ghostly hand. But everything was said. In that short time every argument had been advanced, every possible course explored.

She had to leave. Well, she'd known that from the beginning.

But suddenly, walking across the lawn now, with the lights of the house ahead of her, she thought: Richard loves me.

Nothing could take that from her. It was like the promise of a rock to cling to in a storm, a fire to warm her heart. If she never saw him again in her life, never touched his hand in greeting, never listened for the sound of his footsteps, she'd have that, always.

Richard had stopped. He caught her suddenly by the arm and pulled her around to face him. "Listen, Myra," he said. "We've covered everything. We've argued against ourselves, we've talked and talked and none of it's any good. I suppose we had to talk and argue it out—if only to see how wrong we were."

"Wrong?"

"Dead wrong," said Richard. He laughed with a swift exultance and cried, "None of it is valid against you and me! There's just one thing that's really important. I'm going to marry you."

He shook her a little, his face white against the night. "Do you understand? We're going to marry."

His gaze was caught by something beyond her. He was staring up at the house. He cried, "All those lights! What the hell?" He broke off. He let her go and ran across the dark lawn. She followed. Willie scrambled after her. The house was ablaze with lights; they streamed out upon the terrace.

They reached the steps, Richard ahead. He was still ahead when he came to the French doors into the library and flung one of them open.

A woman was sitting in the ruby chair near the fire. She had tossed a fur coat on the table. She was smiling.

Her golden hair shone in the light. The fire crackled softly. She put back her head and said in a clear, high voice, "Darling, I've come back. I'll never leave you again."

It was, of course, Alice.

CHAPTER 5

If Richard moved or spoke Myra did not know it. She was vaguely aware of someone else in the room, too, a man who rose and came forward. She was vaguely aware of the fact, too, that he was speaking. She heard, or at least sensed, no words. Her whole consciousness was taken up with Alice. Alice's presence in that room. Her small face, her wistful, tired smile. Her fragile beauty.

She could not be there! It was unreal; it was a dream; it could not be true.

It was true.

There was the ruby-red chair in which Myra had sat so short a time ago. There were the papers and the mail Barton had placed on the table. The fire had been replenished and was burning brightly. She had an impulse to touch the table, touch something real and material—the fur coat that lay across the table was real, too; mink, in soft luxurious folds, tossed there by an accustomed hand. How had Alice had a mink coat in prison? Had it been stored somewhere? She had a sudden vision of Alice taking walks in a prison yard wrapped in mink. It was so sharply fantastic that it acted as a restorative. She roused from the first sense of incredulity. Alice had come home; Alice was sitting in the red chair that so set off her beauty; her fair head was dropping back wearily against it, her pansy brown eyes luminous and soft as if full of unshed tears. The man, the strange man in the room was talking. He was coming toward Richard, his hand out. Willie, pushing at her ankles, uttered a soft growl, and crept under a chair.

Richard still had not moved. The strange man, big and jovial in appearance, except for his shrewd and rather cold eyes, was smiling but looked nervous. Myra began to take in words. ". . . am sorry I could not have prepared you for it, Thorne. But it seemed the more merciful way for us to come as secretly and quickly as we could. Mrs. Thorne has suffered too much already from public pillory. I did stop as we came through the village and tried to phone to you but the man who answered said you were out. So we came on." Richard's hand moved as if he had no awareness of it. The big man pumped it up and down.

Alice's voice was as high and sweet as a canary's. She said, "He means I'm free, Richard. He brought me here himself."

Myra would not have said that she could have remembered Alice so accurately. It had been at least six years since she had seen her and then only briefly. But she did remember every curve of her fine, delicately featured face, her round white throat, her soft golden hair, drawn back now from her white low forehead to a large bun on the back of her neck. She wore somber black which set off the lovely curves of her figure against the red chair, and no lipstick. Her eyes looked enormous and there were shadows below them; her small soft white hands lay, palms up, helplessly along the arms of the chair; she was watching Richard.

The big man said quickly, "Webb Manders confessed to perjury this morning. His testimony against your wife was a lie and he has signed a confession to that effect. Consequently, legally, the basis for your wife's conviction was fraudulent. Thank God it lay within my power as Governor to free her, quickly and quietly. I cannot right a great and tragic injustice that was done; but I have done everything within my power to correct it." He stopped and looked at Alice and said rather gently, "Perhaps you'd better take her upstairs, Thorne. She has been through an exhausting experience."

"Yes," said Alice. "Yes."

Richard seemed still unable to move. The Governor said, "Take her, Thorne. I'll explain everything when you come down again. But first see to her. . . ."

Alice rose then, unsteadily, her small hands clinging now to the chair. She said, "My own home. My husband . . ." and held out her hands appealingly, like a child, looking up at Richard.

There was an instant of silence in the room.

Then Richard moving like an automaton went toward her.

His broad shoulders blocked out the view of Alice. The Governor cleared his throat. But Alice did not put her arms up around Richard. He did not bend toward her. Myra wished to look away and could not. Alice slid her arm through Richard's and said in her high, sweet voice, unsteadly now, as if near collapse, "Richard, I—I can't believe it. It seems like a miracle . . ."

The Governor cleared his throat again and said, "I don't want to suggest—I suppose the family doctor—that is, she's not ill, of course, but . . ."

"No, no," said Alice. "I'll be all right. She moved and turned and Myra could see her now, leaning against Richard. Her small lovely face was very white. She said unsteadily, "I can't thank you, Governor. I can't tell you . . ."

"No need," said the Governor gruffly. "No need. Just take care of yourself, dear Mrs. Thorne. Get some roses back in those cheeks. Try to forget. And don't worry about anything. We'll do everything we can about the newspapers. We've kept them out of it so far. No tears now . . ."

She smiled. Her gaze fell on the fur coat. She said, "Tell your wife that her kindness in sending her own coat for me to wear was almost more than I could bear."

"Now, now," said the Governor warningly, smiling. "You've been very brave. No tears."

"I won't cry," said Alice. "I'm too happy." Her soft brown eyes went slowly all around the room, touching every object caressingly. Her gaze reached Myra and fixed itself with a kind of start for an instant and then she said with an apologetic gasp, "Oh, Myra! I didn't realize you were there—I only saw Richard."

The Governor said kindly, "You'd better not talk now; get her to rest, Thorne . . ."

Alice said, "Oh, yes. Yes, I'll rest. My own room again, no bars, no keys . . ." her voice choked. She turned toward the door leaning heavily upon Richard. There was another moment of silence in the room—it was so still that Myra could hear the light swish of Alice's somber yet modish black gown as they walked together to the doorway. Richard did not look back. It was as if Richard were not there at all but a perfectly strange person who moved in Richard's body. They disappeared and Myra's hand was stiff and cramped from holding so tightly to the curtains beside her and the room seemed, in spite of the lights and the fire, extraordi-

narily chill and empty. Then the Governor cleared his throat
again, got out his handkerchief, blew his nose loudly and
looked at Myra.

"That woman's an angel. Very near collapse, I'm afraid,
but too much courage to admit it. However, she'll be all
right now." His eyes sharpened. "See here. Don't you collapse! You'd better sit down." He came quickly to Myra and
led her to Richard's arm chair and put her down in it, talking rapidly. "Good news can be almost as much of a shock
as bad news. Lean back, Miss—er—lean back. Maybe you'd
better have a drink. I could use one myself. Where's the bell?
I'm sorry it had to come as such a shock to everybody, but
the way things were it seemed impossible to do otherwise if
I was to spare you all further notoriety. Now then, Miss—
er—" He was looking around vaguely for the bell.

Myra said, "Lane. It's there beside the door."

"Oh, yes. Yes, I see." He started toward it, stopped suddenly midway, shot her a sharp look and said, "Lane? Is your
name Lane?"

Myra's voice seemed dragged up from some deep distance,
flat and still, without tone or resonance. "Myra Lane."

"Lane," said the Governor. "Well!" He turned, went
quickly to the bell and pushed it and came back to stand before her, his back to the fire. "Are you," he said, "any rela-
tion to Timothy Lane?"

A faraway wonder touched her. What did he know of
Tim?

"He is my brother."

"Your brother!" began the Governor on a note of astonishment and stopped and stared. "Do you live here?"

Again a voice not her own seemed to reply for Myra. "No
—that is, yes, I do just now." His shrewd sharp eyes questioned. She said, "I live with Aunt Cornelia, Lady Carmichael."

His face cleared. "Oh, yes, she was Cornelia Thorne. I do
recall now that someone said she had come back from England to keep house for Dick Thorne."

His eyes were again bright and sharp with question. "I
didn't realize that your brother and you are related to the
Thornes."

She had to speak; she had to reply; she had to explain.

"Oh, we are not. We only call her Aunt. My mother was a

friend of Lady Carmichael's. She died when I was sixteen. I have lived with Lady Carmichael since then."

"I see. In England?"

"Yes, until last fall when we came here."

"I see." He paused thoughtfully and then said: "What about your brother? He went to school here, didn't he?"

"Yes. That is, until he was eighteen. He went directly from school into the army." Why was he talking so much of Timothy? What of Alice's release, her exoneration, her return?

The Governor waited for a moment, with a rather curious look of mingled question and reflection in his face and, in the short silence, Barton came from the hall door. His face was flabby and white with shock, his eyes excited. "You rang, Miss Myra?"

"No," said the Governor. "I rang. I think we could do with a drink, if you please." He looked at Myra. "I think I'd suggest a little brandy for Miss Lane. I'll take a whisky and soda if you'll be so good."

"Yes, sir," said Barton. "Yes, sir." His voice was breathless. He gave Myra an excited look, wavered indecisively in the doorway, said, "Yes, sir. I'll bring it at once," and went away. Willie, puzzled, his tail dejected, crawled out from somewhere and followed Barton soberly.

"Shock to your butler, too," said the Governor. "I thought he'd have a stroke when he opened the door and saw Mrs. Thorne.

"So you're Timothy Lane's sister. Look here, then, you were not in America at the time"—he waved in a broad gesture around the room—"the time all this happened?"

With an effort again, Myra replied. "No. We were still in England. Aunt Cornelia wished to come as soon as she knew; she'd had an accident and couldn't."

"I see. I was sure that neither of you was here at the time of the trial. I was then the prosecuting attorney, you know. Well." He was silent for a moment again, staring at the rug, rubbing his hands together absently.

Alice free; Alice exonerated; Alice at home to stay. What were they saying upstairs, Richard and Alice?

The Governor said suddenly, "I didn't know that you were Tim Lane's sister. I think you'd better know the whole story of Mrs. Thorne's pardon."

Timothy again. This time the allusion was too pointed to

avoid. She said abruptly, "What has Timothy to do with it?"

"Everything," said the Governor gravely. Richard came down the stairs and across the hall. The Governor said, "Well, Thorne. I've taken the liberty of asking your butler to bring me a drink."

Richard was dazed, too. Richard must have the same sense that she had of moving through a dream. He was very white, too; he gave her one swift glance that still did not seem to see her.

He replied to the Governor, in the kind of voice, Myra thought again, she had heard in her own throat, flat and queer, without resonance or meaning.

"That's quite right, sir." He looked around. "Where is it?"

"He's getting it now. I expect you want to know exactly how the thing happened. Did your wife tell you anything of it?"

"She's very tired. A maid is with her." It was as if a stranger spoke, not Richard. He came to stand beside the Governor, his elbow on the mantel. Even his face seemed withdrawn and remote, without emotion or the capacity for emotion. The Governor said, "I'll give it to you quickly, in a nutshell. Webb Manders, as I told you, has confessed to perjury. Consequently your wife's conviction was due to fraud."

"Webb lied!"

"Yes. Thus, in fact, she was, well, framed. She was wrongly and illegally imprisoned. He now admits that he did not see your wife shoot Jack Manders, and that he lied when he said that he did. He has signed a statement to that effect."

"Webb admits perjury!"

"Right."

"But she'd never have gone to prison if it hadn't been for his testimony."

"Exactly. The case against her, except for that, was merely and barely circumstantial. *With* his testimony those circumstances appeared corroborative; *without* his testimony the prosecution had no real case. I know," said the Governor. "I was then the prosecuting attorney, as you'll remember. Nobody knows the case better than I. She'd never have been convicted without the eye-witness testimony of Webb Manders. With it there was a case; without it . . ." He shrugged. "Since it was admitted perjury that sent your wife to prison it was my obvious duty on the facts of the case to pardon her, as quickly and as quietly as possible."

"When . . ." began Richard, but the Governor went on quickly, "She had suffered greatly from publicity. I was determined to avoid any more of that. Telephones, telegrams—somehow, too often, there is a leak. The important thing was to get her out and home, quickly and above all things quietly. I sent for the present district attorney who agreed with me. I wrote out her pardon. My wife, who was the only other person besides myself and the district attorney who knew what I had decided to do, sent a veil and a warm coat along with me in the car. I had my chauffeur take me to Auburn. The warden's integrity and discretion are unquestionable. I told him the whole story. He went himself to bring her to his office. Together we managed to get her out of the place without another soul knowing it. I realized that this would be a shock to you, Thorne; but it would be, in any event, and it seemed to me I had no right to run the risk of photographers at the prison gate, headlines, all that sort of thing." He paused and eyed Richard thoughtfully. "I hope you think I took the right course."

"Yes," said Richard. "Yes."

"We'll have to release a statement, of course. But now that she is safely at home you can take proper measures to protect her."

"Yes," said Richard again.

Barton appeared in the doorway, a tray in his hands, hesitated and came forward.

The Governor said, "It will be only the nine days' wonder of publicity that might really be troublesome to her. My own position is, of course," he paused and his mouth tightened rather grimly, "different. There'll be a field day, especially in the opposition press. However, I followed the only right and possible course, although there'll be plenty who'll say that your money, Thorne, bought her pardon." He paused again for a reflective instant. The grim, obstinate look in his face deepened. He shrugged. "I suppose many men in my place would have delayed, had a hearing, publicized the thing. But that's not my way. Law is law; justice is justice. It is my duty both morally and legally to undo a moral and legal wrong. And I've never been one to let the grass grow under my feet. The papers will be after me, all of them in full cry; but I think I can tackle them. And you can take every possible measure, Thorne, to protect your wife. The police may be obliged to question her but they'll make it easy on her.

"Police!" said Richard sharply.

The tray clattered as Barton put it down on a table.

The Governor said, "Why, yes. Police."

"Do you mean that the case is re-opened?"

"Why, yes!" said the Governor again. "Jack Manders was murdered. Your wife didn't kill him. But somebody did." The big man's shrewd bright eyes went thoughtfully around the room once and came back to fix upon the terrace doors, and then the door into the wide hall. "Somebody stood there —or there—and shot him."

Ice tinkled sharply in the glass in Barton's hands; usually his hands were silent and steady. A log fell with a kind of sigh and sent up a shower of sparks. The Governor's shrewd bright eyes came back to Richard.

"So who was it?" he asked.

CHAPTER 6

The sharp agitated tinkle of ice against glass approached Myra. She was aware of Barton standing beside her, glasses on a small silver waiter. "That one is brandy, Miss," he said. "That one." His voice was unsteady, too, like his hands. She took it, only half conscious of her action. The butler moved on to the Governor. Richard said slowly, "Let me get the straight of this, sir. Is there to be a new trial?"

"Thank you." The Governor looked up directly at Richard. "There will never be another trial for your wife. But naturally her pardon automatically re-opens the case. There will be a renewed investigation; there must be. As I say, somebody killed Jack Manders. Owing to the peculiar and very regrettable circumstances, at my request, the district attorney will take no steps until tomorrow. When he discovers the murderer, naturally there will be another trial for the real murderer, but not for Mrs. Thorne."

"Alice . . ."

"Your wife, Thorne, is unconditionally free. She could never under any possible circumstances be forced to undergo another trial for the murder of Manders. That is the law; she cannot be placed in double jeopardy. A pardon in this instance acts the same as an acquittal. But if I had not been convinced of the illegality and injustice of her conviction I should not have pardoned her. And, to tell you the truth, Thorne, while Webb Manders' testimony was the keystone of my case as prosecutor and it seemed to me then right that she should be convicted, at the same time it did, shall I say, surprise me. I had no doubts of your wife's guilt, but at the same time, instinctively I felt a certain astonishment. I could not reconcile what appeared to be an established fact with my own estimate of your wife's character. It was wrong psychologically, yet God knows a lawyer is only too well accustomed to the infinite variations of the human mind and motives. Her guilt seemed to be a proven fact. I accepted it as such." He drank and said, "You'd better let me give you the details. Miss Lane, too. It was, as a matter of fact, her brother who started the thing."

"Tim!" cried Richard.

"Yes. Timothy Lane. If you don't mind . . ." The Governor glanced around and went to sit in the ruby-red arm chair. He looked extraordinarily big and bulky and powerful sitting there, leaning forward a little, holding his glass in large square fingers. He sighed. "I've got to drive back to Albany tonight. I'll make it brief. Tim Lane came to me yesterday with a—a remarkable story."

"Tim!" cried Richard incredulously again.

Myra's hands were holding hard to the arms of her chair. "But Tim knew nothing about the murder!" she cried. "That is, he knew so little. He saw Webb drive past him toward the house. He heard the shots. But when he reached this room it was all over. He could only tell what he saw then."

"But that," said the Governor slowly, "was very important. Wait, Miss Lane. Let's go back to the night of the murder. You were not here and do not know . . ."

"I saw all the papers. I talked to Tim when he reached England. He knew nothing more than he told . . ."

The Governor put up a hand in a protesting way. "If you please, my dear. We'll talk about your brother's motives in a moment. Indeed—" again the rather grim and obstinate look settled about his mouth—"indeed we must talk of them. But just now I want you to go back to the story Tim told at the time of the murder."

"Tim corroborated Webb's testimony," said Richard. "What has he done now?"

"I'll tell you. Tim came to me yesterday, in the afternoon, late. I remembered his name, of course. He wouldn't say why he wanted to see me—which was just as well. I have a good staff but there are always leaks—at any rate I saw him. He looked rather ill and nervous, sat there twisting his hat and told me a remarkable story. You'll remember his story of the night of the murder."

"Every word of it," Richard said. "He was coming here to spend his last week-end before he went to England with his unit. He met Webb Manders on the train. He'd been drinking a little with the other kids. Webb offered to drive him here, but he said he'd walk, thinking he'd sober up. So Webb went off presumably to the Manders' place—and then a short time later came here."

The Governor was nodding. "Exactly. Webb's story was that he got home, Jack wasn't there, he thought Jack might have come here, and drove back here, passing Tim somewhere along your drive. Tim saw the car; Webb saw Tim in the glow of the car lights but didn't stop."

Myra had read the newspaper accounts over and over; she had never heard the facts told, like that, and suddenly the black and white newspaper print seemed unreal. It was as if she heard, for the first time, the real background for that dark and ugly happening. Perhaps none of it had actually seemed real until now—except Alice and Alice's house.

But what had Tim said? *What had he done?*

The Governor said, "Then, of course, as Tim was walking along the drive, following Webb's car, which, however, had disappeared around the curve and gone on rapidly ahead of him, he heard the shots. He ran toward the house, as you know; got over the wall out there and through the shrubbery and got to the terrace door, over there," said the Governor jerking his head toward the French doors. "And here was

Jack Manders on the floor," unconsciously, it seemed to Myra, he motioned toward the hearth rug, almost at their feet. "Mrs. Thorne had already gone to the hall at Webb's request to phone for the police. Webb—and this is the crux of the thing—Webb was then bending over Jack. That was the picture according to Tim, then, and Webb agreed in every detail. Room empty except for Webb, bending over his dead brother. Mrs. Thorne in the hall at the telephone. Now then . . ."

He paused and drank. The room, the whole house waited, as if it had ears, as if it could hear and waited, listening, to compare the words for which it waited with the truth it knew.

The Governor said abruptly, frowning, "Yesterday young Lane changed that picture. Well, I'll show you." He got up, glanced sharply around the room again as if identifying every detail of its arrangement and furnishings. Then he walked to the other end of the room. There were low bookshelves there with two wide but low windows above them, which were curtained with crimson like the French windows almost directly opposite them. The big man went to the curtains and put his hand on the cord, and looked back at Myra and Richard.

"At the time of the investigation we went over and over the exact layout of this room. I remembered it perfectly yesterday as soon as Tim Lane started to talk. Built out at the end of the house," he said, gesturing with the hand that held the glass, "hall door in the middle, low bookshelves and short windows here, bookshelves all along that wall, then the French doors and the fireplace near which Manders fell, exactly there. The big point, of course, was that Manders claimed to have been walking along the driveway in the direction of the front door when he heard the first shot. He says he thought it came from this room. He stood on tiptoes and could see through *this window*. Thus, he said, he saw Mrs. Thorne with the revolver in her hand—saw, in fact, the murder." He paused and looked at the window.

Richard said in a strained, tight voice, "And he lied?"

"Wait," said the Governor. "Hear me out. He said it was quicker to run around the end of the house than to go along to the front door and back the length of the hall to the library. At least that's what he did. He climbed over that low wall out there, got through the shrubbery and ran up the

steps onto the terrace and reached the French doors—there."
Again he moved his hand, gesturing toward the terrace
doors. "He said that by that time the shots had stopped; they
were in very quick succession naturally; he said that when
he entered the room Mrs. Thorne was kneeling beside Jack
Manders."

Another person was suddenly in the room—two other
people. Alice, in a thin white dress leaning over a huddled
figure of a man on the hearth rug. A thin white dress, Richard had said, with blood on the front of it.

Richard, of course, remembered every small detail. To
Myra it had a new and poignant clarity. Jack Manders was a
man, not merely a name in black and white. Yet she had
known him slightly; she could remember even now his florid,
rather heavily handsome face, his curly black hair, barely
touched with gray, his easy smile. He'd been a tall man,
heavy, good-natured, popular with men. Apparently he'd
had no enemies. Why should anybody shoot him? The only
conceivable motive was the one they had attributed to Alice.

Richard moved, reached for a cigarette, held it in his hand
and forgot to light it. The Governor went on, very precisely,
"Webb's story was that he thought first of a doctor; he hoped
Jack was not dead. He told Mrs. Thorne to go and phone for
the doctor and she got up and went into the hall to do so.
And then he knelt down beside his brother and was trying
to find a pulse when he realized that Tim had come to the
French doors too, and was standing there staring at the scene.
You remember all this, Thorne. But I have to recapitulate in
order to explain to you . . ."

"Go on," said Richard.

"Well, then. According to Tim's (and Webb's) original testimony Tim said, 'What is it? What's happened?' or words to
that effect; Webb replied that Jack was killed. He then told
Tim they must get a doctor and the police. He did not then
accuse Mrs. Thorne—which now is very important. He did
not, in fact, accuse her until after Tim and Mrs. Thorne had
both been questioned and both were on record with their
first, and, as a matter of fact, in both cases, fixed testimonies.
Neither Tim nor Mrs. Thorne changed a word that was important after that first inquiry—until yesterday."

He paused for an instant again. Strangely, in that instant,
the blue paneled walls, the yellow daffodils, the red curtains,

seemed clearer and sharper. Every detail of the room seemed to pick itself out with a clarity and poignancy that were almost painful. Richard's hands were rolling the little white cigarette, twisting it; bits of tobacco fell to the hearth rug.

The Governor said, "Obviously Tim did not realize when he first put himself on record that there was any question of Mrs. Thorne's being accused of the murder. He ran into the hall, found her collapsed at the telephone, took her into the dining room to get her out of the way. It was the nearest room. The police came; they got his statement. Well, the point is, as I told you, the original first picture is changed in an important factor. Some of it remains the same. Mrs. Thorne was at the phone, Jack was dead, there before the fireplace. Webb was in the room. But Tim now says that when he reached the terrace door—wait, I'll show you."

Barton had pulled the curtains together. Now, with a sweep, the Governor opened the heavy crimson curtain. "Webb was not bending over Jack. He was instead in the very act of opening this curtain."

Richard said nothing. The Governor turned and the two men looked at each other across the room, for a long moment. Then the Governor said, "You see what this means."

"Yes," said Richard. His voice was strange, flat and harsh; not like Richard. "Yes."

"It means," said the Governor, "that Webb Manders on the driveway outside these windows *could not* have seen what he claimed later to have seen."

The cigarette crumbled up in Richard's hands. He said, "Webb decided instantly to accuse Alice."

"Yes. Tim says that Webb released the curtain and came, running, to bend over Jack. Tim entered the room. The rest of the story is exactly the same, except in that one detail. But that detail proved Webb had lied." He released the cord of the crimson curtain and came back toward them. "Now, then. First I had to examine young Lane's motives in coming to me with this extraordinary story. And his good faith—or lack of it. I did not know whether or not to believe him. I questioned him; he said he had forgotten the incident of the curtain. I found it difficult to believe that he would have forgotten it. Yet he stuck to the new version of his testimony with such earnestness that I could not fail to test its truth—as I did. I sent for Webb Manders."

He put his glass on the table and sat down and with his hands on his knees looked up at Richard. "I sent for Webb. I kept young Lane waiting. I saw Webb alone. In the interval I had time to think the thing over; it seemed to me that if there was a word of truth in young Lane's present story, there was only one way to extract it from Webb. When Webb arrived I told him flatly that I had evidence to the effect that the curtains had been closed when he claimed to have seen into this room. I made it strong. I told him that this being the fact, the case was automatically re-opened for investigation and that" —the Governor's voice was hard and sharp—"since he had perjured himself, it might go easier with him later if he'd admit the truth then and there. He saw at once that he himself would be suspect, in the event of a new investigation. He saw, in fact, the whole picture. And, to my surprise, I must say, admitted it to be a fact. Tim was telling the truth."

Richard started to speak and stopped. The Governor's eyes were very shrewd and very keen. He watched Richard and said rather slowly, "There is no doubt that it is the truth. I took Webb by surprise. He could not, or, at least, did not, think of a way out of it; and it is a fact that truth is a powerful weapon. In my experience in criminal trials there is often a psychological moment when the sheer weight of truth operates. It did in this case. To make it short, he signed a confession of perjury before he left my office."

"That means," said Richard, "that he did it purposely. He decided to accuse her; he arranged the curtains to fit the story he decided to tell."

"That's right."

"Why? How could he have deliberately planned to send her to . . .?" Richard stopped and the Governor finished, ". . . to the chair. It was a frame. Nothing more or less. Webb says he did it because he believed in her guilt. Because he saw that his brother was dead. Because he wished to make it absolutely impossible for her to escape conviction. He said —then and yesterday—that he waited for a few hours before he accused her because she might confess. When she didn't he accused her, because he believed she was guilty. I think," said the Governor heavily, "that he might be honest enough about that. Provided, that is, he did not shoot his brother himself. As I said, his own position as a possible suspect was an inducement to his confession of perjury. He knew his danger, had known it all along, and hoped to induce a more lenient view on our part."

"It could have cost . . ."

Again Richard stopped. Again the Governor finished for
him. "It could have cost her life. But if he is honest in saying
that he sincerely believed in her guilt, that is a comprehensible
motive for his accusation of Mrs. Thorne, both because Jack
was his brother and he may have wished to avenge him, and
because of his own sense of justice. If actually *he* killed his
brother, then it is even more easily understood as a motive for
his lie for Mrs. Thorne's conviction would automatically save
Webb."

"Did he do it?"

The Governor did not reply for a moment and, when he
did, his manner had changed. Up to then, except for the extremely searching look in his eyes when he watched Richard,
his manner had been open and candid; there was now a certain reservation. Yet his words were frank enough. "I don't
know. I'm inclined to believe not. Yet certainly we are right
up against the whole question again. If Mrs. Thorne didn't kill
him, who did?"

Suddenly Myra wondered if Richard too had sensed that
rather ominous change in the Governor's manner. She
thought that he had, for Richard's own face seemed to close
up. His voice, too, had a certain reservation. He said, "There
were not many suspects."

"No," said the Governor so deliberately that there was a
kind of indefinable significance in his tone. "No, there were
not many suspects. I should say there are not many suspects."

After a moment Richard said almost as deliberately,
"Along what lines will the investigation proceed?"

"The usual lines, I should say." Again there was an element
of reservation, almost of evasion, in the Governor's manner;
yet again his words were prompt and apparently frank. "Opportunity, means, motive."

"I see. Presence in or near the house, possession of the gun
. . ."

"Your gun," said the Governor.

"My gun," agreed Richard. "But what about a motive? Has
anything new developed in that direction?— If I may ask?"

"Certainly you may ask," said the Governor. "There
is nothing new. Indeed, there was never a proved motive to

attribute to Mrs. Thorne. The obvious one, indeed, the only one that seemed logical at the time was, well, an affair, a very serious affair, between them and a quarrel. As you'll remember there were instances which seemed to support that theory. Oh, it's true, there was never a letter, a scrap of paper, a witness of anything that was"—he cleared his throat and seemed to substitute words—"a witness of any particular value or significance. But there were, as I say, instances. He was an intimate friend; he was frequently seen with your wife and with you; he was a constant visitor here at your house." He put up his hand as if to prevent Richard's speaking, and added quickly, "Oh, I realize that this could have been the most ordinary and innocent of friendships. There was nothing to suggest anything else except the circumstances of the murder itself. His presence here at night when you were away seemed, in view of the murder, very significant. Webb's false testimony to the effect that he had seen the murder seemed to clinch it. Yet actually it could have been exactly as she said. Jack had strolled over here simply because he was alone, because he wanted to chat, he wanted a book to read. It was Webb's testimony, Webb's perjury, that gave the fact significance."

Richard said slowly, "What about Webb?"

"What does the district attorney intend to do, you mean? Well, he's to be charged for perjury, of course. He's to have until tomorrow to get his affairs in order. I promised him that. What happens later depends upon the progress of the investigation, upon Webb himself, the district attorney, the jury."

Richard tossed the shredded white ball of the cigarette into the fire. The Governor sighed and sat down in the red chair again and said, "Now Tim is a different problem. It is difficult to believe that he forgot, until now, so important a fact. Yet, if he did not forget, if he intentionally withheld it until now, why?" He turned directly to Myra. "I cannot believe that he'd wish to hurt Mrs. Thorne. I think, on the contrary, he would have lied to save her if he had been able to do so. Maybe I'm wrong. I don't know the boy. But he impressed me as the kind of youngster who'd act impulsively—and perhaps more chivalrously than truthfully. But in this case it's reversed. If he'd told the bare truth in the first place, including this very important detail he claims to have forgotten until now, Webb could not have gotten anywhere in accusing Mrs. Thorne."

Richard said, "Tim wouldn't knowingly have injured Alice or me."

"But he did substantiate Webb's story. He has now recanted. His claim that he forgot Webb's opening of that curtain is very difficult to believe. And if it is not the real reason for his inconsistency, what is the reason?" A kindness which rang sincere and regretful crept into his voice. "I've been thinking about this all the way over here, trying to get every angle on it. I don't want to be too hard on the boy—nobody does. And there's been a cruel injustice already in this case. I cannot have that repeated in any sense. I like the boy; he seemed to me honest. But if there's something there that he's not told me, what is it?"

He paused as if Myra already knew or could guess what that something was. And she would not guess. She would not follow the path of his reasoning. She would not look ahead to the precipice to which it led.

Yet she knew its nature.

Richard knew it, too. He moved over to stand beside her.

The Governor said, "I said that there are only a few suspects. I cannot overlook the fact that Tim *might* have come to the house sooner than anyone knows; that he certainly had countless opportunities to take the gun. I cannot suggest a motive. But conscience," said the big man slowly, "is a very powerful force. As irresistible and almost as explosive as gun powder."

"Tim Lane didn't kill Jack," said Richard.

The Governor said, "No. I don't think he did. But I don't think Webb killed his own brother, either. And if by any chance—mind you, I'm only saying *if*—young Lane did kill him, it would explain a lie in the first place. It would explain his coming to me now, in remorse, trying to get Mrs. Thorne released without actually making a confession to murder himself. Certainly the murder was unpremeditated; certainly it was the result of a quick and unexpected impulse; all the circumstances point to that. If Tim did it, if he seized the first story that came into his head to clear himself, if he felt then he had to stick to it, if even—I'm only saying if—he felt that no jury would convict a woman of Mrs. Thorne's position, beauty, wealth and all that, therefore, she was in no real danger, if indeed that aspect of the case, that is, the possibility of Mrs. Thorne's being accused, did not so much as occur to him at that moment and, as I say, later he was afraid to retract his first statement . . ." he shrugged. "If some or any of these suppositions are correct, it would explain everything. Manders was murdered. The only three people we know to have been on the spot are Mrs. Thorne, Webb Manders and"—he looked at Myra again—"and your brother, Miss Lane."

CHAPTER 7 ▪

So that was the precipice at her feet, unhidden. Myra said, "Tim couldn't have done that," and knew that her words to the big man watching her were mere words, what he had expected.

Richard said, quickly and forcefully, "Look here, sir. I know that boy. I've known him since he was really a kid. He's been coming to this house for school vacations, weekends, since he was thirteen or so. This was like home; he had no other home. My aunt, years ago, took both Myra and Tim under her wing. She took Myra to London with her; she put Tim in school here . . ."

"I know," said the Governor nodding gravely. "Miss Lane told me."

"Oh. Well, the point is, I really know Tim. He's incapable of murder. And even," cried Richard hotly, "if Tim could murder, as he couldn't, he would never knowingly give evidence involving Alice." He checked himself abruptly as if he realized that reason was of more force than angry denial. He went on more quietly and very seriously. "I wish you could know Tim as I know him, sir. There's not a mean or a cowardly shred in him. The thing you've suggested is simply all out of line with his character. I tell you, I know him."

"You are also prejudiced, Thorne," said the Governor. "I liked the boy myself, but at the same time—well, in war things happened. People react very differently and very—

unexpectedly. Nerve strain does odd things, especially to a youngster. It's one of the ugliest parts of war that our youngsters take so much of the rap. But that's beside the point, just now, too, except that—well, say a boy of Tim's nature, rather nervous, I should say, high strung, his whole present and future swept up by something he doesn't wholly understand, his entire outlook and thoughts turned from—well, football and tennis to war and killing. It seems to me, frankly, that almost anything in the way of unexpected reactions might occur."

Richard shook his head. "Not murder. Not lying to save himself at the expense of my wife. Not Tim."

The Governor's heavy shoulders lifted. "In that case, Webb Manders would be, so far, an alternate suspect. Do you really believe that he did it?"

Richard said slowly, "I'd be far readier to believe him capable of it than Tim."

"Capable of killing his own brother? That's a very terrible thing to believe, Thorne."

"Murder is terrible," said Richard. He stood for a moment, deep in thought, and then turned to Myra. "Look here," he said, "shall I ring up Sam Putnam?"

Sam Putnam, of course, was the lawyer who had defended Alice. If Richard wanted to call him, then it was really serious, really true, Myra thought with a kind of inner gasp of horror. The Governor said, "That's a good idea. I'd advise that—if you don't mind my saying so. I've got to get started back home. It's been a long day." He got up, shaking his trouser legs down and sighing wearily. He said, "Miss Lane—Thorne—I do want you to understand that I am not accusing young Lane. Or anyone . . ." A rather curious look came into his face, something shrewd and hard and implacable. ". . . or anyone," he said, looking at Richard, "just now. I don't intend to have another miscarriage of justice. Certainly I don't want anybody charged merely to present the public with a murderer. But I do want the investigation to discover whoever it was that shot him. I've been frank with you about the entire situation; I owe that to you." He came to Myra and took her hand. His shrewd eyes were suddenly very kind, but also very direct and determined. "Prove that your brother didn't do it, Miss Lane. Sam Putnam is a very able man. He'd have got Mrs. Thorne acquitted if it hadn't been for Webb Manders' point-blank, eye-witness testimony. It is now—or will be tomorrow, out of my hands. I don't know what the district attorney will do, or what angles he intends to explore. But I don't want this boy to be accused if he's not guilty."

A just and righteous enemy has more power than an unjust and unrighteous one; the Governor was not an enemy, he was fair and he pitied her and he pitied Tim, but he was the opposition, he was actually just now an enemy. His eyes, set so shrewdly in his wide face were kind and honest—they were also in a sense implacable.

"Thank you . . ."

The Governor patted her hand lightly and put it down. Richard said suddenly, "This means that there'll be police again. Questions, reporters, all that."

"I'm afraid it does, Thorne."

"Beginning tomorrow?" said Richard.

"Beginning tomorrow. Now then, I think my coat is in the hall." He turned in that direction and said with a start, "Oh! Mrs. Thorne! I didn't know you were there."

Myra leaned forward to follow his look. Alice was standing at the foot of the stairs, her hand on the balustrade, the long flowing lines of her flimsy pink dressing-gown clinging to her graceful body; her face was pale and tired, her dark eyes enormous, her fair hair was hanging over her shoulders like a child's. Richard had whirled around, too. He said suddenly and rather harshly, "I thought you were resting, Alice."

"I wanted to say good-bye to the Governor." Alice came forward across the strip of hall and through the wide door into the library. She put out her hands to the Governor and said with a catch in her high, musical voice, "I can't thank you—I thought I'd try to—I can't."

"I only did what was right," said the Governor. He took her hands, though, in his big powerful clasp. He said to her, "It seemed the more urgently my duty, because in a way I owe my election to office to the fact that you were convicted."

"Oh, no . . ." said Alice.

"That intention was not in my mind," said the Governor. "It was later that I decided to run for the governorship. But because of the wide publicity of the case and perhaps because many people expected you to be acquitted owing to your youth and"—he smiled briefly—"your beauty and wealth, rather than the legal angles of the case, I was on the crest of a wave of public approval. I had prosecuted, I had secured a conviction. It was a triumph for American democracy and justice and I was the focal point of it. In a sense the hero of it. It proved in their minds that I was above bribery and coercion. Not that so far as I know you attempted to bribe anybody, Thorne. . . ."

"No," said Richard. "We did not."

"But in a rather definite sense I went to Albany because Mrs. Thorne went to Auburn. Consequently, it was the more urgently my duty, as I said, to act as I have done."

And it would increase his determination to push the investigation, thought Myra. Clearly he would have to supply the people who had put him in office with the reasons for this pardon; clearly he needed to present them with a new and this time a true conviction. And as clearly, and somehow ominously, he was obviously an honest man, almost a zealot for the law and the correct interpretation of it, and rigid in adhering to the responsibilities vested in him.

She could not but respect him and she could not but fear him, for he threatened Tim—Tim who had been, as the Governor so truly said, snatched from normal boyish interests and put to the grimly precocious business of killing. But millions of other men, young and old, had been forced by Germany and Japan, two bloody-minded nations, to undertake the same bloody business, the more merciful in direct proportion to its apparent mercilessness. It would be no just excuse for Tim. But Tim, she thought again with that quick sharp inward horror, had not murdered Jack Manders. Tim could not have placed Alice in such horrible jeopardy with a flat and cowardly lie.

Richard was talking, the Governor was talking, Alice was talking. She had not heard their words. And the Governor was on his way toward the hall. Richard was walking along beside him. Alice stood, watching them, small and defenseless, a handkerchief crumpled up tightly in one hand. Alice who had come home, whose place in that house Myra had wished to take.

In the very moment before Richard looked up and saw all the lights blazing in the house he had with a kind of passionate truth rejected all their reasons for denying their love for each other; had dismissed the whole fabric of logic by which she had refused to supplant Alice and he had agreed to it. In another moment the entire situation would have reversed itself—in another second, she would have surrendered to what seemed now the inevitable truth. She loved Richard and he loved her and that was of far greater importance to them than anything else.

But now Alice was proved to be innocent; Alice was pardoned; Alice had come home.

So it wasn't true, after all, that Myra's love for Richard and his love for her was the most important fact in their lives.

There was only one thing for her to do. Myra saw it then with pitiless clearness.

The men's voices and footsteps were receding along the hall, past the great stairway with its tall carved pineapple newel post and shining mahogany balustrade, along the floor toward the great front door which was set into an angle at the very end of the long, wide hall.

Alice said in a wondering murmur, as if to herself, "Nothing is changed. Everything's the same." She looked lingeringly all around the room and then went slowly to the bowl of lilies of the valley that Mildred Wilkinson had brought.

"Lilies," she said, half whispering.

The word and the gesture shook Myra inexpressibly. Both disclosed a vista of Alice's life during those months of unjust and horrible imprisonment. Pity made her voice unsteady. "Mildred brought them this afternoon."

Alice's fingers, almost as soft and white and fragrant-looking as the lilies, paused for a second. "Mildred . . ."

"Mildred Wilkinson."

Her profile was as delicate and fine as if it had been done in porcelain; only her long soft eyelashes moved. "Oh, yes," she said then. "Of course. Mildred." She left the lilies and went toward the daffodils as if drawn by flowers. Again the gesture was revealing in a way that made Myra's throat ache with pity.

Yet it was strange too, to feel pity for Alice—Richard's wife. For the first time, perhaps, in Myra's life she recognized the fact that a complex and contradictory blend of emotions may exist at the same moment, fighting each other, in the human heart. In the deepest sense Alice was her rival, her successful rival, returned after what amounted to martyrdom to her rightful position as Richard's wife. Myra knew that, and recognized its whole significance to herself—and at the

same time Alice's gesture toward the lilies wrenched her
heart with pity.

One should hate one's rival, instinctively; she could never
hate Alice.

Her fair hair fell forward, like a child's, over the golden
daffodils. "That's the right bowl for them. How did you
know, Myra? But I suppose Barton arranged them. Barton
would know."

"I arranged them," said Myra. "It was obviously the right
bowl."

"How clever of you to know!" Alice lifted her head and
drifted over to the tall old secretary. The key to the glittering glass doors was in a drawer and she felt for it, without
looking, took it out, unlocked the doors and swung them
open.

"There's my cupid," she said, and took out the delicate,
lovely figurine and held it, smiling a little, in her hands, turning it. She glanced at Myra. "I found him myself," she said.
"I spent far too much money for him. But isn't he charming?"
She stared at Myra and cried suddenly, almost wildly, "I can't
believe it! That I'm home, I mean! Yet . . ." Her pansy-
brown eyes sought Myra's pleadingly. "It seemed to me that
it had to happen. Some time. I felt that all the way through
the trial, through everything. At first I couldn't believe that
they'd accuse me. I couldn't seem to comprehend it. Any of
it! It was unreal, fantastic. It seemed to me that everyone
must see I could not have done that. Even in prison, day after
day and night after night, I could not understand their *not*
seeing it!" She waited a moment and said more quietly, "I
was sustained, I think, by knowing that some day they would
see how wrong they were. That the truth must come out.
Still—now it's happened I can hardly believe that either."

Her soft brown gaze shifted. Richard's footsteps were
coming back along the hall, toward the library. Alice said,
"I'll go back upstairs. I promised Richard that I'd sleep." She
replaced the small cupid carefully and locked the doors and
slid the key back into the drawer as Richard came into the
room.

"You'd better rest now, Alice," he said very quietly.

"Yes. I'm just going." She hesitated, looking at Myra.
"You've been so good to us, Myra." Her voice broke a little.
She held the handkerchief tighter in her hand. "You came to

a house with a pall upon it. You stayed here, all this time for
Aunt Cornelia—and for Richard. None of us can thank you
enough but I am more deeply indebted to you, Myra, than
anyone else. You've been—wonderful."

I've fallen in love with your husband, thought Myra. If
you had been one hour—one minute—later in coming home,
I'd have consented to take your place. I'd have fought to take
your place. And still in my heart I want it and I want your
husband, and I've got to fight, all my life perhaps, against that
longing.

Richard's face was white. She glanced at him and, with
anguish in her heart, away again. He knew what she was
thinking. He said, "Myra has been more than loyal; so has
Aunt Cornelia. You must go, Alice. You can talk tomorrow."

"Tomorrow," said Alice, "in my own home. Every tomorrow—yes, yes, I'm going. But I can't sleep. I told Francine
to have Barton serve dinner in my room for both of us. You'll
come up then, Richard?"

Richard's lips tightened. "Yes, Alice."

She smiled and gave a little, childish wave with the crumpled handkerchief and went away. The soft rustle of her
silken robe, the light sound of her footsteps diminished. Richard stood, watching her. Myra watched as she reached the
stairway and started upward, so small, so slight and delicate
a figure against the dark panels and the solid steps. Neither
of them spoke until Alice had disappeared up the wide steps
and around the turn of the broad landing.

Then Myra turned and looked up at Richard and he was
looking at her.

"Richard, you heard her!"

"Yes."

"Thanking me!"

There was pain in his eyes and something else, something
queerly like anger. Even through her own complex and mingled pain and self-reproach she saw that and was touched
with question and a resultant small dismay because she did
not and now never would know and understand his every
look and every word with the dear accustomedness of marriage.

He said in a strained, almost angry voice, "You must not
reproach yourself or me. Nothing has happened that could
possibly be prevented."

"We had no right . . ."

"Stop!" He interrupted her with a harsh note in his voice as if the anger in his eyes had flared into a spark. But then immediately, if that was true, he controlled it. He said very quietly, but with great earnestness, "Listen, and remember this always. We do not require justification, either of us. That is not specious reasoning; it is fact."

But her own pain drove her on too quickly. "People always say that!" she cried. "It is always possible to justify some way a mean and shoddy . . ."

He came to her and took her by the shoulders hard. "You are not to say that! There is nothing mean and nothing shoddy between us."

As suddenly as it had come the self-anger and wave of bitter self-reproach left her. "I was wrong to lash out at you like that, Richard."

His hold on her shoulders relaxed. She wondered briefly whether or not he had stopped what amounted to hysteria on her part. He said, "Yes. But I knew why."

"I felt ashamed and angry with myself. Until I saw her, I did not realize she was just the same. It was as if—the murder and the trial made a difference in her, as if it put her in another world, as if she wasn't Alice. I never knew her well. We'd met a few times before I went to England with Aunt Cornelia. Somehow she had become—removed, a name. Not Alice."

"Yes, I know."

It had to be said, before the courage to say it was quite gone. "Richard . . ."

His eyes quickened at the change and gravity in her voice. He waited, and she said, "Everything is different now."

"Nothing between you and me is different."

"She is your wife."

"She is no more my wife than she was an hour ago! No more my wife than . . ." he stopped, released her quickly, and turned toward the mantel. He said in a different, quieter tone, "I really mean that exactly as it sounds. You are right of course, Myra. She is my wife and—this—does change things. Outwardly, that is; there are different things to consider. But she has been proved innocent, pardoned. Therefore," he paused but went on, "therefore divorce . . ."

How could they have been so blind! "We were wrong! We didn't realize what a divorce would mean to her. We can't do that. Not now . . ."

He was looking into the fire. She could only see his dark head, bent. He said slowly, obliquely, "I love you. Nothing real has changed between you and me; nothing can change."

Tears suddenly threatened her. She said, unsteadily, thankfully, longing to go to him, touch him, feel his arms holding her, shielding her, and knowing that she must not move toward him, "I'll remember that. Always."

He whirled around. "What do you mean by that? Listen, Myra! I don't know what's going to happen right now, or how it's going to happen. I wasn't expecting this. There are—angles, things to think of. But you and I cannot change . . ."

She stood, holding the chair, to look directly into his face.

"I can't argue, Richard. Both of us knew that anything between us had to be forgotten, as soon as we saw Alice. It's so—*different*," she cried. "Now that she's home. We cannot add to the cruelty she's already unjustly—so horribly unjustly—suffered."

She went to him then and put her hands upward, against his shoulders.

"Richard, dear Richard—we will forget . . ."

He did not reply, only looked at her with pain and again something like anger (With fate? With the way life arranged itself?) in his eyes and presently she put her head lightly against his shoulder, her face turned away from him so she looked at the ruby-red chair and the tall mahogany secretary. The Capo di Monte cupid smiled placidly at her.

She said, slowly, pausing between the scattered words, aware of his nearness, too, and that, never again perhaps could she stand like that, leaning upon his strength and tenderness almost as truly as she leaned against his shoulder and felt the warmth of his arms holding her, "There is no other way. Alice is like a person who's been sick and must have care. Like someone shipwrecked who must have safe harbor. We'll forget, Richard, because we have to. I'll go to stay with Tim. Perhaps—some time—the friendship we had in the beginning, Richard, will come back, without the—the other . . ." Her voice died away as she faced, in her mind, a bleak and arid space that lay ahead.

Richard said nothing and gradually she became aware of his silence. She turned in his arms.

His face was as blank as a wall; it was as if he had retreated behind that wall.

He said, from an incredibly remote distance, "It would be

better for you to stay here for awhile, Myra. Until things are more settled. Until, well, somebody murdered Jack Manders and they're going to try to find out exactly who it was. And they have three suspects. Webb. Tim. And me."

CHAPTER 8 ■

It was, as a matter of fact, salutary, like cold water in the face of a distraught and half-hysterical person. It drew her instantly from the future to the urgency, and indeed the threat, of the present. "You!"

"Well—yes. I'm sorry, Myra. I thought you knew that."

"Not about you! Not . . . Is that why the Governor looked so—so . . ." Hard? Implacable? "*Suspicious!*" she cried.

"I thought you knew," said Richard again.

"No, no. I only thought of Tim. Oh, Richard, they *can't* suspect you!"

"I wish I hadn't told you. But then you'd know tomorrow when the D. A. gets around to us. Or as soon as you had a chance to think. And you must believe me there's no real evidence; they have to have suspects, that's all, and . . ."

She cried sharply, "But they never questioned you."

"Oh, yes. They questioned."

"But why? Because they thought Jack and Alice . . . ?"

"That was the theory. My wife, my house—my gun. But I didn't kill him, Myra, and neither did Tim. So I promise you I'll not let either Tim or me be railroaded . . ."

Again she brushed away his attempt to reassure her. "You were not here! You were away! You didn't come home until after the murder. The police were already here. You had an alibi. . . ."

"I had an alibi of sorts. The conductor on the late train I

took out from New York thought—rather vaguely—that he remembered having taken my ticket. I got here to the house after twelve. Jack was shot about ten-thirty. I *could* have come home about then, shot him from the hall or the terrace without Alice's seeing me, escaped through the woods, and later returned home again, arriving this time openly and boldly at the front door. To find the police already here. It could have been done."

"Did they say that? Did they accuse you of it?"

"It was suggested and I was questioned. But you see then Webb told his story. He said he had seen Alice kill him. That was the big, the important factor. Nobody after that was really suspected by the police."

"Nobody could believe that if you had killed him you'd let Alice go to prison."

"You heard everything the Governor said. I think that the verdict was a surprise in an odd way to everybody because they had expected her to be let off, whether or not she did it. I might have reasoned, you see, the same way. That I, in a trial, wouldn't have a chance, but that she, a woman, young, beautiful, would never be convicted." Suddenly he smiled. "But I didn't. So put all this out of your mind."

She said somberly, "Is it—horrible? The investigation, questions . . ."

"It isn't nice, but they'll not question you."

"But you had no motive, no . . ."

"There was no provable motive for Alice to have killed him. If there *had* been anything in the nature of an affair between him and Alice, why, then I'd have had a motive, according to them."

It was merely hypothetical; it wasn't fact; but even as a motive it had been strongly enough supported by the existing circumstances (and mainly by Webb Manders' fraudulent testimony) that in a trial, in a court of justice, the jury had considered it so likely and substantial in its claims that they had accepted it, and had sent a woman to prison for life.

Richard said abruptly, "But believe me, Myra, it was not a theoretical motive that convicted her. It was Webb's lie. That was the keystone to the whole arch of evidence against her. I *could* have come home, leaped to conclusions that because Jack was here she'd been having an affair with him, and shot him and got away with it. But I think any prosecuting attorney would have a hard time proving it." He looked at her soberly. "I think anybody would have an even harder time proving that Tim was implicated."

Tim! "Tim could not have shot him, Richard. I don't know why he has done this. It does seem improbable that he could forget anything so important but . . ."

"We'll ask him," said Richard. "He may not have realized the importance of the curtain. He may have forgotten. Or— well, we'll ask him. But whatever he says or doesn't say, he's doing what he thinks is right. Believe that too, Myra." He took both her hands. "Wait till you talk to him."

His face had suddenly a close resemblance to the portrait of his father that hung in the long, formal dining room—a fighting face, stubborn and a little arrogant, square-jawed, with deep-set eyes. "I don't like Webb Manders; but I don't think he killed his own brother. I don't think Tim killed him. I am certain about myself. So far we are the only suspects. But a fourth suspect—unknown, unseen, but a suspect would be a great help."

She said half-puzzled, half-credulous, "Was there such a person?"

He waited for a moment again, looking down at her. "Why not?" he said. And suddenly put his hands around her face and, holding it, said, "Wait, Myra. Don't think, don't try to make decisions, don't do anything. . . ."

"I've got to go away, Richard. I can't stay here."

Again for an instant his face looked like his father's, stubborn, implacable. He said: "All right. But you can't leave this minute." He took his hands from her face and turned and started for the hall. She said, "What are you going to do? Where are you going?"

"I'm going to phone for Sam. We'll have to get hold of Tim, too. Where is he?"

Tim—of course. She told him the number quickly and then rose and followed him to the library door. "Let me talk to him, Richard, when you get him."

"All right. I'll phone Sam first. He may be hard to find."

Along the hall, just under the great stairway was the niche where the telephone, an extension, stood on its table. She could not see Richard, but she could hear his voice. She stood there waiting, while he tried one or two numbers and then apparently at the third was told to wait. No one was in the hall. On some surface level of her mind she wondered where Barton was, what the servants were doing about dinner, and then remembered that Alice, rightful mistress of the house, had already given orders about dinner—her dinner and Richard's, shared together over a small table, alone, in Alice's wide, beautiful room with its silk and lace cushions and its scent of lilac sachet.

She moved sharply. She turned back quickly into the library as if by sheer physical movement she could escape thought.

Someone, of course, would have to tell Aunt Cornelia. Or had they already told her? Had Alice already gone to her to be welcomed with all of Aunt Cornelia's staunch loyalty and feeling for family?

It was darker. The window above the bookshelves, where the Governor had swept back the red curtains, glittered against the darkness. She started automatically to close the curtain and, as she did so, someone tapped quickly at the terrace door and opened it.

It was Mildred Wilkinson. Her elaborately curled and coiffed hair looked disheveled. Her long, thin face was pale and her light eyes had bright, wide black pupils. She was wearing a dinner dress, a long, pale green chiffon with a light tweed topcoat slung around her shoulders. "Myra," she cried, and came into the room quickly, closing the door behind her. "Myra, is it true? Is Alice home?" She saw the answer in Myra's face. She cried excitedly, "I saw the car! I was sure it was Alice sitting in the back. But I couldn't believe it. I simply couldn't. I was just at the entrance of my own drive. . . . I'd stopped to see Dottie Campbell after I left here and I was turning into my own drive when the car passed me, and it looked so like Alice, somehow, veil and all. I watched and it turned in here, but I still couldn't believe it. I went on to my house and changed for dinner and kept thinking, could it have been Alice and what happened! Finally I had to come! What happened? Is she ill? What has happened?" She was panting, her words and movements jerky and rapid. She stopped to catch a quick breath and Richard came back along the hall.

"I've got Sam," he said. "He's coming straight out. But Tim . . ." He saw Mildred and stopped, and Mildred cried shrilly, "Is it true? Is Alice home?"

For an instant Richard did not reply. He was thinking quickly, Myra knew, trying to cover all the contingencies that Mildred's unexpected appearance and knowledge might evoke. He said then, directly and very gravely, "Yes. It's true.

But I must ask you not to tell anyone yet, Mildred. The statement has not been given to the newspapers yet and won't be until tomorrow."

"Oh, I'll not tell a soul," promised Mildred hurriedly. "But what happened? Is she sick? What's happened?"

Again Richard seemed to think hard and quickly for an instant. "She has been pardoned. She'd want you to know."

"Pardoned!" Mildred's face was a queer blue-white. She caught her breath with a rasping sigh. She stuck her head forward greedily, so the cords of her thin neck showed up sharply. She's older, thought Myra suddenly and queerly, than I knew. Mildred cried, "Pardoned! What has happened? Why . . ."

"Webb Manders has confessed to perjury."

"Webb! But he saw her kill him. . . ."

"He says he did not see it. He says he lied. It was all a lie. He has signed a confession to that effect."

"Confession! Of murder? Webb . . ."

"No, no. Of perjury. Webb is to be charged with perjury. They'll open a new investigation."

Mildred's drooping, rather limp green chiffons seemed to waver limply, too, for a moment, as if deprived of support. She said, "Investigation . . ."

"Yes."

"All that? All over again?"

"I suppose so. Mildred, you must keep this to yourself for the moment. We depend on you."

"Oh, of course, of course!" Mildred stared at him unblinking for a long moment, then she cried, "I must see her."

"She's very tired, Mildred. She's resting. . . ."

"Oh, of course." Two red spots had come into her ashy face. She cried, clutching tremulously at her chiffons and her beige tweed coat with her long, thin fingers, "I can't wait to see her. I'm her best friend. I only want to tell her how glad I am. But I mustn't tire her. I'll go now and come back when she's rested."

"I know she'll want to see you then."

"Yes, yes. How wonderful it is! I'll go now." She wavered toward the door, waved excitedly and hurried out. Her green skirts and flat-heeled gold sandals flashed along the terrace and disappeared. Richard said, "She was always crazy about Alice. Well, I got Sam, Myra. He'll be here as soon as he can make it. Tim's out somewhere. At least I couldn't get him."

"Where is he?"

"I don't know. He'll turn up. Don't be frightened, Myra. He's all right. And he'll be all right. You'll see."

"Why would he do it, Richard?" she cried again. "He couldn't have really forgotten. He must have understood how important it was!"

"You saw him in England, didn't you? Later?"

"Yes."

"What exactly did he say of the murder? Can you remember?"

CHAPTER 9 ▦

She went back in her mind to that cold, wet London day. Tim had had a short leave. She had come up from Aunt Cornelia, still in the nursing home, in the country, to meet him. They'd met at Paddington Station, blue and dimly lighted, sandbagged, bombed, crowded with service men and women and small sandwich bars. He'd been nervous then, she'd thought—thin and white and fine-drawn. He'd come hurrying, only one of the many in blue or khaki-colored uniforms until something in his walk, something in his thin face and tall, slender body identified him as Tim. They'd met, almost casually, concealing emotion, and hurried. Always hurried. It was one of the things she remembered most clearly about the war. There was never enough time for the trains with their fantastically interrupted service, for taxis, for the long queues.

They'd only said a word or two and pushed their way through the crowds and managed to get seats in a bus and eventually reached the Claridge and had tea. Tim had searched around in the pockets of his A.A.F. uniform and got out some sugar he'd brought her; possibly half a cupful.

He hadn't wanted to talk of the murder or of the trial. He hadn't really, she thought suddenly, wanted to talk to her. Yet he seemed to reach out toward her, too; he'd seemed to want to be with her. It was as if he'd needed a kind of re-assurance. She'd thought then that it was because of the war, because by then he was going, as one of the gunners, on almost nightly missions.

She said slowly to Richard, "He didn't say much. It was hard to talk, somehow. We hadn't met, you see, for nearly three years. He'd grown up so much, yet he was just the same, too. Except we couldn't—we didn't have time—to—to get acquainted again. We had so little time really. He had to get a train back and so did I. He thought then that he might get a week's leave later. He talked about the training; he talked about the bomber crew—some. He talked about London. I could see, then, that he didn't want to talk of the trial. He asked if I'd read the papers. I said yes. Then I said something about his part in it. I said I had wanted to be with him."

"How did he seem?"

"Hurt. Sick. Hating to talk of it; hating to think of it. But"—she caught herself quickly—"not as if he were guilty, Richard. I felt it was because it had happened here; it had happened to you and Alice. That was what he hated. And because he'd had to testify against her."

"Did he tell you anything about the inquest?"

"He said—what I already knew—that they'd subpoenaed him; that they'd had his leave extended by his commanding officer; so he came later, with another unit. But that was sort of—oh, by the way—when he was talking of the rest of the crew. He said that they had been strangers to him when he arrived. He was a replacement, but they'd taken him in as if he weren't a stranger. It was not direct—the allusion to the inquest and the trial, I mean. Then, when I asked him directly about it, he—well, again I saw that he hated to talk of it. I wished I hadn't asked. He told me only what was in the papers."

"Tell me," said Richard.

"Well, Tim had been drinking a bit, and when Webb said he'd give him a lift as far as the gates here, he refused because he wanted to walk. Webb then later, after, I suppose, he'd reached home and then come back here, passed Tim on the drive but didn't stop. Oh, it's just as you and the Governor said—Tim followed him, heard the shots, ran around the end of the house and on the terrace, reached the door and Jack was dead and Webb was bending over him and Alice was in the hall, phoning. That's all."

She could see Tim saying it, crumbling up his sugarless, butterless muffin, not looking at her, darting quick glances about the room, lighting a cigarette with nervous, thin young hands.

"But you thought he was telling the truth?"

Had she? "Why, yes. Yes, I thought so."

"Did you feel then that he realized fully the importance of his corroboration of Webb's story?"

"Yes. I think so. He seemed sick, Richard, unlike himself. Part of it, I thought, was the war, the nerve strain, the job he was doing. But underneath, basically, it was the trial, Alice's conviction. Yes, I think he realized his own share in the evidence that convicted her. I remember trying to tell him that he couldn't have helped it, that it wasn't his fault, that he must not feel that he could have changed anything."

"What then?"

"That was all, really. He looked at his watch, and I could see that it made him miserable to talk of it. I—put out my hand across the table and he put his on it for a minute and then he gave a sort of start and said he'd better hustle along. So he did. I had to go to the London house. The east wing had been bombed and I wanted to see that it was boarded up properly, and then get some things from Aunt Cornelia's room in the west wing. He took me there and then he had to go on. He wrote. He's not a regular correspondent but he wrote whenever he could. But then he was sent home and then out to China and kept there. I didn't actually see him again until he got out of the army."

"Has he talked of the trial or of Alice to you since he came back?"

"No. Not once."

"I suppose it was this thing, working up to a climax, that was on his mind last week-end."

Conscience, the Governor had said. So strong that now that he was at home, back at Thorne House for his usual visits, in familiar surroundings, yet made so horribly unfamiliar in Tim's eyes by the absence of Alice, its force was unable to be withstood. Secretly making up his mind to go to the Governor.

Richard saw the terrible speculation in her eyes. He said, "That boy might have killed Jack, but he wouldn't have let Alice take the rap. So that alone proves he didn't kill Jack. We'll get hold of him and he'll explain. He'll have a good reason . . ."

Barton came in the door. "I beg your pardon . . ."

"Yes, Barton."

"About dinner, sir. It's rather late."

Dinner. Myra looked at the little French clock. Long ago, in another world, she and Richard had gone for a walk and he'd said, there's time before dinner.

Barton, looking old and flabby, and still white with excitement, said, "Madam sent word I was to serve her dinner and yours in her room, sir."

"Yes," said Richard slowly. "Yes. That's right."

"Yes, sir. And may I say, sir, that Lady Carmichael learned through one of the maids of Madam's return and sent for me to inquire. I took the liberty of replying to her questions so far as I was able."

"That's right, Barton," said Richard again. "Will you tell her, please, that I'll see her as soon as I can?"

"Yes, sir." He started toward the door and then turned back to Myra. "Should you care to dine with Lady Carmichael, Miss?"

Myra hesitated. She only wanted to be alone. Aunt Cornelia's eyes were too wise, too perceptive. Yet she could not dine alone at the great polished table in the dining room with the candles flickering in their enormous silver holders, with Thornes of other generations looking down from the walls, regarding her, an intruder, an interloper, the other woman sitting at Alice's table, in Alice's place where she'd sat now (and felt so curiously happy, so secure) for so many months. She said, replying, "Yes, if she wants me. You might ask her, Barton."

"Yes, Miss Myra. I'll serve your dinner, sir, then, immediately in Madam's room." He glanced around the room, saw that the short crimson curtain above the bookshelves at the other end had been pulled open, made a soundless gesture with his lips, and waddled toward it and, as he did so, Tim opened the French door.

"Tim!" cried Myra.

Richard jerked around to look. Tim said, "Hello, Myra, Richard. Hi, Barton."

"Tim," cried Myra again, with almost a sob in her throat, and Tim sauntered very casually (although with a touch of defiance in his manner) into the room.

He was tall, very thin, brown-faced, with sharp and un-youthful lines which fatigue and grilling hours of grim responsibility had creased into his face like tissue paper. He was in civilian clothing which didn't fit. He'd been impatient, desperately weary of uniform. He'd obviously snatched his sagging topcoat off the rack. His dark hair was sleek and neat but his thin body looked as if it moved about restlessly inside his loose-fitting clothing. Barton had turned too. He said, "Mr. Tim! I didn't see your car, sir. I didn't hear you ring . . ."

"I didn't ring. I walked from the station and came in this way."

Richard said, "I'm glad you've come. We tried to reach you by phone."

"Oh." Again there was a hint of defiance in his face, but he grinned nervously. Barton closed the curtains with a swish and click that sounded loud in the silence. Then Tim said, "Oh. I see. You've heard then?"

"Tim, *why* . . ." began Myra, and Richard said quickly, "Mr. Tim will be here to dinner, too, Barton."

"Yes, sir." Barton went to the door and turned back. "Shall I tell Lady Carmichael?"

Myra, staring at Tim, scarcely heard him. Richard said quickly, "Yes. Yes, certainly." Barton disappeared. Richard too was looking at Tim.

Tim who wouldn't return their look. Tim who slid out of the loose topcoat he wore and tossed it on a chair. His ill-matched and ill-fitting tweeds looked suddenly like a masquerade costume. He ran his hands over his hair nervously. He said, "Well, what are they going to do? Did they tell you?"

"They've already done it," said Richard slowly. "The Governor brought Alice home."

Tim did not speak. His eyes were fixed upon Richard, his young face suddenly sober and white. Richard said, "She's home now."

"Alice—here!" said Tim then.

"She's upstairs. He pardoned her."

There was a rush and patter of footsteps along the hall and Willie charged into the room and upon Tim. He bent and gathered him up. Richard said, "They're going to charge Webb with perjury."

Tim's head was bent over the wriggling, leaping little black dog. His brown hand ruffled his ears. "I knew that," he said indistinctly. "He made me wait. He told me Webb had confessed to perjury."

"All right," said Richard. "How did you happen to remember that about the curtains, Tim? Was it your coming back here and seeing the house? Or what?"

For a moment Tim did not reply. Myra made a step forward toward him, and Richard, waiting, his face very quiet, glanced at her so she stopped and waited, too. Tim said, his face still bent over the dog. "Is anyone around?"

"Why, there's only me and Richard . . ." began Myra, but Richard said quickly, "The Governor's gone. Alice is upstairs. I'll see . . ." He went to the doorway and looked along the hall and came back. "No one can hear," he said in a low voice. "What is it, Tim?"

Again Tim hesitated, stroking the dog. Then he looked up. "I made it up," he said flatly.

"You . . . *Tim, what do you mean?*" cried Myra.

Richard put his hand on the boy's shoulder. "It's all right —go on . . ."

Tim eyed him rather doubtfully and, again, defiantly for a moment. Then he said, "Well, I'll tell you exactly. But, for God's sake," he turned to Myra, "keep this under your hat, Sis. I— Well, it's as I said, I made it up. I decided it might not get Alice out but it certainly would cast doubt on Webb's story, and it was his story that convicted her. So, legally, there'd be a question, it seemed to me, and it might—it just *might*—do something that would help her. I've been thinking about it naturally all this time."

The half-defiant look left his face. He was all at once terribly, almost tragically serious. "You see," he said, "I'd told the truth in the first place. They questioned me right away, that night. I never dreamed of their accusing Alice or even suspecting her. I was pretty well stunned when they did and when Webb said he'd seen her shoot him. I . . ." A slow flush crept up over his thin cheekbones and receded. He said steadily, "Alice had been awfully good to me. Alice . . ." He stopped and bent again over Willie's black little head.

Richard said gently, "You felt that Alice couldn't have shot him."

"I didn't see how Alice could have done anything that wasn't—like Alice," said Tim. "She . . . I damned near died when I saw that my testimony backed up Webb's. I couldn't change it. I had already told what I'd seen. At least," he swallowed hard and looked up at them and said, "at least I didn't see a way to change it until later. Months later. Then during the war I—well, of course I'd kept thinking of it, and turning it over and over in my mind. It was horrible. Alice . . . I couldn't get away from it. I decided that if I ever got back here I'd do something, I didn't know what, to get her out. Then last week-end I was in here, sitting right over there," he nodded toward the sofa facing the low windows, "and I suddenly saw the way to do it. So I went to the Governor . . ."

"Wait a minute," said Richard. "You mean, exactly, that you invented that story you told him?"

"*But Webb* . . ." began Myra, and Tim said, "Yup. I invented it. I looked at those curtains and I thought and thought, and all at once I knew that all I had to say was that I'd come up on the terrace and stopped there in the doorway before Webb saw me, and that he was pulling those curtains open and they'd been closed before, when he claimed he'd heard the shots and stood on tiptoes and looked into this room. It was as simple as that. And then, by golly—it was the truth."

There was a moment of utter silence. Neither Richard nor Myra moved or spoke. The fire sighed. Tim's thin brown hand tugged Willie's ears, the little dog gave a leap up toward his face. Tim said suddenly, "You could have knocked me over with less than a feather when I came back into the Governor's office after he'd seen Webb, all prepared to stick to my story come hell or high water and then—by golly, I was so surprised that I damned near gave it away then and there. It was the truth and Webb admitted it. Of course, my weak point was having to say that I'd forgotten it and only now remembered. But it was the only excuse I could think of. I thought they might charge me with perjury or some damned thing, I didn't know what, but I didn't see what they could do if I stuck to it. Except, of course, it might not have worked. The Governor might have seen through it; maybe he did."

And he thinks, thought Myra sharply, that you may be a murderer.

Richard stood quite still, his hand on Tim's shoulder. Tim said, "I wish to God I'd thought of it sooner. Alice . . ." He looked at Richard and at Myra and swallowed rather hard again and said, suddenly shedding the years of forced adulthood and becoming very young and very boyish, his eyes shining, "Alice *didn't* kill him."

"You mean," said Richard gently, "that you had been afraid that she had. . . ."

"Well, I didn't see how she could have done it. She's so—so good," said Tim. "But then I thought maybe Manders—well, maybe he was a heel, you know. A well-mannered, well-washed heel. Maybe she'd, well, had to shoot him. You hear of things like that. Maybe—oh, I thought of all kinds of things. Crazy things. I even thought, what the hell! Suppose she did shoot him! Whatever Alice had to do was—was *right*. What's the use of making such a fuss over a fellow like Jack Manders! That's what I thought. But . . ." Again his face was young and boyish. "But she didn't! If I'd had the sense then to think of a way out, she'd never have gone to prison."

There was another short silence. Richard gave Tim's shoulder a reassuring pat as he released it and then turned and walked the length of the room and back again. He sat down in the arm chair.

Tim said, "The most I hoped to do was stir up something, cast reasonable doubt on Webb's story. The weak point was my pretending to have forgotten all this time. Anybody would know that I'd have done everything I could to get Alice out of it. But I thought I might—just *might* accomplish something. It'd be my word against Webb's and Webb was prejudiced. Well, of course, so was I. But now . . ." He lifted his face again and grinned a little. "It's swell, isn't it?"

"Yes," said Richard. "Yes. Look here, Tim, as I remember it, Webb swore in his testimony that he had passed you along the drive. You were walking and he was in his car."

"Yes, that's right."

"Did—well," said Richard carefully, "did any other cars happen to pass you along the road? Earlier, I mean, while you were walking from the station and before you turned into the driveway?"

Tim's face was instantly sharp and alert. He put the little dog down on the chair beside him. "I don't know. That never came up. I saw Webb, as you know. He went on past me. He saw me. At least he said he did then. What do you mean,

Dick? Wait a minute," said Tim slowly, "I guess I know what you mean."

"If you can think of anybody else who might have seen you it would be a help. Just to nail it . . ."

"You mean," said Tim, watching Richard, "that a new investigation is underway?"

"It will be. In the morning."

"I see. Yes. And they . . ."

"You are in the clear, Tim. You didn't shoot him. It's only a question of getting things straight before the police and the . . ."

Tim said, "Have they questioned you?"

"No. I'm in the clear, too; that's beside the point. Just now, before Sam comes, let's try to . . ."

Tim interrupted sharply again. "Somebody shot Manders. So they'll not give up till they find out who it was. Yes, I see. You've sent for Sam?"

"Yes, but only . . ."

"I know what that means. Well . . ." His face was intent, his eyes suddenly adult and wise. "Well, there's only you and me and Webb. And you'll be their choice. Your gun, your house, Alice . . ." Tim said slowly, "How do you know I didn't shoot him? How do you know he didn't deserve it? I've probably had my share in killing a lot of people. It wouldn't bother me much. How do you know Alice didn't know that I killed him—and wouldn't tell it because of her— her loyalty to me. How do you know . . ."

Barton, in the doorway, cleared his throat nervously. All three jerked around to look at him. How much had he heard? How much would he remember? How much . . ."

He put one hand over his mouth and coughed and looked at Richard. "If you please, Madam wishes you to know that your dinner is served. She is waiting for you, sir, in her room."

"Tell her I'll be up at once." Barton coughed again and waddled away. Richard said, "Sam will be here soon. We can talk over the situation and see what we can do. Only understand one thing, Tim. I'm not going to have any nonsense on your part. I'm not in any danger of being charged with murder. So get that out of your head. If you've got any notion of trying to distribute the suspicion so as to clear me, forget it. I'll not have it. Understand. Now then . . ." He reached for a cigarette; he lighted it rather slowly. He said, without looking at Myra, "Sam will be here soon. I'll be down when he comes," and turned, still without looking at Myra, and walked out of the room. She watched him go as she had watched Alice, in spite of herself, across the hall and up the stairs. Where Alice in her silken, scented room—beautiful Alice—his wife, waited for him.

Tim said abruptly, "It was his gun, you know. A Smith and Wesson, thirty-two. I've seen it many times. He kept it in a drawer of that table. His gun, his house, Alice . . ."

"Richard couldn't have killed him," cried Myra rather desperately. "You couldn't have killed him. Neither of you would have let Alice go to prison."

"Wouldn't we?" said Tim. Again the look of taut, knowledgeable adulthood was in his face. "I'll tell you this," he said in a queer, faraway voice, "I've seen a lot of better fellows die. When are they going to unleash the police?"

"Tomorrow."

"Tomorrow. Well, I'm going up now and wash. See you later."

He was already halfway across the room. He made a kind of backward wave with one hand and ran across the hall. Willie leaped off the chair and followed. Tim did pause for an instant there, his hands on the tall newel post and looked back at her.

"I don't suppose I could just see Alice for a minute?"

"Why—why, yes, of course . . ."

"No, I'd better give her a chance to rest. I—yes, I'll wait." He turned and ran up the stairs. Almost as if to escape her and her questions.

Tomorrow. Police. Reporters. Questions. Suspects.

Alice's exoneration was complete. But the fact of murder, unsolved, lay within that house, within that room, a grim and dreadful presence, awaiting its revenge.

Who had stood in that doorway leading to the hall, or in the open French door upon the terrace and held Richard's gun in his hand?

It was very still. She felt extraordinarily alone, somehow, in the mellow, gracious room with its crimson curtains and books and flowers, Mildred's lilies on the low table, Alice's daffodils.

Alice's cupid, still watching her, with its small, pretty smile.

She'd better go, too, and change. She turned toward the

door, saw Tim's coat where he'd dropped it on the chair and went back for it, scarcely thinking of what she was doing. She went into the hall.

There was no sound anywhere. Upstairs behind a door that she must soon pass Alice lay back against the lacy, fragrant pillows and smiled at Richard. Alice who had returned and resumed her rightful place.

And the place that was to be—had to be—forever her own.

Myra reached the stairs and started up them and tripped on the third step.

It might have happened any time—any night, any day, any hour—since the hot June night when Jack Manders had been killed. It happened then.

Because Myra was carrying Tim's coat, because she caught her heel in a dragging fold of it, because she fell backward and flung up her hand and caught at the newel post, hard, pushing backward and up with all her weight in order to save herself from falling, she found the gun.

The tall, sharply pointed top of the newel post, carved in minute detail like a pineapple, its point upward, gave a silent kind of tug and the whole top, down to the square post, came loose and fell and clattered downward loudly on the rug. A gun lay in the unfinished wooden hollow of the post directly under Myra's eyes.

The clatter reverberated hollowly through the hall and stopped.

The house again was still and silent.

Myra was quiet, too, frozen into stillness as if she would never move again. A gun, a revolver—a Smith and Wesson, thirty-two.

The gun. The gun that had never been found. Richard's gun.

CHAPTER 10 ▇

It was, of course, obvious why the police had not found it.

To tear the house apart had not meant literally to tear it timber from timber, brick from brick. If there had been secret hiding places, hidden cupboards, hollow panels, the police would have found them. If there had been loose bricks around the fireplace, a wobbly flagstone on the terrace just outside the library windows, a hollow secret space in the old secretary, they'd have found that. But blank and solid walls, floors, balusters—a newel post, had offered no hiding place.

But the newel post *had* offered a hiding place. And someone—who?—had known it.

That someone had known that it was loose, had known that below the wooden top, carved in the shape of an up-ended pineapple, there existed an unfinished, raw wooden hollow which was big enough and deep enough to hold a gun.

That someone had fastened the pineapple—who? when? —so solidly upon its base that when the police came the night of the murder, and when they searched, and in all the time since, until now, no one else had known the gun was there. Indeed it was unlikely that anyone who did not know would so much as consider the newel post as a possible hiding place. Myra herself had assumed, if she thought of it at all, that it was a solid piece of wood, carved and ornamented, but one solid piece. And even if, during the police investigation, anyone had tentatively tried to move the pineapple-carved top, it fit down so solidly into its socket that it resisted the pressure of such a hand. And indeed only the strong upward lift she had accidentally given it would have, in all probability, dislodged the ornamental top.

Her mind was racing. She forgot to listen to the house, listen for sounds, listen for the swish of a skirt in the hall above or the padding footsteps of Barton away off in the dining room.

When had it been hidden? Almost certainly the night of the murder and before the police took over and searched every inch of the house.

Who then had hidden it? The murderer? Who else could it have been?

Who had known of that hiding place? Webb? Richard? Tim? Alice?

Webb could have known about the loose post and the hiding place it provided. It was at least within the realm of possibility that if he were a fairly frequent visitor to the house he could have discovered that it could be moved, loosened, lifted entirely. It was not likely but it was possible.

Alice might have known. Tim might have known. Richard might have known. Could anyone else have known? Aunt Cornelia—possible. Barton—possible, or his wife, the cook, or Francine, the middle-aged French housemaid. Or even Mildred Wilkinson.

But none of them had been in any sense suspects.

She was standing on the lower step. Suddenly she felt as if she were spotlighted, as if the whole house watched her— listened, aware of what she had found. She looked along the hall. There were lights in sconces against the dark paneled walls. A great, rose-shaded lamp stood on a table against the wall beside the door to the ivory-and-gold drawing room where Alice's portrait, in her wedding gown, reigned, so beautifully and surely mistress of the house. That room was darkened. It was never used. There was a light coming from the arched dining-room door wider than the others, at the end. Nobody was near; nobody could see her. She took the gun in her hand.

She did not then think of fingerprints, either her own or any others. The gun was cold to her touch and felt, somehow, clammy and sweaty. She concealed it in the folds of Tim's coat. She moved, crouching to take up the carved mahogany pineapple with its delicate diamond pattern and tracery of stiff pointed leaves, in her other hand.

It was not as heavy as she had expected. She felt a slight sensation of surprise on lifting it.

Again she glanced up along the stairway—down along the

hall—and then carefully replaced the carved top upon the hollow post. It settled down firmly into the socket that was made to receive it; so firmly that when she tested it, it would not move.

Holding the gun under Tim's coat, she went back quickly into the library. She moved away from the hall door, out of sight, dropping Tim's coat on a chair. She knew how to break a gun; Tim had showed her one time with his service revolver. The gun felt unclean in her fingers, owing probably —and merely—to the thin film of oil upon it, unrubbed and unwiped, collecting a faint coating of dust. She broke it.

It was a revolver. It was made to hold six shells; there was one left in it. And instantly, long-ago headlines, long-ago print leaped before her eyes as if she were reading again those creased and folded newpapers which had crossed the Atlantic with their ugly news.

Jack Manders had been shot five times. Five slugs in the body of the murdered man. Five . . .

A Smith and Wesson, .32. She turned it, looking at it, examining it, hating it.

If it was not Richard's missing gun, it was like it.

If it was not the gun that had been used for murder, it was like it.

So she had to give it to the police, who would be coming the next day to resume investigation into the murder. To question Tim. To question Richard. His gun, his house— Alice.

Richard could have hidden it there, if he had come home, secretly, earlier than anyone knew then, or later, if he had shot Jack, if he had escaped quickly through the hall so no one saw or heard him.

Tim could have put it in the post. There was time and opportunity after he came into the library. Webb was terribly engrossed, bending over his brother's body. Alice was at the telephone under the stairs; she could not have seen the newel post from there. Tim could have hidden it and neither Webb nor Alice would necessarily have known. Tim knew where Richard's gun was kept, he had said so only a few moments ago. Tim could have taken it, at almost any time.

There was no motive for Tim to have shot Jack.

But what about Richard? "You're their first choice," Tim had said.

What couldn't the police make of the gun in a case against Richard?

She made no conscious decision. She did not think of her own fingerprints on the gun; neither did it occur to her that the gun was potentially dangerous—that there might in that silent house lurk elements of danger, a mind that remembered the gun's hiding place, a hand that once before had tested its terrible efficiency. She removed the remaining shell. She held it in her hand and it seemed unreal, its cold, small weight perfectly harmless and innocent, a thing out of a fantasy.

She slid it in the pocket of her gray jacket. She closed the gun and the click of metal sounded remarkably loud. Where could she hide it?

Behind the books? Along some remote shelf? In a drawer of a table or the tall secretary? She was frightened, cold, despairing. She must get it out of the way before Tim came running downstairs again and found her with the gun in her hand. Before Barton came to tell her that dinner was served upstairs in Aunt Cornelia's room, before Richard . . .

Richard. Deep in her consciousness, very obscurely, there was something like the snap of an invisible switch, cutting off a line of thought. It was a line of thought she must return to, a path she must explore, but, she thought, almost in panic, *not now!* Hide the gun! Hurry!

Where would it be safe from the police? Where *had* it been safe all that time? The French clock struck a half hour briskly, as if it, too, said hurry. Hurry!

The sweet fragrance of Mildred's lilies of the valley was almost sickening, it was so strong. The fire had gone to red embers. Barton would come in presently to replenish it with logs. Barton had an instinct for the exact moment when more logs were needed.

But he was not in the hall; no one was there or on the stairway.

She looked first, holding the gun concealed.

Then she went softly across the hall and quickly, very carefully replaced the gun in the newel post.

Quickly and carefully, yet when she stepped back from it her hands were trembling, her heart pounding in her ears. The post—looking so blank, so obviously one solid, unobtrusive piece of wood—caught a dull gleam of light from the lamp in the library behind her.

She went back into the library. There had been something that she had intended to do, some action she'd begun. Oh, yes, Tim's coat. She went to pick it up and, as she did so, the terrace door rattled and opened and Sam Putnam came in. "Hello, Myra."

"Sam, I didn't know you were there!" *Had he seen her examining the gun?* She glanced swiftly at the red curtains but they were tightly drawn over the long French window. She glanced, too, thinking of the driveway with its view of the room, toward the other end, but Barton had drawn those curtains, too. Sam, his usually taciturn, sallow face now pale and excited, did not appear to notice her involuntary glance over his narrow, brown-clad shoulders He said, "I just got here. I came as soon as I could. Luckily I'd driven out from town early. I was at the club. Where's Dick?"

"Upstairs."

"With Alice? How is she?"

"Tired, of course." It was with a physical effort that she replied. It was as if the discovery of the gun had plunged her into a morass from which she could not extract herself.

Sam had dropped his topcoat and was hunting nervously through pockets for cigarettes. He was not watching her. Instead, his quick glance was going here and there about the room, fastening for a moment on the narrow curtains at the further end. He found cigarettes with one wiry hand and settled his tie with the other.

Sam Putnam was an old friend of Richard's. He had gone to school with him; he had been Alice's lawyer and had defended her with tenacity; usually unemotional, with an icy, rather cold intelligence, he had infused his defense on that occasion with an emotional and fiery appeal which, had it not been for Webb's direct and forceful testimony so strongly and necessarily corroborated by Tim, would almost certainly have swayed the jury in Alice's favor. He was thin and dark, with marked, sallow features and a bald spot, circled with thin black hair. He was devoted to both Richard and Alice and, like Mildred Wilkinson, had been a faithful and frequent visitor since the trial.

He said, darting a quick look at her, "What in God's name is the matter with Tim? Dick says he claims to have forgotten the curtain. How *could* he forget! Is he here?"

She answered the last question, "Yes. He came a few minutes ago."

"I'll talk to him." Luckily, she thought, he left that question. There was no reason why they should not, all of them, confide anything they knew to Sam, yet she did not wish to tell him Tim's real explanation herself. Let Richard and let Tim decide that. Sam said, "Well, thank God, Webb buckled up and admitted it. A confession of perjury was something to get. I have to hand it to the Governor. He's a smart guy. Always was. He'd never have got Alice convicted without Webb's testimony and Tim's; that was the stumbling block from the beginning. That and the fact that Alice simply —obviously told the truth. There was no defense in her story; even if she'd shot Manders in self-defense there'd have been something for me to work on with the jury. But as it was there was only her denial. . . . Well, you say she's all right?"

"Yes."

He was speaking, as was his habit, rapidly, rather nervously. Myra said suddenly, "You never believed that she had shot him, did you, Sam?"

"Did I . . . ?" His eyes turned to her and went blank; a kind of opaque veil seemed to come over them. He said, "I knew Alice pretty well. I'm very fond of her. I expect you knew that. No, I never believed it. Naturally, I was sincere in my defense. That is—if she *had* shot him for some reason, I'd still have been on her side, and not because I'm a criminal lawyer and I'll take only clients in whom I can have a reasonable belief—not because of that at all! But because I know Alice. She always said she didn't kill him and I believed her but, nevertheless, *if she had shot him,*" he shrugged, "I figured he deserved it. Dick says they're starting a new investigation."

She nodded. He swept on with his usual nervous, jerky rush of words. "It's going to be tough—no use dodging that. The Governor has got to justify his action. Plenty of people will say he rose into his job on the strength of this case and the wide publicity it had—and now that he's safely elected he has turned around and let her out. He's an honest man. I have to give him credit for it. A lot of men in his position would have been afraid to release Alice until he had somebody else as good as under arrest in her place. Although

—maybe they are pretty certain of being able to make an arrest soon. Did he say that he'd got any new leads?"

"Richard asked him if there were any new angles; he said there were not."

"He'd say that whether there were or not. He's a politician, don't forget—cagey. I wonder what's their idea. I can't think of anything that might have turned up that would be new. Except an eye witness—another one and I imagine that's out. Or, of course, the gun."

He said it casually, lighting the cigarette he'd been holding in his thin fingers. She was momentarily thankful for that and that he was not looking at her with those sharp, trained eyes. The shell seemed to weigh down her jacket. She had a fantastic impulse to glance downward and make sure that there was no betraying outline of it visible. Yet Sam was their friend; Sam was on their side.

But she did not intend to tell him about the gun. Not now. Not yet.

There was no time for a thought-out, carefully considered decision; no time to analyze reasons which were deep and instinctive, but she had to know certain things. She said, "Oh, yes. The gun . . ."

He got his light and snapped the lighter. "Dick's gun. It completely disappeared. That helped Alice's case; I made as much as I could of it. That gun saved her life, as a matter of fact." He spoke tersely and in too off-hand a way, so, somehow, she knew that even now, there was terror in the thought of what might have happened. He covered it by adding too hurriedly, too offhandedly, "She simply couldn't have disposed of it outside the house. Webb got on the scene too fast. He insisted then that he didn't see the gun at all. The police turned the house inside out—grounds too, for that matter, but either Webb or Tim were with Alice almost constantly from the time Webb got into that room. Definitely she didn't have it then—even Webb admitted that."

He paused for a moment, and Myra thought, but she could have hidden it, so easily, so quickly, running back into the hall to the telephone; while Webb, according to the true situation, was opening the curtain and making his ugly plan to accuse her. The newel post was visible from where Myra stood now. From the narrow, important window at the other end of the room it would not have been visible.

Sam said, "I suppose Webb was afraid to say anything about the gun for fear it would be discovered somewhere outside the house later and thus tend to disprove his whole story of Alice. If he said, for instance, that when he came into the room, and Alice ran across after she shot Jack and was kneeling beside his body, she then had the gun in her hand—he'd have had to explain what she did with it during the next few minutes, certainly not more than two or three, if that, between the time he sent Alice out of the room, ran across himself and pulled open those curtains and got back and there was Tim. He sent Tim right out after Alice. No, it wasn't safe for Webb to make any statement about seeing the gun."

She said slowly, "If whoever shot him stood there in the doorway to the hall and escaped that way, he could have taken the gun with him and disposed of it . . ."

"Dropped it in the Sound," said Sam. "Right. And I always thought that's what happened. Unless Webb hid it himself."

"Webb! How could he have hidden it? Why?"

"Because it didn't have Alice's fingerprints on it, naturally," said Sam, looking at her as if she ought to have known the answer herself. "He could have found it, where whoever shot Jack dropped it, picked it up while she was out of the room, hidden it . . ."

"Where?" whispered Myra.

"Anywhere. Somewhere outside, I should say."

"Tim would have seen him."

"Not if he worked fast. It would have been easier for Webb to hide it somewhere here, in this room, but the police could never find it. If Webb did hide it, he's going to want it now." He smoked and said, narrowing his eyes, "If the gun is in the Sound, it's safe. But if it is merely hidden somewhere, then whoever hid it is going to want that gun."

"Why? Is it so important?"

"Important!" Sam stared and gave a short laugh. "If I had that gun I'd . . ." he stopped, brooding.

"What would you do, Sam?"

"What would I do?" he laughed shortly again. "I'll tell you what I'd do. I'd set a little trap. A very neat little trap."

"Trap . . ."

"I'd let everybody know how important that gun is. I'd talk about it, I'd stress it, I'd scare hell out of whoever shot Jack and got rid of that gun. Then I'd watch. It's simple.

That is," he said, with a kind of sigh, "if the gun were hidden somewhere and I knew where. But it can't be done."

"Why not?"

"Because there's no gun. To all practical purposes. There was a gun. Dick's gun. But it's at the bottom of the Sound. Or somewhere equally safe."

It's in the newel post. It's scarcely twenty feet from where you're standing. She caught back her thought with a kind of terror lest Sam could pluck it, unuttered, from the air. She said, "But if it was hidden then, that night, temporarily, whoever hid it has had plenty of time to remove it. To dispose of it, finally. Why, Sam, it's been nearly two years."

"Well," said Sam. "Webb couldn't have, not if it's in this house somewhere. Alice couldn't have, even if she knew. Tim couldn't have . . ."

"But he . . ."

". . . I was about to say even if he knew that the gun was here. But there's no use talking of it, Myra. No use trying to find it . . ."

"But what could anybody prove if it was found? Fingerprints . . ." Her own were there now; but she'd been in England; she was not suspected of murder. How strange that fingerprints on a gun were real, too. Fingerprints, things you read about in newspapers.

"I could prove who killed him," said Sam.

Almost in that moment, she gave him the gun. But then he said slowly, "I'd hate to have the police get it. Dick's gun. And most certainly Dick's fingerprints on it."

CHAPTER 11 ▮

He looked slowly and with a kind of longing around the room. His sharp, nervous eyes shifted back to her. Again with an effort she tried to make her face blank, her eyes unrevealing. He said, "Why are you asking so many questions about the gun?"

Terror again, with neither form nor mind, nevertheless, laid its touch upon her. "You spoke of it, Sam."

"Yes, but . . ." His eyes probed. "You haven't seen it around anywhere, have you? Any kind of gun?"

She said, surprised at the ease with which an evasion came from her own cold lips, "I don't think Richard has another gun. Sam, I'm frightened, I think. Who . . . ?"

"Who killed Jack? Everybody's scared. You're not the only one."

"What will they do?"

"Do you want it straight? They'll pin it on Dick."

And Richard's gun would help—*Don't tell him; don't tell anybody about the gun!*

She said aloud, fighting for self-control and fighting instinctively for Richard, "But you said the Governor was honest . . ."

"Oh, he's honest. So's the new district attorney. But he's got to have a conviction. The Governor's got to have a conviction."

"But you said *pin* . . ."

"The man was killed. Somebody killed him."

"Not Richard . . ."

Nothing in Myra's life had prepared her for the thing Sam then said. Yet she had known already that a path—a dangerous and dreadful path of thought—had to be traveled.

Sam said slowly, "If Dick did shoot him, Myra, he was probably within his rights."

"*He could not have killed him!*"

"Why not? Look here, Dick's my friend. Don't misunderstand me. Neither he nor Alice ever told me that Dick killed Manders, or ever said anything that would have led me to believe that Dick killed him. But if he did, it's the same as with Alice, in my mind. Manders deserved it. Don't look at me like that, Myra. Good God, I'm here to help Dick."

She'd been right not to tell him!

Her lips were cold and stiff. Her hand, she realized with horror, had gone of its own volition into her pocket and closed, tight, on the shell. She said, "Richard would not have let Alice go to trial. Richard didn't kill him. . . ."

There was a short silence. Then Sam said, "But you see, Myra, you weren't here. You couldn't know, but the fact is nobody expected Alice to be convicted. Legally of course, there was nothing else for the jury to do; but actually nobody expected, especially in the beginning, that any jury would convict her. Suppose Dick thought that."

"No."

Sam said rather gently, "It's all new to you, Myra. It's not quite real yet. Dick said we've got till tomorrow."

"Yes."

"I wish we could get some sort of new line on it before then. If only there was somebody, somewhere, who wanted to get rid of Manders. Well, I went all over that at the time . . ."

"What sort of man was he? Did you know him?"

"Oh, I knew him. Casually. Not very well. I never liked him much. Yet there was never anything I could put my finger on. If he was a polite heel, as I always felt he had the capacity for being—and a brute and a bully as well—still I could never prove it. Heaven knows I tried. There must have been women in his present or past life, but, if so, nobody knew anything that was of any use to us. I worked on that angle. If I'd found anything at all I'd have tried to get Alice to change her story, say that she shot him and plead self-defense. It wasn't the truth, but it would have given her a better chance."

He looked away from Myra, fumbled in his pockets, reached out to touch one of the lilies of the valley. He said (not like Sam; not like an able and skilled trial lawyer, accus-

tomed to speaking to that most intent of all audiences, twelve
men and women in a jury box), "I'd have shot Manders myself if I'd walked into the hall or up on the terrace and Alice
had needed . . . but I didn't. I was here that night. I mean,
staying at the club. The police phoned. The first thing that
shot into my mind was that Manders—drunk maybe—had
made a pretty violent scene and Alice had panicked and shot
him. Or that Dick had come in and saw red and . . ."

He stopped abruptly. His sharp eyes went toward the hall.
There were voices on the stairs. She turned.

Barton had appeared from the dining room and was
waddling anxiously forward. Miss Cornelia called over the
banisters, "Will you get out my chair, please, Barton? I
decided to come down."

"Yes, Madam, certainly. You didn't tell me," said Barton
rather reproachfully, but hurrying toward the wheel chair
under the stairs, near the telephone.

Tim said, "Easy now, Aunt Cornelia. Just because you look
sixteen you don't have to act like it." His voice was rather
nervous and unnatural. Miss Cornelia had changed for dinner.
She wore black lace and pearls, and her head was high. Her
jeweled hand rested on the carved top of the newel post.

Myra's heart gave a kind of lurch.

Yet Aunt Cornelia couldn't have murdered Jack. She
couldn't have hidden the gun; she was in England: She was,
as a matter of fact, lying on a narrow, high bed in a nursing
home, with her broken hip in a cast, at the time the murder
occurred.

And Aunt Cornelia's pearls, the way she held her head told
her that Aunt Cornelia too had considered all the im-
plications that followed Alice's release—and she was going
to face it out. She had looked that way, she had behaved that
way, during the blitz, when her own adopted country was
undergoing horror. Her eyes lighted on Sam Putnam. She
cried: "Sam! I didn't realize that you were here. You can't
have had dinner. Barton . . ."

Barton, pushing the chair toward her, was not perturbed,
although there was a subtle, resigned something in his manner that suggested that nothing, that night, would further
amaze or confuse him. "Yes, Madam. Do you wish to dine
downstairs, after all?"

"I've made you extra work. I'm sorry."

"Not at all, Madam. Now then, if you'll just steady the chair, Mr. Tim."

Barton, of course, knew exactly how to lower Miss Cornelia into the chair. Tim, helping, looked down at her. "Okay?"

"Oh, quite. I'll just hold to the newel post . . . Ah, that's right . . ."

Myra quite literally held her breath.

The small old hand relinquished the newel post.

"Thank you. Now, Tim, push me into the library." They came through the doorway, Tim's head bent, intent upon the chair, Miss Cornelia erect, her eyes bright and resolute. She said, "Sam . . ." and put out her hand which he went forward quickly to take. "It's good to see you."

"Dick told me over the phone about the pardon."

"I have not yet seen Alice. I feel she should rest and be alone for a bit."

"Any other woman would have collapsed," said Sam.

"I fancy she is very near it." She looked suddenly rather bleak. "We ought to be a very happy and thankful family, Sam. Indeed, we are, except . . . Sam, what does a new investigation mean?"

"Why, only that, Miss Cornelia." His tone was carefully unperturbed.

"Does it mean—will they arrest anyone else?"

Again he tried to reassure her. "Not necessarily. So far as I know there's no new evidence."

"I see." She looked at him steadily for a moment. "New evidence, such as what, Sam?"

"Well." Sam shrugged and said as he'd said to Myra, "If, for instance, they got hold of the gun."

"Have they?" asked Miss Cornelia, directly.

"Not so far as I know."

"But that was . . ." she paused to catch an uneven breath. "But that was Richard's gun," she said, suddenly cold.

"Dear Miss Cornelia, whoever killed Manders got rid of the gun forever, that night. Or certainly if not that night, since then. I only . . ."

"Sam, will they say Richard killed him?"

Tim put his hand on her shoulder. Sam cried, "No, no . . ."

But her eyes, so suddenly old, silenced him. "Tell me the truth."

Myra said, in a voice that sounded in her own ears half-suffocated. "I'll go now and—and change."

Miss Cornelia did not look at her. Sam, taking the old woman's hand, began to talk gently, reassuringly. In spite of herself, bent on escaping, Myra still had to linger in the doorway to hear him. "Believe me, Miss Cornelia, if that gun has turned up, the only thing that could incriminate Dick would be—well, the place, say, where it was hidden, or—oh, fingerprints."

"Richard's fingerprints?"

"Anybody's fingerprints."

"But Dick's would normally be there; so would mine," said Tim suddenly. "We'd used it, target shooting, only a few weeks before the murder."

"Would fingerprints last nearly two years?" asked Miss Cornelia.

"Not," said Sam forcibly, "if that gun is where I think it is. That's in the middle of the Sound."

Myra had reached the stairway. Her hand went out involuntarily toward the unobtrusive piece of wood. The small gesture frightened her. She went quickly up the stairs, aware of the continued murmur of voices in the library. Too much, she thought suddenly, had happened, too fast—like a tidal wave sweeping unexpectedly out of a calm summer sea, taking all before it, toppling towers and laying waste and so destroying familiar landmarks that it was difficult to know the way.

One road alone emerged clear from all the debris, and that was actually two roads, one for her to take, and one for Richard. She passed the door to Alice's room.

It was closed. There was no sound from within, but she hurried past almost for fear she would hear something—Richard's voice, Alice's, mingled in quiet talk.

She reached the wide, pleasant room she had used now for so many months. She entered it and closed the door and the false strength which had operated like a hypnotic spell, sustaining her, collapsed.

She leaned back against the wooden panels of the door. The windows were open as she'd left them late that afternoon when she went downstairs to wait for Richard to come home—telling herself then that it was for the last time.

Ironically, it had proved to be the last time but not as she had then foreseen it.

The sound of the peepers was shrill and musical through the open windows. The book she'd been reading that afternoon lay open on the low table beside the chaise longue. How strange it would seem if she picked it up again, how far away and uninteresting the characters. How incredible it was that a page of black and white print, a paragraph, a sentence, could mark so great a change!

The shrill sweet whistles of the peepers seemed sad now, full of longing. She'd stood down there on the shore, in Richard's arms, hearing that distant thin treble. Good-bye to Richard, good-bye to Myra, good-bye to love.

She caught that thought back. It was silly—melodramatic, self-pity. And true!

Whose hands had last touched the gun?

Whose fingerprints besides her own were upon it?

"If Richard had come in and saw red . . ." Sam had said. And she had replied, "He wouldn't have let Alice go to trial. . . ."

It was a terrible, swift debate, as if she were two people.

In order to escape it, as she had escaped the library, she made herself go to the windows and close them. She slid out of her suit and blouse and her little satin girdle and brassiere. She peeled her stockings with, since the war, habitually careful hands. She pulled her dark hair up tightly and turned on the shower in the adjoining bathroom.

What could she do with the shell? The police would arrive the next day. What wouldn't they make of Richard's revolver, she thought again, despairingly! Suppose, this time, they found it!

Sam had said it was at the bottom of the Sound. It occurred to her for a wild instant that she might row out in the night, drop the gun in deep water.

She put the shell eventually in her small evening bag. Later, when it was dark, she'd get rid of it somehow, outside. It was curious how indestructible so small and inanimate a thing might be.

She got into a long dress, choosing the first one that came to her hand, white with a scarlet jacket and scarlet fold that came to the hem; she was brushing her hair, smooth and close back to the soft, Grecian knot of loose curls at the back of her head, vaguely aware of the whiteness of her face in the mirror, the enormous darkness and anxiety in her eyes, when someone knocked.

She thought for an instant that it might be Richard. It was not. The parlor maid, Francine, stood in the doorway. Her dark hatchet face was sharp with excitement and curiosity; her narrow eyes were avid. She said: "Madam wishes to speak to you, Miss Myra."

"Madam . . ." For a moment she thought only of Aunt Cornelia.

"Mrs. Thorne, of course. Oh, Miss, isn't it exciting! Barton says it gave him such a turn when he opened the door and there she was on the step cool as a cucumber. As if she'd been away only for a week-end." The maid's eyes were delving, curious, sharp.

"Tell Mrs. Thorne I'll be there in a moment."

"Yes, Miss," Francine hesitated, plucked at her apron and went away.

She made herself take time, she put on lipstick, choosing the shade that went with the dress as carefully as if it mattered, fastening her scarlet, highheeled slippers, touching hair and wrist and throat with perfume. The woman in the mirror looked strange to her, older, more matured. She forgot the small gold evening bag and went back to get it.

She went out of the room and along the hall to Alice's room and knocked. Would Richard open the door?

He didn't. Alice's high, sweet voice called out, "Is that you, Myra? Come in."

The room was already a bower. Flowers were all over it. The windows were open, letting in the cool spring night. A small fire crackled within the oval, pink-marble mantel. Richard was not there. Alice, in pink satin and lace, her fair hair still down her back so she looked like a rather luxurious but very beautiful Alice in Wonderland, was lying back in the chaise longue. She smiled rather nervously. "Come in, Myra. How nice you look. Red and white is becoming to you. Please sit down. . . ."

Her eyes were gentle, half-hidden by long soft eyelashes. She was very small and very frail-looking, lying there with the blue shadows of fatigue in her eyes. Myra felt tall and strong and earthy, somehow, beside her. But her knees were trembling. She sat down in the green slipper chair near Alice, who stretched out one hand pleadingly and said, "I had to talk to you. About Richard and you—and me."

CHAPTER 12 ■

Had Richard told her?

But that would have been too cruel, something that Richard could not have done.

Well, then, had she guessed? Had there been something in the air, something intangible, untetherable and yet present whenever Myra and Richard were together in the same room, breathing the same air, allowing their eyes to meet, no matter how swiftly, nor how impersonally.

The fire sighed softly. Lilac sachet lay in a fragrant cloud in the room. Alice twisted her small hands together; on one of them shone her wedding ring. "I wish you would say something, Myra. It's so hard to try to do this alone."

Myra said slowly, "You are very tired, Alice. Can't we talk later?"

Alice's eyelashes swept upward for a fractional second in a glance that was half-frightened, half-bold, like the bright inquiry of a bird peering from underbrush. She leaned forward, speaking rapidly and unevenly. "We haven't ever known each other very well, Myra. But I know so much about you, you see. Tim adores you. So does Aunt Cornelia. And then you've been so very kind to Richard and to Aunt Cornelia since you both came back home, in spite of the horror that happened here."

"Don't think of that."

"Yes, yes. That's what the Governor said to me. Try to forget. Resume your life as if you had only been away for a time. He said that. I will."

But she turned her head, nevertheless. She put her chin upon her hand and looked into the fire and added, in a musing voice, "I must pretend it never happened. I must make a new life. I must try to be firm and determined. I must build up self-confidence. I must be the kind of wife Richard wants. That's why"—she turned to Myra—"I had to see you tonight. I can't rest, I can't sleep until I know what you are going to do."

"What I am going to do?" repeated Myra with a kind of astonishment.

"About Richard, of course," said Alice.

So Richard must have told her. What had he said?

Alice went on with that weary swiftness and breathlessness. "I thought we could talk about it alone together. He needn't know. He mustn't know. You see, I'd heard so much of you from others, that I felt we could talk about it honestly and frankly, the two of us." She leaned forward, a soft lock of her hair fell over her Dresden china-like face. She brushed it back and said, "I don't blame either of you. It was bound to happen. I expected it even sooner."

"You expected it!" Myra was caught again in amazement as if Alice had spread a soft net about her which had tripped and entangled her.

"I knew he'd be lonely. I knew that there are always attractive girls—and, of course, you are extremely attractive, Myra, in that sensible, crisp way of yours."

Something very feminine, very swift and very absurd in the smallness of its resentment stirred in Myra. Was her claim to feminine charm that of being sensible?

The wide, gilt-framed mirror over the dressing table with all its glitter of gold and crystal, reflected them, and oddly, quickly, both women glanced in that mirror. Yet they did not observe their own faces for their eyes met in the mirror, met and held inquiringly, like the exploring glance of two strangers meeting for the first time.

And then as swiftly, again at a shared impulse, both women looked away from the mirror. Alice said, with a rather nervous laugh, "That mirror is too dark. I must have it changed."

She leaned forward again toward Myra. "You were here in the house all these months. Propinquity is always the answer, really. Neither of you could possibly have expected me to come home—like this—back to Richard as his wife. I don't blame either of you. And I don't want anybody to be hurt. Yet—yet . . ." said Alice and stopped and put out both her hand appealingly again toward Myra.

The net was so soft that Myra could barely recognize its presence and yet it lay all at once all about her, as gentle and as pervading and persistent as the scent of lilac. And its meshes were imperceptibly drawing themselves together. Myra got up and went to the window and let the cool night air blow on her face.

"Please look at me, Myra," said Alice softly. "I've hurt you. I'm sorry. Please look at me . . ."

Myra turned reluctantly. "Has Richard talked to you?"

Alice hesitated. She bit her small perfect lip and then said, "No. Not—directly. No."

"How did you know?"

There was for a bare instant a fixed, set look in Alice's face. She said, "It is true then!"

Again astonishment touched Myra. "But you already knew?"

Alice's soft dark eyelashes lowered quickly. "Oh, yes. I knew. I—guessed. It was in the air somehow between you, Myra. Nobody told me. But I—knew. One does know those things. Of course I—I'd better tell you the whole truth, Myra. I had feared you. I knew Richard would be lonely. I would have offered to release him, if he had asked for it. If he had asked for it while I was in prison," said Alice.

She paused and waited and then went on. "What else could I have done? I could not have expected Richard to live out his life alone. Yes, if he'd asked me then for a divorce I'd have consented. If it—broke my heart . . ." said Alice and leaned her head back against the lace pillows.

Again to Myra the very complexity of her feelings was bewildering. She could not grudge Alice her freedom and her exoneration. She did not. *And Alice was in the right.* That at least was clear and unquestionable.

Well, she had known that from the beginning. She must tell Alice, she must end this terrible interview. And Alice said, "I am not a practical person. I've never been. Yet—well, there is a practical, and, I admit, a selfish view which yet I must make myself consider. You see, it is true that if Richard leaves me now people will say that I killed Jack Manders, that Richard believes that I killed him."

"Oh, no!" cried Myra, shocked. "No one can ever say that of you, Alice."

Alice put her hand across her eyes. The wedding ring on it caught a gleam of light. "I dread the next few months.

Myra, I need Richard. And I have to ask you this. Do you think that perhaps—I don't mean to hurt you—but that perhaps Richard might have fancied himself in love with almost anybody? That sounds so cruel!" she cried in sudden compunction. "But wait—Richard loved me. He adored me. We were married a month after we met—one summer in Paris. Mildred Wilkinson introduced us. He had graduated only two weeks before and was having a holiday before settling into the harness that he'd always known was waiting for him. He adored me," she said again softly. "He gave me everything I wanted. I hadn't a cent, you know. There was barely enough to send me to a good school. Luckily for me, I met Mildred there—she gave me the trip abroad. And I met and married Richard. It was love at first sight. And always, even through the trial, even when everything went against me, he still loved me. He proved it. He was loyal all the time, every minute. Don't you think it possible that now that I'm free he'll turn back to me? Don't you think that he may even now be a little—well, embarrassed—by whatever the situation has been between you?" Again she cried swiftly, "I sound cruel. I—all of us, are very much in your debt. But sometimes it is kind to be cruel."

"Alice, you need not have said any of this."

"What do you mean? It is true, isn't it?"

"I am going to leave. I told Richard that before you came home. There is no question of divorce; there is no question of Richard and me marrying. There never will be. Now then . . ." She moved swiftly toward the door. "They are waiting for me. Is there anything I can do for you? Do you want Francine?"

"No . . ."

"I'll go downstairs then. . . ."

"Myra," said Alice, "when are you going to leave?"

Myra whirled around, for the last time astonished by that wholly astonishing interview. Again Alice's gentle, pale face, her pathetically weary eyes were disarming.

"I don't know. I can't go immediately because the investigation is to be reopened, as you know. . . . "

Alice sat up suddenly. "Reopened!"

"I thought you knew."

"They're going to try to find out who—murdered him?"

"Yes, naturally. I thought you . . ."

"I didn't realize that," said Alice sitting back. "I didn't think—I—it's all so horrible to me, you know. Does it mean police, questions, everything all over again? I thought they were only going to try Webb!"

"They'll try Webb for perjury. You'd better rest, Alice. Try not to think of it."

How strange it was that she could hate Alice and feel sorry for her at the same time. Hate her? But she did not hate her. It was impossible to hate Alice; and Alice was in the right. It always came back to that.

Alice said, "I thought Webb killed him! Nobody was here except Webb! And then Tim . . ." She broke off to stare at Myra and cried suddenly, "They *can't* suspect Tim! Tim wouldn't hurt anything!" Her face sobered. "Tim . . . I must see him, Myra. Tell him I must see him. I want him to know that I understand everything. He didn't mean to hurt me; he suffered, poor Tim. No matter how important the curtains were he couldn't help forgetting. Why I — even *I*, Myra—couldn't have said whether they were open or closed when the shots came. They asked me that night. I didn't know. Why should I? Tell Tim I understand and I want to see him."

"But Tim didn't . . ." began Myra and realized that Richard hadn't told Alice of Tim's lie which had so success-fully and unexpectedly proved to be the truth. Why not? Because Alice might, unintentionally, tell it?

Alice said curiously, "Tim didn't what?"

"He didn't mean to injure you," said Myra slowly.

"I know that," said Alice. "I must tell him . . ."

Someone knocked, Myra opened the door and Francine, eyes glittering, said, "If you please, Miss Cornelia says they are waiting, Miss Myra."

Alice said quickly, "Darling, I've kept you! Go on down to dinner. I shall be quite all right. You might just build up the fire, Francine."

Myra closed the door behind her.

The present pattern, the immediate path lay directly ahead of her. Some time she'd forget; some time pain would be only a memory of pain.

She went down the stairs. This time she kept herself from touching the newel post. The others were in the dining room, around the table, the candles lighted, the silver and crystal glimmering. Miss Cornelia in her wheel chair sat at the head of the table. Richard was not there. But then he'd already had dinner with Alice.

Miss Cornelia smiled and nodded toward the vacant chair. "We didn't wait." She turned to Sam, continuing their conversation, frankly, it seemed, before Barton, because he already knew so much. "Are we, do you think, to expect a perfect deluge of notoriety?"

Myra slid into the chair. Tim, silent, was opposite her.

Sam said, "We can't escape a certain amount of it. The police may help us there. Indeed I'm surprised there is not a police guard already here." He went on to talk of past experiences, nervously, watching the door.

Myra listened, hearing only the words. How swiftly and unerringly Alice had guessed the truth, and then as unerringly had gone about it to prove or disprove her suspicion. "*It is true then*," she had said.

That perhaps was the really astonishing part of their astonishing talk. Alice's instantaneous efficiency and courage in grappling with the situation in the very moment, practically speaking, of her return. Yet she had always been swift thinking and efficient, and, in spite of her fragile look, very courageous. Even the reporters, writing of the trial, had complimented her composure and dignity—understandable now. She had had the support of her own knowledge of the truth.

They were talking again of the investigation. Sam replied to some question of Aunt Cornelia's and part of his reply caught Myra from her thoughts of Alice. " . . . the district attorney may have a new angle. A new clue."

"A new clue? Such as"—Aunt Cornelia faltered but finished—"Richard's gun."

Sam nodded. "But of course I may be wrong. Perhaps he has no new angle so consequently is fishing for one."

"Fishing?" inquired Aunt Cornelia sharply.

Sam explained. "Suppose they have no new clues, suppose there is no angle they haven't already covered. So suppose the district attorney says to the Governor, release Alice. Tell everybody there is to be a new investigation. Scare the hell out of them if you can—and see what happens."

Tim's sleek head jerked up. "A new round?"

"Exactly. Give everybody a new set of chips and see," said Sam deliberately, "who bets, and how many cards they want and . . ."

Richard returned. They heard the heavy slam of the door directly across the hall and all turned. He was bareheaded and a topcoat was slung over his shoulders. He walked across to the dining room, gathering them in one quick glance, meeting Myra's eyes, but so swiftly that the fleeting look told her nothing. "Hello, Sam."

Sam rose and went to meet him. "Hello, Dick. I came straight from the club."

"I've been to see Webb."

"Webb Manders!"

"He's coming here. He'll be here in a few minutes."

A number of things happened all at once. Barton came in with peaches on a silver dish. The front door opened and closed again heavily. Aunt Cornelia's hands clenched hard on the lace cloth, her sapphires glittering. Tim got up and dropped his napkin. Mildred Wilkinson crossed the hall behind Richard and stopped, peering over his shoulder.

Sam said to Richard, *"Why did you do that?"*

Mildred said, fluttering, "I came up the drive just after you, Richard. I didn't ring. . . ."

Tim said, "If Webb shot him, what did he do with the gun?"

Myra saw every detail and heard every word but in the same moment a question, a frightening and terrible project came into full being in her mind.

Perhaps it had been there for some time unrecognized. Perhaps it had been planted by Sam.

If Sam could make a trap of the gun—could she?

Mildred, peering, fluttering, said, "I hope I'm not intruding. I simply can't wait any longer to see Alice. Have I come at the wrong time?"

Aunt Cornelia unclenched her hands deliberately and looked at Myra. "Please take Mildred to Alice," she said.

Her look said, "Get this woman out of here."

CHAPTER 13

But Mildred lingered, letting her coat drop, stooping, fumbling to pick it up, delaying long enough to hear Richard's reply to Sam's question.

"I thought we'd better talk. All of us."

"You and Webb and Tim . . ."

"Webb has admitted to so much of the truth; maybe he knows more."

Sam asked slowly, "Do you think he'll tell it?"

"He might—if you question him, Sam."

Mildred had the coat up nearly to her shoulders and dropped it again, her face blank with listening. Sam said, "How did you get him to come?"

"Told him facts. Told him we had till morning to pool what we knew. The truth is somewhere, Sam."

"If Webb killed him he's going to keep a close mouth."

"But if he didn't we're in the same boat, Webb and I . . ."

"I'm in there, too," said Tim. "Only, I don't see how Webb could have killed him, even if he wanted to. I saw his car pass me, I heard him shut off the engine, and then only seconds later the sound of the shots. There simply wasn't time for him to get out of the car, get around the library wing of the house and across the terrace in time for that."

Aunt Cornelia said suddenly, "Tim, I never asked, I never thought—perhaps they asked you then. But are you sure it *was* Webb in the car?"

Mildred got her coat over one bony, freckled arm. Tim said, "It was Webb's car, and when I got to the terrace Webb was there in the library."

"But did you see him?"

"Not actually—no. The lights of the car were in my eyes. He said he saw me walking along the driveway."

There was a short silence. Sam said, "Everything's different now; the whole set-up is different. Well . . ." he paused again, his dark eyes narrow and thoughtful.

Richard said, "That's not why he's coming though. He's coming because he's scared . . ."

"Aren't we all," said Tim.

". . . and wants to know what we intend to do."

Mildred's coat started to slide again and this time Myra caught it and said, "Alice will want to see you. . . ." She led the way along the hall and up the wide stairway. Mildred followed reluctantly, still, Myra thought, straining her ears toward the murmur of voices from the dining room. It was so strong an impression that she turned and Mildred had actually stopped and was leaning over the banister, her hand on the newel post.

Again Myra's heart gave a sickening lurch. Mildred? But Mildred knew nothing of the gun. Mildred had never in any way entered the case. But, in spite of herself, Myra watched.

Sam had said, a new round, new chips, new bets. He'd said the gun was important. It had been safe during Alice's imprisonment; it had endangered nobody.

It was different now.

Mildred knew that Myra was watching her. She saw recognition of it come into Mildred's face. She saw Mildred turn her head slowly to meet Myra's eyes. She could not read the look in Mildred's eyes, but her hand slowly let go the newel post. She said, "How terribly bewildering it all is! Webb—how could he have killed his brother?"

Her face in the dim light seemed very drawn and white. "Perhaps he didn't."

"Someone killed him," said Mildred, and started up the stairway again, her limp green chiffons trailing after her.

All of them said and thought that: someone killed him.

They reached Alice's door and knocked and Alice told them to come in.

"Mildred!" she cried.

She was still in the chaise longue, and already, like a child, looking at her possessions, her jewels. A square leather jewel box stood open on the foot of the chaise longue and odd pieces of jewelry littered the table and Alice's lap. She cried,

"Mildred . . ." and put out her arms, her hands full of jewelry.

Something dropped, a linked bracelet, with a tiny jewel watch. Myra picked it up as the two women embraced, and put it on the table. Alice had always loved jewelry and wore it constantly.

Mildred sat down in the little green slipper chair beside Alice, and slipped off her coat again.

"Alice, how wonderful you look. What was it like? How terrible it must have been! And here you are back in your own beautiful room after that cell . . ."

"Well, it wasn't exactly a cell, Mildred. It was a—a sort of room, you know. Quite sunny really and very clean . . ."

"So unexpected! Not that I ever believed you did it. You know that, Alice. How *could* Webb have lied so horribly! Alice . . ." Mildred bent to pick up another piece of jewelry that had dropped—a small locket, old-fashioned, in black enamel and pearls. Myra murmured something about leaving them and opened the door. Mildred, her voice sharp and avid said, "Alice, what is this? I never saw it before. . . ."

"What? Oh, that, I've had it ages. . . ."

"Where did you get it?"

"Why, I suppose Richard gave me so much . . ."

Even at the moment of their reunion Mildred's curiosity operated. Myra closed the door and walked slowly back toward the stairway.

She must make a decision about the gun. And she must explore—quickly—the path of speculation she had instinctively wished to avoid. Well, then: first it *was* Richard's gun and, above everybody else, Richard was suspect for the murder of Jack Manders. So she could not give the gun to the police or to anybody except Richard himself. It might conceivably clear him, but that was too dangerous a risk to run. It was far more likely to bolster their case against him. His gun, his house, his wife—and the gun had been safely hidden in his house probably all the time since the murder.

But then, she thought, wouldn't he have removed it? Wouldn't the police see that?

It was dangerous, too, to take that risk. Besides, they'd say it *was* safe, so long as Alice was in prison. Or would they say even that he had expected that very fact to operate to prove his innocence and Alice's guilt—in case of the exact shift in circumstances which now confronted them? It was a tortuous line of reasoning; yet ominously clear, too. No, she'd not give it to the police.

And she could not give it to Richard, for suppose—only suppose—Richard had put it there.

It was, of course, the frightening curve in the path, beyond which she would not look and now must look. Well, then: Sam had said suppose Richard came home and found Alice and Jack and saw red. His gun, his wife, his home that he loved. If he had killed Jack, suppose there had been provocation.

Instantly a passion of denial rose against that. He couldn't have killed Jack because he wouldn't have let Alice go to trial for it. Not Richard.

The debate had this time a conclusion; it had to have. Leave the gun where it is; it is unloaded, it is safe; see what happens.

Sam would have done it; it was what he had meant. Why shouldn't she do it, when so much was at stake? Sheer faith and love demand courage; courage, indeed, was better than blind and unreasoning faith. That suddenly seemed clear, like a debt she owed to Richard. She went slowly down the stairs, doubting, nevertheless, her own decision.

Aunt Cornelia was at the foot of the stairs with Barton and Tim preparing to carry her up. She said, as Myra reached her, "I'll stop and speak to Alice. I'll get Mildred out of the house; it's better." Tim said, "Steady her a minute, Myra. Now then, my lady, here's a chariot."

She slid again upon their linked hands. This time no one touched or seemed at all aware of the newel post.

Sam and Richard were in the dining room talking. Myra went slowly through the library where Barton had built up the fire, and out upon the terrace.

It was much colder yet below the chill there was still the mysterious earthy promise of spring. Gradually her eyes adjusted themselves to the night. There were a few stars and a scattering of swiftly moving clouds. The balustrade, rimmed below with a thick growth of shrubbery, loomed up solid and black before her. She walked toward it, her slippers making little taps along the chill flagstones.

The night was still, in spite of the scudding clouds, with only intermittent breezes. Almost, she thought, she could hear the slow swell of the tide along the Sound far below where she and Richard had stood and talked, argued and lost the case against themselves, and then—for a moment, for an instant, there at the break in the hedge not far below her had thought that they might win. So briefly, so shortly . . . "There's just one thing that's really important. I'm going to marry you. . . ." Richard had said, and had looked up and the lights of the house were blazing, and Alice was waiting in the warm and lighted room.

Myra shivered a little under her thin red jacket. Suddenly she realized that the thing she clutched so tightly in her hand was her own evening bag. She had planned to get rid of the shell and it was now simple. Dig a little hole somewhere, under some hedge, along the path, anywhere out of sight, push leaves over it.

As suddenly the thing that Sam had suggested about the gun, which had seemed so tremendous, so intricate, so impossible for her, Myra, to achieve, seemed almost as simple.

The gun was in the newel post. Someone had hidden it there; now that there was a new set-up, a new round of poker, somebody might have to get rid of the gun. All she had to do was watch.

It would not be Richard.

A night bird rustled somewhere. Perhaps it was Willie on a night prowl.

Behind her the terrace doors opened and a rectangle of light shot out upon her and then vanished as the door closed again. "Myra," said Richard's voice, "I thought you were there," and came toward her.

His face emerged dimly from the night, yet she knew it so well that every line seemed clear to her. He sighed and put one foot up on the balustrade and leaned on his knee. "Myra, I told Sam just now the truth about Tim's action in going to the Governor. I was of two minds about doing it, but Sam insisted that Tim *couldn't* have forgotten the curtain. He suggested that Tim had shot Jack and then, kid-like, got scared. So I told him. But I don't want anyone else to know—not even Aunt Cornelia or—Alice . . ." He took a long breath and got out a cigarette and lighted it, tossing the match down in the deep black shadows below the balustrade.

It was again for an instant very quiet, so night sounds made themselves manifest—a faint rustle in the shrubbery, a soft breeze away down in the pines where she and Richard had walked so short a time ago. Richard said abruptly, "I talked

to Alice. Not much—while we were having dinner. I think
she knows about us, Myra."

"Yes . . ." began Myra and remembered Alice's plea for
secrecy. Richard needn't know, he must not know, Alice had
said. But that was unfair! Myra had every right to tell Richard of that interview, even though nothing she or Richard,
or even Alice, could put in words, could change or alter
facts.

But without marking her hesitation, Richard went on, "It's
just as well, perhaps. God knows what this thing is going to
do to us all, or where it will end. But when it does end . . ."
His cigarette, scarcely lighted, made a small red arc out over
the balustrade, across the darkness below. He turned and
took her suddenly and closely in his arms.

The breeze stirred the pines and the dark, thick growth
below the terrace. The flagstones felt cold under her slip-
pered feet. Richard said, "I love you. I'll always love
you. . . ."

Sam stood in the doorway. He could not have heard. He
must have seen the closeness of their figures. He called,
"Webb is here."

"All right," said Richard but held her.

Sam closed the door.

Quite slowly and deliberately Richard turned her face and
put his own hard cheek against it for a moment. Then
abruptly he released her. "Will you come in? You don't have
to listen, you know. And I don't know whether or not we'll
accomplish anything. Even if Webb knows anything he may
not tell it."

She had to have time in which to quiet the uneven pounding of her heart. She had to veil the look that must be in her
eyes before others saw it. "In a moment," she said.

"All right." He took a long breath, seemed to square his
shoulders and went back along the terrace, in at the lighted
door.

She stood quite still. The clouds had drifted so fully across
the sky that only a few stars now showed through. The
hedges were like lines of soldiers, black, standing solidly at
attention. The clipped privet was outlined in dense black
humps. Her small gold evening bag was cold in her fingers.
Somewhere down there she'd hide the shell. She walked
slowly across the terrace in the direction of the steps and

then down into the mingled shadows below. Willie apparently heard her. He came in a scramble from somewhere, waggled happily when she spoke to him and attached himself to her.

The new spring lawn was soft and damp below her slippers. As she drew nearer, the entrance to the path became clearer, the outline of the hedges sharper. She reached the path between the hedges and entered it, glancing along its length down toward the pines and up at a gradually ascending slope which it took along the house and at an almost parallel line with it, until it turned and gave upon the graveled driveway, fairly near the front entrance. Empty now in both directions, as far as she could see, the path ran like a gray ribbon between the two sharp black lines of the hedges. Willie followed her and stopped when she stopped.

It was much more difficult to bury the shell than she had thought so small and simple an act could possibly be. The soil was loose and damp. She used a twig and then her fingers to dig with, and finally opened her bag and got out the shell itself and pushed it deeply into the loose little space. She covered it carefully, stepped on the loose soil to flatten it and dug around into the roots of the hedge for leaf mold and raked it over the spot. But it was her feeling of stealth that was difficult—something like guilt, as if it were a small and terrible grave. She looked quickly along the path again before she rose from the deep shadow. Nothing moved anywhere except Willie who had watched her with interest, sniffing at the leaves. She stood, her breath coming fast. No one would think of looking for a shell. The gun, perhaps, but not a shell.

Her scarlet silk jacket was thin. She shivered and, merely because it was then a nearer approach to the house, started along the path in the opposite direction from the pines, toward the driveway and the front entrance. Willie, bored, disappeared somewhere in the shadows again.

The turf was soundless and seemed cold and damp. Her skirts whispered lightly against the black walls of the hedge.

Perhaps Webb would confess. Perhaps Webb, really, had murdered his brother and then tried to escape by accusing Alice!

She reached the end of the path and came out upon the graveled space, lined with thick black clumps of laurel, which lay around the stately, pillared front entrance to

Thorne House. A light shone over the steps and spread outward to the white gravel. There were three cars parked
there. Sam's of course, and Webb's, and the old, enormous
Cadillac custom-made, majestic, bought by Mildred's father
years ago and used now by Mildred. Anything the Wilkinsons ever bought was the best that could be bought and they
used it, determined apparently to get the last cent out of it,
forever. And quite suddenly the lights of the car were turned
on, full and dazzling in her face.

She caught her breath and put up her hand to shield her
eyes and instantly the lights blinked out again. The car door
opened so the interior of the car lighted and Mildred said,
"Myra—Myra . . ."

She'd been crying. Her pale-blue eyes were rimmed with
scarlet, her eyelashes wet, and her face, in the cruelly sharp
downward glare of the lights, was streaked with tears and
was old-looking, with lines showing under the rather thick
make-up she habitually used, and her lipstick was blurred.
She clutched her coat around her thin throat and said, unsteadily, "Myra, I saw Webb Manders come. What are they
going to do?"

"I don't know." She was shivering so her own voice was
uneven. "Is anything wrong, Mildred?"

"Wrong!" said Mildred and laughed in a high, half-hysterical way and stopped and cried. Her mouth stretched in a
sobbing grimace. "*Wrong!* Oh, no, no! It's only—only Alice.
It hurts me to—to see her like that." She steadied her lower
lip with her teeth, and stared at Myra. Her eyes had bright,
sharp black pupils. She cried, as if Myra had turned away.
"Wait a minute, Myra. I wouldn't think that Dick would let
Webb enter the house. I can't see why . . ." She stopped and
sucked in her breath and cried again, "What are they doing?"

"I don't know."

"You do know! I can see it in your face. I can guess—why,
of course!" Comprehension flashed across her distraught,
blotched face. "That's it, of course! They're trying to patch
up something all together that will hold against the investigation. To protect each other. Richard and Webb and—why,
Tim! Your brother! He was here that night, too."

"They're not trying to patch up something, Mildred. Please
don't say that to anyone. It's not true."

"No, no, I won't! Trust me. I—I didn't mean to ask questions. I—it's only that seeing Alice again has upset me. I sup-

pose it seems strange to you, my feeling for Alice, I mean. But you see . . ." Suddenly she turned away from Myra and stared ahead across the shining dark hood of the car. Her hands beat softly on the wheel. She said jerkily, "I haven't had many friends, Myra, not really. I don't think I'm the kind to make friends somehow. I—it isn't easy for me. And then I've always been so hedged in with all that money, with being a Wilkinson. Now I'm alone and—life has gone by somehow—and the money doesn't give me the pleasure I thought it would. Alice . . ." She took a long, uneven breath and said, "Alice was always so beautiful."

Myra had never heard Mildred speak so earnestly. She had never, in fact, heard her speak without a certain flavor of affectedness and artificiality. The years-long devotion of a plain and lonely woman for a woman who had everything that to Mildred seemed desirable, was both moving and pathetic.

Mildred went on slowly. "We've been friends a long time, you know. She was always pretty and popular. She has the gift of charm. I was plain and rich and unpopular, but I loved her. I never believed she killed Jack, of course, and I never believed she would be convicted. They told me she wouldn't. Everybody said the jury would never convict a woman so—so beautiful," said Mildred with a curious, sad wistfulness.

Myra said quickly, "Mildred, nobody could have been more loyal than you. All this time you've remained a friend to all of us. You've come here faithfully, you've never let anything shake your friendship with Alice."

Mildred laughed again. It was a short, abrupt, laugh. She said, "I'll go now. Good night, Myra."

She reached for the ignition. She turned on the engine and its sedate heavy throb woke the silent night. In the act of closing the car door she leaned out and said loudly over the throb of the engine, "Tell Alice I'll be back."

The door slammed and the light inside the car went out. With a jerk of the gears the car began to move backward, around the semi-circle, in reverse. Myra, puzzled by Mildred's sadly revealing words, puzzled by her return, puzzled more than anything by that short, abrupt—and bitter?— laugh, watched the big, sedate car come to a stop, start forward, swerve and then go out of sight beyond the curve of laurels.

The sound of the engine gradually died away. Myra turned

and walked back to the steps. The massive front door, with the great old knocker which had felt the pressure of so many hands, was unlocked. That was lucky, she thought, shivering in the cold. She would not have to ring for Barton. She went into the hall.

She was so chilled that she was trembling a little. She stood still, gathering warmth. The lights were still on in the hall, but the dining room was dark, the table cleared. Lights and the low and indistinguishable murmur of men's voices came from the library, at the other end. She walked slowly in that direction. The newel post again drew her like an evil magnet. As she passed the stairway, she could not help looking at it. She had to resist an impulse, again, to touch it. She stopped in the library doorway.

Richard was standing at the fireplace, his elbow on the mantel. Sam was sitting on the edge of a table, swinging one leg and staring intently at the knifelike crease in his brown trousers. Tim was smoking.

And something had gone wrong.

Everything had gone wrong.

CHAPTER 14 ■

She knew it even before she entered the room, before she saw Richard's face and before Webb Manders spoke—Webb who had been only a name to her then, not a personality, not a man who lived and breathed and walked, and had sent Alice to prison. She took a step forward and stopped. She had seen Jack casually a few times, while she and Aunt Cornelia were preparing to go to England years ago. Thus she remembered him when the incredible news of the murder came. She had never before to her knowledge seen Webb. He stood in an aggressive attitude, like defiance and anger, just before the terrace door. He looked like his brother and unlike him; he was tall, too, but more slightly built, with Jack's thick, curly black hair and blunt, thick features. Webb had a lantern jaw, however, the jaw of a despot or a zealot, a narrower, more angular face and just then a look of cold anger. His lips, curved and full like Jack's, were, however, pale and drawn into ruthless lines. Jack might have looked like that, thought Myra suddenly, ruthless and rather cruel, if he had so wished.

A flicker of Webb's eyes in her direction showed that he saw her and knew who she must be. He said suddenly, "So we have nothing to say to each other. I came because I was curious. I wondered why you came to me and why you wanted me to believe that you were friendly and that you thought we might get together to our mutual benefit. Mutual benefit . . ." said Webb with a kind of fury of scorn and anger. "Your benefit! You're only trying to save your own neck, Dick. You and Sam hoped to pin a murder charge on me. Well, I'm not having it. As for you, Tim, some time maybe you'll explain why you've done this. If I'd known yesterday that the only evidence the Governor had was your little story I'd have . . ." He stopped and drew in his lips and said, "I'd have taken a different line."

Sam laughed shortly. "You remembered witnesses barely in time, Webb. A few more words and we'd have made you regret it."

"Oh, no, you wouldn't," said Webb. "You're too good a lawyer to try threats, Sam, or to lose your temper."

Richard said, "Okay, Webb. If you don't want to talk . . ."

"I've told everything I know a hundred times."

"You've told some things you didn't know, too," said Sam.

Webb's face flushed angrily. Richard said, "Skip it, Sam. All right then, Webb. But you *were* on the scene of Jack's murder immediately. Will you answer one or two questions?"

"I don't know. You can ask them."

"All right. Between us, aside from your feeling about Alice, did you see anyone else that night? In the hall—on the terrace—anywhere?"

Webb waited a moment as if exploring it for traps. Then he said, but still angrily, "No! I didn't have any reason to believe there *was* anybody else. That doesn't give you or Tim a clean bill of health, though, Dick. It was a dark night. I was running. Somebody *could* have got away without my knowing it. Any other questions?"

Sam started to speak. Richard said, "Wait a minute, Sam. Yes. The gun. Webb, the story you've admitted was not true is out now. Actually—in fact—*did* you see the gun?"

Webb hesitated again. This time for a long moment or two while he stared at the lilies Mildred had brought. Finally he said, "No, I didn't."

"Did you look for it?"

"Not then. Later, yes. After . . ." his angry eyes went to Tim. "After Tim got here. Tim with his convenient memory." There was in his face suddenly a puzzled look. "I'm an honest man, so I'll tell you something. I'd trade anything I knew, right now, for the truth from Tim. Why did he corroborate what I told in the first place and now, nearly two years later, come out with this? He said that he forgot the curtain. Obviously he's going to stick to that explanation. I don't believe it. I don't think the Governor or district attorney or anybody else believes it. But I'd like to know the truth. I'm an honest man and . . ."

"You, honest?" said Sam, lifting his thin black eyebrows. "A man who sent a woman to prison by swearing to a lie?"

A slow, queer flush crept upward again over Webb's face. "All right. And I'm going to be charged with perjury. But I'm not going to be charged with murder." He looked at Richard. "You'd like that, wouldn't you? You saw the jam that you and young Lane are in. You said to yourself 'I'll be smart; I'll get Sam Putnam, he's smart. We'll all get together and work something out of Webb and fasten the thing on him. We'll cross question him; we'll trick him.' Oh, sure, very smart. Only I'm not having any."

Richard said slowly, "No, that's wrong, Webb. I'm not trying to fasten a murder charge on anybody. I told you the truth. You were here that night before anybody else. It seemed to me it might profit us all to survey the situation together. That's all."

"Profit you, you mean," said Webb.

With an impatient gesture Sam got up from the table and, as he moved, saw Myra. "Oh, Myra, I didn't realize you were here." Tim jerked around as Sam spoke. Richard looked at her too and said, "This is Mr. Webb Manders, Myra. Miss Lane—Lady Carmichael's ward."

"I know." Webb gave her a quick hard glance and a nod.

"I've heard that you were living here, Miss Lane." His eyes went to Richard and back to her and yet so swiftly and so coolly that if there was significance in it, it was not overt. He said as coolly, "If you can get the truth out of that brother of yours, Miss Lane, you'll be doing us all a favor."

"He has righted a great wrong," said Myra, "for which you were responsible."

A flash of anger came into his eyes. His lantern jaw thrust forward. "But you do realize," he said, "that Tim *could* have killed my brother."

"Not according to your own testimony, Webb," said Richard shortly. "You said that you passed him on the driveway, that you were in a car and he came in after Jack was killed."

"But my testimony," said Webb, "was perjury. Don't forget that. When this new investigation gets under way they aren't going to neglect me. Oh, no."

"They're not going to credit any story you now tell," said Richard wearily. "You may as well tell us anything you know."

Webb said coolly and distinctly, "I did not hear or see anyone in the hall or on the terrace. You may have been there, Dick. I'm not saying you weren't. But I didn't see you, if that's what you're scared about. And I never saw the gun. I don't know anything about it. But if you want to know where it is, ask your wife."

Richard's fists doubled, Webb drew back a step quickly, and Sam, as quickly, intervened. "I warned you, Dick, to keep your temper. He's leaving. . . ."

"Oh, I'm leaving!" said Webb at the door. "That's right! But get this straight. I came in this door and there was Jack —where you're standing. Alice was kneeling there beside him—his blood on her dress. *And on her hands.* I believed it then and I still believe it. *Wait*—I knew he was dead. And I knew that I'd have to prove that she did it. Juries are too soft-hearted with women—pretty women, rich women. I was on the driveway when I heard the shots. I had tried to see in that window, over there, and I couldn't because the curtains were closed. So that was clear in my mind. I could think fast. As soon as I saw what had happened I sent Alice to the telephone. I ran across and pulled open one of the curtains and ran back to him. I didn't hear or see young Lane . . ." There was a look of venom and hatred in his long face. "When he backed up my story I thought merely that he was telling the truth, that he'd come up on the terrace and reached the door only after I'd got back to Jack's body. I lied, sure, I lied, but because I believed that she shot him. Because I intended to accuse her, and intended to make the accusation stick. And I still believe she killed him."

Tim was nearest him. He had been gradually moving over toward him, although Myra did not realize it until he swung at Webb, quietly, really, and in a businesslike manner. Webb saw it coming and ducked. Tim's fist struck him along the jaw and sheered off. Richard was across the room in one movement, Sam after him. Suddenly all of them were separated, and Webb, rubbing his jaw, shouted angrily, "Sure, three of you against one. Well, I'm not going to fight anybody. But I'll tell you. Suppose Alice and young Lane made an agreement."

"*Agreement!*" said Sam.

"Sure. Alice says if young Lane will do the shooting, she'll take the rap for awhile. Then young Lane is to remember some evidence which will get her out of the clink. See? So he goes to war and probably the two years seemed a long time to Alice. But he does come back, and he does get her out."

"You're crazy, Webb!" said Richard.

"Oh, no, I'm not. Suppose that's why there isn't any gun found; suppose Jack was actually shot with Dick's gun half an hour before I got here; suppose Tim or Alice got away with the gun, Tim hurries away from the house and Alice or somebody fires the shots I heard . . ."

"This is fantastic, Webb! There are a hundred loopholes," said Sam.

"Okay, what are they? The biggest argument against it is the danger that Alice would get the death penalty and Alice was pretty sure she wouldn't. She's too pretty."

"Why?" said Richard. "Jack didn't threaten Alice. An elaborate plan on her part—and Tim's—to get rid of him is nonsense."

"Nonsense? Okay. But young Lane would do anything for your wife, even to murder . . ."

"Webb, you're . . ."

"No, I'm not! But he's crazy about her. Always has been. Sure, call it puppy love if you want to. But this puppy was trained to kill."

Sam caught Richard's arm and shouted, "Tim don't . . ."

But this time Tim did not move and Webb backed hurriedly out the door. "I'm leaving! I'm not going to fight Dick or anybody! But you can't pin a murder charge on me."

His long face vanished, his footsteps thumped along the terrace. Sam's hand on Richard's arm gradually relaxed. The thumping, angry—and frightened?—footsteps diminished and in the strained silence the little French clock began to strike energetically, with a musical nonchalant briskness which was all out of character with the scene it had marked.

The little French clock which also had marked the moment of Jack Manders' death!

It struck twelve times and Richard said with a heavy sigh, "I was afraid it would do no good. He doesn't know anything about the gun."

"He does if he shot Jack," said Sam. "If that gun is still anywhere around, whoever used it is going to get rid of it. It's the only thing, now, that can prove or disprove anything. Too much time has passed; too many things have been forgotten or destroyed that might have been clues. The gun is the big piece of evidence that has never been produced. But honestly—I don't think it can be produced. Nobody would be such a fool as not to get rid of the thing." He sighed. "Dick, I'm your lawyer. We've got only till tomorrow. And I'm damned if I know what to do."

"Neither do I," said Richard. "It's late. We might as well go to bed."

Tim said suddenly, "Webb was right about Alice, Dick. I mean the way I feel about her. But it's okay, you know. I mean . . ."

"Oh, Lord, I know it's okay, Tim."

But Tim had to go on. He spoke easily and frankly, without even a tinge of embarrassment. "I was always crazy about her. Not that she ever knew it. I mean—well, she'd have been upset."

Richard said, "I know, Tim."

Tim said, "She's—Alice. She wouldn't have touched Jack with a ten-foot pole. She . . . Of course, I'm crazy about her! But that doesn't mean that I don't—that *you* aren't— well, hell," said Tim, "you are just as important to me as Alice. Only . . ." he stopped, and Richard said, "You're all right, Tim. Forget it. We'll all be all right, once we get through this business tomorrow." He turned to Sam. "You'll stay of course, Sam. I told Barton to put out pajamas and a razor for you. You're in the room next to Tim."

Richard was suddenly banking the fire, arranging the screen as if it was any night. As suddenly they were all moving toward the stairway.

"Anybody want a highball?" said Richard.

Nobody did. Sam was at the bottom step. Again to Myra the newel post seemed endowed with magnetic powers. Sam's hand touched it, lingered, while he turned to say something to Richard. She had to watch, testing, in spite of herself, the strength of the pressure against the post. But then he lifted his hand as if unaware of the thing it had touched and went on.

At the top of the stairs the corridor stretched along wide and empty and gracious—as if it too knew no secrets. Somewhere was a floating delicate fragrance of lilac, a tangible soft reminder of Alice's presence in that now opened and warmed and perfumed room. And the silence, some impalpable prohibition, seemed to lay itself upon them all, so their voices lowered, their footsteps were restrained and quiet. There was no chance for a word alone with Tim, no chance for a word alone with Richard. He went past his own room, however, along with Tim and Sam. "I'll show you," he said, although Sam knew the way.

Tim bent and kissed her cheek when she reached her own door. Sam took her hand briefly, and then in a rather puzzled way gave her fingers a quick scrutinizing glance before he released it.

Richard said, "Sleep, Myra. Don't worry . . ." His voice was tired; his eyes said nothing.

She closed her door behind her. The lights were on, the bed neatly turned down. She looked at her hands. There were still traces of crumbly soil and leaf mold around her slender nails. Sam, of course, had seen them.

But it didn't matter; nothing so small and unimportant mattered.

She did not hear Richard return along the hall. She did not, in fact, hear anything but the high, neverending whistles of the peepers. She stood for a long time at the open window.

But all questions, everything, simmered down to one; that one had a terrible urgency which superseded all the others.

Suddenly it was not simple. It had seemed easy, listening to Sam. Actually there was nothing simple about it.

What *could* she do about the gun?

Wouldn't whoever hid the gun believe, and have every reason to believe in the safety of that hiding place? It had once—and for nearly two years after—been perfectly safe, even at the time of the most pressing police search for it. So why should that person now secretly remove the gun?

And in spite of the talk of it, so Sam and Tim and Richard —yes, and Webb, and even perhaps Mildred and Aunt Cornelia, were all strongly aware of its importance, would any of those people remove it?

So short a time ago, in anticipation, the project of making a trap with the gun had seemed simple; now it was not. How did anybody make a trap?

What would Sam have done? Warned everybody, certainly, stressed the importance of the gun as new evidence. But that in effect, was done. And then what? Would he have watched? All night, all the time, every minute, from one of the darkened rooms along the hall?

Could she do that?

It seemed in an odd sense theatrical, and impracticable in real life to crouch in waiting silence and darkness, watching the newel post, listening for steps from the terrace, or down the stairs. Mainly it seemed now unsound in practice and unlikely to prove anything. Besides if anyone did come stealthily out of the night and remove the gun, exactly what could she do?

In any case, whatever she did, she'd have to be sure that the house was quiet, that no one was still about to see—and question.

She undressed slowly. She got into a dressing gown, red wool with a slender basque-like top and full long skirt so it looked, somehow, medieval, and was very warm. Red, Alice had said, is becoming to you.

She turned out the light and went to lean upon the wide window sill. Clouds had now fully covered the sky. The terrace and lawn below were a solid depth of blackness with no patch of light from some yet lighted window anywhere. The great house all around her seemed to sleep.

And her project seemed fantastic. Alone, in the weariness and darkness of the night, all her doubts as to her own wisdom returned. She waited—thinking.

And someone walked along the terrace.

It was a cautious little tap, tap of sound but perfectly clear.

Then the footsteps stopped. There was a moment of silence. It lasted so long that she began to think she must have been wrong, that no one walked in the night and darkness, that no one stood there waiting—doing what?—in the black shadow below.

Then she heard a quick spatter of sound; it was an odd sound like little pebbles falling. That stopped too and after another moment of silence came again.

And then quite sudden and sharp there was a whisper. Words came distinctly out of that well of blackness. Scattered words, clear and lost, and clear again. "Come down . . ." She heard those words distinctly. "Come down —come down . . ." And then ". . . talk to you . . ."

It was peremptory, sharp.

After that there was nothing.

No footsteps, no whispers, no sound of a window or a door being opened or closed; no further sound of rattling pebbles.

She listened and listened and could only hear the hard, exasperating pound of her own heart.

Pebbles—spattering on the terrace—flung at somebody's windows, of course. Whose? Richard's room, Alice's, Aunt Cornelia's—two or three guest rooms all had windows facing out over the terrace and the Sound.

The voice was a whisper; it could have been anybody's. She did not recognize it; and she could not tell really, on that troublous night of calm and shifting sudden breeze, with clouds covering the stars and a distant murmur of the Sound and pines, whether it was near or far from her.

The silence lengthened; it might never have been broken. Still no door opened along the hall, or if it did, she didn't hear it. No steps and no rustle crept past her door.

Had she dreamed the thing?

She knew she had not.

Who was it, then? And why?

Later, which was in its terrible way unfortunate, she did not know how long she stood there, straining her ears to hear. She did not know either what time it was when she made her way, groping in the darkness, to her own door.

Who had come to that house where murder once had walked as softly and as furtively?

She held the bronzed handle of the door carefully, so the latch would not click. She listened and the house was perfectly still, yet it seemed to have a kind of sentience, as old, much-lived-in houses do have at night when the house itself takes over. The hall was empty and night-lighted.

Her dressing gown rustled against the wall, making a soft, susurrant echo. The corridor beyond the turn was empty, too. She reached the stairway.

The hall below was dimly lighted, exactly, she thought, as they had left it an hour or two—or longer—before.

She gathered up the folds of her long red skirt and went down, a step at a time, nervous lest the little heels of her mules click upon the steps.

She reached the newel post.

The library was dark ahead of it; glow from the remaining embers made only a dim patch of twilight within that cavernous blackness. Her hand was on the newel post. She listened and still there was no sound anywhere, no sound at all.

She put both hands upon the carved top and lifted and pulled it upward. There was a faint small sound of the wedged and solidly fitted wood, rasping dully against wood. The pineapple came away, cold and smooth in the darkness, and she held it and groped in the hollow with the other hand.

The gun was not there.

Her hand explored the whole rough wood cavity; there was no gun; there was nothing.

She replaced the pineapple. Then she saw what she had not seen up to then. Along the hall on the terrace side of the house, opposite the stairway, there was a thin sharp line of light, the width of a door.

It was the door to the gold-and-ivory drawing room. It was blank and closed. There was only that thin, bright line below it.

Murder had once been in that house.

She moved down along the hall. She was some distance from the door but she could hear a sudden rustle of motion behind it; and the quick murmur of a voice. And then again complete silence.

Nothing moved in the dimly lighted hall. No current of air crept from the library or down the stairwell. Again she tried, in a tense, queer exasperation, to quiet her own heart so she could hear. Could she creep nearer? Could she open that door? Who was there—and why?

Then quite suddenly but very definitely it seemed to her that there was a peculiar, tense quality in that silence.

It lasted perhaps as long as she might have counted half a minute, thirty slow pulse beats.

It was broken in as peculiar a way as its own singularly tense quality of stillness. There was a sharp, clear click, like metal upon metal, and almost immediately a laugh.

A hysterical, loud and rather long laugh.

And that too ended abruptly. There was a sudden rush of motion, a high, rapid rush of words, another broken, thumping sound as if something falling—and the door quite suddenly flung itself open.

The room was lighted—there was a swift view of gilded, French arm chairs and ivory panels and a great gilded mirror at the other end, between the long windows. Then Mildred Wilkinson half stumbled, half fell through the doorway, and Alice, fair hair streaming down her back ran to kneel beside her. "Mildred—Mildred . . ." she screamed frantically. "Don't . . ."

Alice looked up and saw Myra. She cried wildly, "Stop her—stop her—help me. She's taken poison."

Mildred had both hands at her throat and, as a matter of fact, died in the posture.

Alice cried, screaming, sobbing, "She said she would—I couldn't stop her—Myra . . ." She lifted her hands from Mildred and flung them backward, horror on her face. "It's too late! She's already dead . . ."

Behind her a wandering small night breeze again stirred across the terrace and billowed the lace and silk curtains at the end of the room, at one side of the fireplace.

Someone was running along the corridor above and then plunging down the stairs.

"She killed him," sobbed Alice. "She killed Jack. She said she killed him."

CHAPTER 15 ◼

It was Richard plunging down the stairs, around the newel post, across the hall to kneel beside Mildred. Alice, incoherently, half-sobbing tried to tell him. "She killed herself. She took poison . . ."

He did not appear to hear her. But after a long moment he got up. "She's dead." He looked swiftly at Alice and at Myra. "How did it happen?" And as Myra turned dizzily from the sight of Mildred's disheveled hair and dreadful hands, he took a quick step or two toward her and caught her in his arms and held her, so her face was upon his shoulder, her eyes hidden.

Alice cried, "I tried to stop her—I couldn't—it was poison. Mildred killed Jack. Richard, Mildred killed him."

"What do you mean? Tell me . . ."

Myra moved and lifted her head. His shielding arm released her.

Alice was standing flattened against the wall, her hands flat against it, on either side of her slight figure, as if they alone supported her. Her fair hair fell like a child's, on either side of her face. She said, "Mildred was in love with him. He was tired of her. She killed him. She killed herself."

Without speaking Richard went to kneel again beside Mildred.

His broad shoulders and dark bent head hid Mildred. The gray flannel folds of the dressing gown he had flung over his shoulders swept outward, like a merciful curtain. It seemed a long time before he rose slowly and started toward the telephone.

"Where are you going?" said Alice.

"To call the doctor."

"She told me she was going to do it. She said it was cyanide."

Richard went on, back past the stairway. He did not, however, stop at the telephone but instead turned into a passage that ran back, parallel with the dining room. He disappeared and Alice gave a sobbing, small moan, and flung her hands over her face. "Myra, get me something—anything—brandy! Hurry . . ."

"You'd better sit down, quick . . ."

"Yes . . . Yes . . ." There was a chair near the open door, just inside the ivory-and-gold room. Alice moved past Mildred and sank into the chair.

"I'll get brandy," cried Myra.

It was a long way to the dining-room door. The hall stretched endlessly ahead of her. Richard, hurrying along the small corridor, had reached a narrow coat and golf-club closet. As Myra passed the entrance to the corridor she caught a quick glimpse of his dark head and gray dressing gown. He entered the coat closet and she hurried on to the dining room and fumbled for lights. There was a cupboard near the pantry door where a supply of liquor was kept. She ran across and opened the doors and fumbled among the bottles. Aunt Cornelia's sherry; port, which in a sedate and old-fashioned way was still served the gentlemen after dinner at Thorne House; brandy; she must have a glass! She ran into the butler's pantry and turned on lights there, too. The gleaming expanse of chromium steel and glass shelves glittered. She snatched a glass and ran back through the long, stately dining room with its great hooded fireplace, its portraits of Thornes of other generations, its massive, old furniture. She came into the hall, and Richard, a coat over his arm, was at the telephone. He did not see her. His back was turned to the hall and he was talking. "Doctor, this is Dick Thorne. Can you come right away? No, it's not Aunt Cornelia; it's Mildred Wilkinson. She's dead. . . ."

Alice had not collapsed. She had moved again into the hall and was listening to Richard at the telephone.

"Here is the brandy," said Myra. "I'll pour it."

"Oh, yes, yes!" said Alice. She came to. She put up shaking small hands. Myra went to the table that held the lamp. As in a dream she uncorked the tall bottle and poured out brandy and gave it to Alice who clasped the glass as obediently as a child. Richard's voice stopped abruptly. They heard him put down the telephone. He came back, and, kneeling down again, deliberately and gently, he spread a coat over Mildred. One of his own coats. Myra looked at it with minute attention, as if it mattered. He adjusted it very carefully, so it covered Mildred's face, her hands, her hair. Then he stood.

"Now then," he said, "Tell me exactly what happened, Alice."

"She told me. She said she killed him. Then she took poison. She wrote a confession. It is in that room. . . . On the desk —the little French desk. She wrote it there . . ."

Richard settled the dressing gown around his shoulders and then began to put it on, shoving one arm through one sleeve and then the other. He went through the open door, past Mildred.

For a moment, to Myra, it was as if all the silences of the world had been rolled into one. Neither she nor Alice moved; there was no sound from upstairs. No one else apparently had heard—Sam, Tim, Aunt Cornelia, none of them. Richard probably had been awake, thinking, planning—listening, perhaps, as Myra was listening. He must have heard the sound of their voices.

He came to the door again. He paused to close it as far as it would go, moving a fold of his coat in order to do so. The door would not quite close but it sheltered the thing that lay under the coat. He had a white piece of paper in his hand.

"It's a confession. This is what she says." He held the paper under the light and read slowly:

"'To the police: I wish to make a statement in order to clear anyone else who may be accused of murder. I shot Jack Manders. We had been in love for a long time. I killed him because he intended to leave me . . .'"
He stopped. "That's all."

Alice said, "She stopped there. She was so—so proud. I think she could not bear to go on. She stopped there, and took the poison."

"Tell me everything. . . ."

"I will. Yes—Yes, I will." Alice took a long breath. She put down the brandy and locked her hands together. "She came tonight, Richard. I was awake. She threw pebbles up against my window and I heard it and went to the window. She was on the terrace. She whispered—I could hear distinctly. She said she had something she must tell me. She said for me to come down. I came and she was here. She had come in through the terrace door, the library door; but then she led me into that room. She turned on the light and closed the door as if she didn't want anyone else to hear." She caught her breath unevenly.

"Go on, Alice."

"She told me she had shot Jack. I—I didn't believe her. I thought she'd got some sort of twist in her mind. She'd lived alone too long. She brooded. She was always—queer, you know, ingrown, like all the Wilkinsons. Moody and strange. Her eyes, though, looked—oh, Richard, they looked as if she meant it. And then—and then she showed me the poison."

"What was it?"

"She said it was cyanide. She said it would take only a minute. She had a little evening bag with her. She took out the poison and showed me. It was in a pill. She had brought her own pen. . . ."

Richard glanced back toward the half-closed door. "Yes, I saw it, on the desk, beside this."

"She'd brought the paper, too, her own paper. She sat down at the desk and started to write and I could not stop her. I told her she didn't realize what she was saying. I told her she couldn't have killed him. And she said—she said—that she'd been in love with him. . . ."

"Mildred! I can't believe it. . . ."

"I asked her why she shot him. And then she said that he was tired of her. He told her it was over. She couldn't bear it. She was beside herself, desperate, so she did not know what she was doing. She didn't say how or when she got the gun or how long she had planned it. She followed him here. She didn't know that I was in the room when she shot him. She didn't realize it. She must have been beside herself—mad. She said that and I believe it. And then she said, with the sound of the shots she seemed to—to come to herself, and realize what she had done. She said she was going to kill herself, too, then, but she lost her courage. And then later Webb accused me and she could not make herself confess. Until—now."

"She was afraid of the new investigation."

"Yes—yes . . . But she wanted to clear you and me before she took the poison. She . . ." Alice's voice broke. "She asked me to forgive her. And she wrote those few lines and then could not go on. She reached for the poison. She said, 'It's cyanide; it won't hurt.' I hadn't really believed her until then. I ran to her but she put it in her mouth and pushed me away. I tried to get it out of her mouth and she got to the door and pushed me back and then—then she . . .''

She flung her hands up over her face and sobbed. "I couldn't stop her, Richard! I couldn't do anything! There wasn't time!"

Richard looked again at the paper in his hand. He read the few words over and over and then looked up at Myra, "You were here, too?"

Myra shook her head. "I heard Mildred on the terrace. That is, I did not know that it was Mildred. But I came down . . .''

Alice said, "Richard, do you doubt me? Are you asking an outsider, Myra, whether or not I am telling you the truth?"

"Myra is not an outsider," began Richard, and Alice said suddenly, "No. I realize that. She is in love with you. Isn't she, Richard?"

Richard's dark head jerked upward. He gave Alice a long, straight look. "We'll talk about that later, Alice. Just now . . .''

"No," said Alice. "Now. If you love each other, I won't stand between you. I promise you that."

Richard's face had no expression. Alice turned to Myra. "I was wrong when I talked to you before. I hadn't had time to think. It was a blow to discover that the thing I had feared was true . . .'' She looked at Richard, who stood, watching her, his face still unfathomable and quiet. "I told Myra I had guessed you were in love. I talked to her. I asked her to give me a chance to . . . But now I see—after I've had time to think—that I was wrong." She came to Myra, and stood so near that a faint fragrance of perfume rose in a small cloud between them. She said, "I was wrong, Myra. I had no right to come between you. I see it now."

Her brown eyes were soft and shining with earnestness; her beautiful face was like a flower rising from the lacy folds of her pink dressing gown.

The great, paneled hall seemed suddenly cold and the huddle below Richard's coat too near them. Myra shivered a little and Richard saw it and said abruptly, "It's cold here. We'll go into the library. I'll build up the fire."

He went on ahead of them and turned on lights. It was warmer there as if, Myra thought suddenly, the chill in the hall had a center, an uncomfortable focus from which they had removed themselves.

Richard put Mildred's letter on the table, laying an ashtray upon it for a paper weight, and went to the fireplace, and put on logs and kindling. He stirred the embers until the kindling began to smoke and then to blaze. The ash tray, green glass, enlarged Mildred's desperate, sprawling handwriting. Myra, staring down at it, could make out through the wavering glass, certain words—"killed Jack. He intended . . ."

The handwriting was big and sprawling, and looked hurriedly, wildly written. She turned away from it, appalled by the vision of Mildred it induced—hagridden by conscience, by remembered heartbreak and frenzy, and now by fear.

Alice was standing beside the ruby-red chair, her hands linked, her face pale and determined. Richard stood and looked down at the fire, and then turned and Alice said unexpectedly, "I meant what I said, Richard. If you want a divorce . . ."

Richard said directly, "Yes, I do, Alice. I meant to tell you later. But perhaps it is as well for us to understand each other."

"Yes," said Alice. "Yes . . ."

"About Jack Manders, I mean," said Richard.

"Jack! But Mildred confessed. . ."

"That isn't what I meant," said Richard slowly. "I didn't believe that you killed him. Wait—let me tell you, Alice. Whether or not you had killed him, I'd still have done everything I could to help you. If you shot him—I'm only saying if . . ."

"Go on," said Alice. "Go on . . ."

"Well, then, if you killed him there had to be a motive. I never really liked Jack Manders. I never knew quite why. Certainly with other men he behaved as—they did. But there was a phoniness about him; it always seemed to me that he was on the make. I knew that he liked and wanted money. And I thought he had the capacity for being both stupid and ruthless."

"You invited him here. You were his friend . . ."

"You invited him here, Alice," said Richard slowly. "Often."

Her small, beautiful face was white, she leaned forward. "Are you trying to tell me that you thought that I was having an—an affair with him?"

Richard said flatly: "I didn't know. I didn't think so. I'd never known you to lose your head over any man."

"Richard, how can you take that tone! It was always you I loved. From the time we met. I was so young . . ."

"We were both young. We won't go into that. I did not know whether or not you were having an affair with Manders. . . ."

"I was not . . ." whispered Alice.

". . . but if you were, and he had angered you, then I was afraid that you might have shot him . . ."

"No, no," moaned Alice in a distraught way. "No . . ."

He looked at her for a moment, rather curiously, as if she were a stranger to him. Then he said gently, "You are now cleared, Alice. Mildred's confession will close the case. It will stop the new investigation. It will close the thing forever. From now on, Alice, nobody will think of you with anything but pity for your terrible and unjust conviction, and with respect for the way you have borne it. You do not need me any longer."

The kindling crackled; flames shot upward. Alice's fingers dug into the red-satin upholstery. Her face was white and stony, like a perfectly chiseled marble mask. Her brown eyes went to Mildred's letter on the table below the green glass ash tray and then to Myra and her gaze had the stoniness, the frightening blankness that was in her small face. She looked back at Richard who was watching her, who had not moved. She said, "There are two of you. You are stronger than I. Is that why you built up the fire?"

"*Alice* . . . !" cried Myra.

She went on swiftly, panting. "One move from either of you and that letter would be gone in flames. Either of you can do it. I can't stop you. That—or a divorce. That's what you mean, isn't it? You can both say I murdered Mildred. You can say anything you like; everybody will believe you. They believed Webb . . ."

Myra, horrified, cried, "Alice, no! I'll tell the truth. I'll tell them exactly what I heard . . ." She turned to Richard. "I heard voices—I could not hear words. Mildred was hysterical—I heard her laugh. I heard them at the door, and it came open and I saw Alice trying to help her, trying to stop her . . . I saw it!"

Alice's clenched hands slowly relaxed.

Richard said, "You are wrong, Alice. Nobody is trying to blackmail you. Our own situation has nothing to do with this. We'll talk about divorce and a settlement later. . . ."

Someone was coming down the stairs. All of them heard it and looked and Sam came hurrying into view. He was in pajamas that were too big for him, Richard's, and a topcoat. His narrow sallow face was sharp with curiosity. "What is it . . . ?" he said. "I thought I heard somebody . . ."

He stopped, caught by their looks, their attitudes. In the short silence, away off toward the back of the house, a bell rang and rang. And then Richard went to the table and picked up Mildred's letter and gave it to Sam.

"She killed Jack."

"*Mildred* . . ."

"She killed herself a few minutes ago. Her body's in there. She took poison. That's the doctor at the door. I'll let him in. . . ."

Sam was reading the letter again, his face waxen, like a yellow candle. The bell rang distantly in the pantry, and Richard started toward the door. Sam said, "You'll have to phone the Governor, too. The district attorney. You'll have to get the police. You women had better get dressed. They'll have to question all of us."

"Yes," said Alice. She moved toward the door, passing Myra so near that she could hear the light swish of her dressing gown. As Alice passed she lifted her eyes and met Myra's in a brief, yet curiously deliberate, glance. She went on into the hall.

The fire was burning brightly. Yet, quite suddenly the chill from the hall seemed to seep into the room.

Alice had been lying. All at once Myra knew it, as certainly as if Alice had admitted it.

Her soft, brown eyes were implacable with purpose. She had no intention of giving up her claims upon Richard; she only wanted him to believe so.

CHAPTER 16 ■

Alice's slender figure went on ahead, her dressing gown whispering softly. What, actually, did Alice intend to do?

Or rather, how did she intend to accomplish her aim: to dispose of Myra, somehow, some way, and reestablish herself in Richard's house? And in his heart?

And again Myra thought, her own heart sinking, that Alice was in the right. Her house—her husband.

She followed Alice slowly up the stairs. Below, at the end of the hall, the front door opened. Myra heard Richard's low voice, the doctor's shocked exclamations and the sharper, higher voice of Sam at the telephone. She could see Richard and the doctor, short, grizzled, bald from that angle, trotting beside Richard, swinging a shabby leather case. They reached the ivory-and-gold room and the door resisted a little, as if the thing that lay there held it against intrusion, demanding mutely the dignity of death.

There would be now no new investigation. Tim was safe, and Richard. Alice was cleared beyond all question. That much, at least, was settled.

But the situation between Richard and Alice and herself, Myra, was unchanged. Even if Richard was determined, even if whatever Alice planned to do failed, even if Richard's love for Myra was like a fortress, impregnable to approach of any kind, could Myra—*could* she—let him insist upon a divorce? There were glimpses certainly of a marriage which was not well-built. It would have been too easy for Myra to let herself build upon those glimpses.

And besides, suppose Alice's plan, whatever it was, succeeded!

Alice had turned to glance back curiously. "Why are you stopping?" she said. "What are they doing?"

"Nothing. The doctor has come. I think Sam is telephoning the Governor and the police . . ."

"Oh," said Alice blankly. She put her hands up again to push back her hair. "Oh," she said and went into her own room.

Myra went on. She aroused Aunt Cornelia; she aroused Tim. Rather she intended to arouse Aunt Cornelia. Actually Aunt Cornelia was sitting upright in bed, in an elegant white fur bed jacket, smoking nervously and pretending to read. She had heard voices, she explained, and listened while Myra told her.

"Mildred!" she said, her face old and bleak. "Mildred! I'm going to get up!"

"But the police . . ."

"That's why. No, no, don't wait to help me. I can manage. I'll ring for Barton to help me downstairs."

But as Myra moved toward the door Aunt Cornelia said abruptly, "Wait, Myra. I think I have something to say to you. Come here."

She went back to the bed and the old lady reached up to take her hand. Her touch was gentle, her old, deep-set eyes were very bright and compelling. She said directly, "You're in love with Richard. Aren't you, my dear?"

It was useless to deny it. Besides, there was no reason for denial. "Yes," said Myra.

"That's why you are going to leave me?"

"Yes."

"I thought so. He loves you." It was a statement, not a question. She waited a moment, her wise yet anxious gaze seeming to search Myra's. Then she said, "I'm going to meddle further. I'm going to tell you to do something which seems contrary to what I—so much older than you—ought to tell you. The things we call old-fashioned are new-fashioned, too, based on simple principles of right and wrong. But if you love Richard, fight for him."

Her searching eyes, her forthright manner, and her long and tried love for Myra made it possible for Myra to reply as directly. "No," she said, "I can't."

"Because of Alice, of course."

There was no need to reply. Aunt Cornelia said, "Yes. Alice. I have not seen much of Alice really. Richard brought her to me in England shortly after their"—her voice was a little dry—"after their whirlwind courtship and marriage. I saw her again when I came to America to get you, Myra. I stayed here for a couple of months, waiting for you to finish your school term. But I believe that under no circumstances could I know Alice," said the old lady deliberately, "better than I knew her in the first fifteen minutes of our acquaintance. But that isn't the point. Myra, listen to me: Mildred has confessed—Alice is free and now fully exonerated. Richard was loyal to her, during her need, but now . . ."

"Perhaps he still loves her," said Myra. "In his heart."

"I see," the old eyes delved mercilessly into her own. "I see. So you're going away. You'll leave them together. Let time and propinquity work. I should warn you that Alice is a very shrewd and a very—" again her tone was dry—"a very determined woman. Also very beautiful."

"And she's his wife," said Myra.

There was another short silence. Then the soft, withered yet strong old hand released her own abruptly. "I've taught you too well," said Aunt Cornelia rather irritably. "All right. We'll say no more about it. Go and get dressed."

Fight for him? thought Myra, hurrying to Tim's room. Cornelia Thorne Carmichael, with all her years and wisdom, knew as well as Myra that she could not fight Alice.

Tim was sound asleep and so was Willie, a black little shadow on the foot of his bed. Neither proposed to be wakened.

She had to shake Tim and call him and shake him. But when she told him, he was instantly awake and out of bed. "Have they called the police?"

"Yes."

"Get out. I want to dress." But he stopped and looked at her and said, in the stunned and exploring way that Aunt Cornelia had spoken, "Mildred!"

Willie yawned and stretched and yawned. Tim said as she left, "We'd better phone to Webb, too."

Webb, however, was not at home. Sam had already tried twice to reach him when Myra, dressed now in the gray country suit and sweater she had taken off so long—*so long* ago, she thought incredulously—came downstairs again.

But the police had already arrived. The village police, a sprinkling of state police, and eventually some men in plain clothes.

It seemed a long time that they were in and out of the house, in and out of the ivory-and-gold room, mysteriously busy, talking in elliptical undertones to each other—and less elliptically, very definitely and specifically, questioning Alice, questioning Myra, questioning Richard. They wanted to question Webb, too. They wanted to ask him if he had known of his brother's "friendship," said one of the men in plain clothes, clearing his throat, with Mildred Wilkinson. Again Sam telephoned Webb's cottage, and again there was no answer.

Willie, by that time too widely and vociferously awake, had been shut in the kitchen, where Barton and his wife, Francine, and the other servants apparently gathered. Even the gardener, in his cottage away back of the garage, had been aroused by the cars and the commotion and had come to the main house to inquire. Myra, looking into the hall, saw him standing, pale-faced and goggle-eyed, beside Barton in the door of the dining room.

The village police, of course, knew Richard and Alice. They knew Mildred and the gloomy old Wilkinson house; they knew all the circumstances. They were respectful and they showed their sympathy for Alice and Richard. The others were more businesslike but obviously felt that a great wrong had been righted and their job was to tie up the ends of it quickly and with as little further grief and publicity to the Thorne family as was humanly possible. At the same time, in view of rigid instruction from the district attorney who, himself, by telephone, took a hand in the case, it was also their obvious job to leave no loose ends dangling. It was the district attorney, too, who undertook to keep reporters out of the case. "Until morning," he said. "I'll be there before they get there."

Sam gave the police the letter which was itself all the evidence that was needed. Alice told them the story of Mildred's suicide.

She had combed her golden hair smoothly away from her white forehead and coiled it again in a shining bun at the base of her neck. She had put on a pale-blue dress, simple as a schoolgirl's, with a short pleated skirt and a round white collar and cuffs. Even when Alice was never again to return to Thorne House, all her clothes had been kept, as if ready for her wear, in the great dress closets off her room. Except for her pallor, the blue stains of fatigue below her eyes, and the sad droop of her mouth, she looked like a child in the demure blue dress.

The police questioned her and Myra only once and seemed satisfied. One of them, a tall boy who stood as if he'd had military training and probably was barely out of the army, made rapid notes on a shorthand tablet.

And there was not much, really, for either Myra or Alice to tell. "She called me," said Alice. "She was on the terrace and she threw some pebbles up against my window."

"She knew your window?" said one of the plainclothesmen.

"Oh, of course," said Alice. "She was my oldest friend. This house was like her own home."

"Go on, please, Mrs. Thorne."

Alice, in the ruby-red chair, took a long breath. All of them listened. The library was for a moment like a courtroom, like a stage. Aunt Cornelia in her wheel chair, Tim standing beside her, his hand on the chair, Sam roving the room as if unable to stand still, smoking constantly, Richard standing again by the mantel, leaning his elbow upon it, the groups of uniformed police, the dark figures of the plainclothesmen with their noncommittal faces and alert and watchful eyes—all of them were suddenly transformed to an audience, watching Alice, listening. Alice braced her hands upon the arms of the chair. "She asked me to come down. I couldn't hear exactly what she said, except I knew it was Mildred and that she wanted to talk to me. So I came down. Here, to this room. She was here."

The boy with the shorthand tablet scribbled quickly. The plainclothesman standing near Alice said encouragingly, "What did she say then?"

Alice lifted her soft brown eyes. "I don't know. I think she said something about wanting to tell me something. Then she led me into the room across the hall. She turned on the light and closed the door. I thought that she closed the door because she didn't want anyone to hear. Then she went to the desk. She had a little evening bag with her. . . ."

One of the policemen nodded. Alice went on. "She took out the poison—it was a pill—and put it down on the table. Then she took out a paper. Her own paper and her pen and then she"—Alice bit her lip and said unevenly—"then she began to talk wildly. In a rush of words. I couldn't hear. . . ."

She stopped and put a small, lacy handkerchief to her lips.

Sam said quickly, "Take it easy, Alice. You can tell them later if it is too much for you now."

"No, no . . ." Alice steadied herself. "I'll go on. I couldn't hear everything she said. She was excited and almost incoherent. But then I began to understand that she was accusing herself of having killed Jack and of having sent me to prison. I didn't believe her. I tried to reason with her. I—but then she said she'd write it and she did. I still didn't think she had killed him. I thought she had brooded too much about it. I didn't know what to think, except I didn't believe her. And then . . ." again she looked up with troubled eyes. "It all happened so fast," she said, catching her breath. "All at once she flung down the pen. She said she couldn't bear to write any more; that everybody would read it, it would be in the papers, everything. And then, before I could stop her, she snatched up the pill. She told me what it was. She said it was cyanide and it would take only a minute. I still thought that she was hysterical, laughing and crying at once, but then, just as she put the pill in her mouth, I was afraid she meant it. I screamed then, I think. I don't know what I did. But I ran to her, I struggled with her, she pushed me away. Then she fell and . . ." She was trembling, ashy white.

Sam said, "That's enough. Isn't it, Lieutenant? Mrs. Thorne has been through a terrible experience."

"Yes, yes," said one of the men in plain clothes. "Thank you. Now, then—Miss Lane?"

The spotlight shifted. The small intent audience swerved its attention to Myra. She was sitting on the sofa at the end of the room, below the fateful, narrow red curtains. She knew that Richard had glanced at her encouragingly. She knew that Tim was nervous by the way he didn't look at her. Alice sat very straight in the red chair, her beautiful face quiet, and again, Myra thought, meeting Alice's eyes, stony. But Alice, Myra realized with a kind of shock, was afraid of what she might say! Webb had once accused her falsely. Suppose now Myra accused her! Alice, herself, had suggested it. She had said. "You are stronger than I—both of you—you can throw that paper in the fire—you can say I killed her. . . ." Alice who had to learn to trust again!

Myra was aware suddenly of the waiting silence. She looked at the man Sam had called Lieutenant. "I came downstairs only a minute or two before it happened."

"What exactly did you see, Miss Lane? Take your time. We only want to have a full report."

"It's as Mrs. Thorne says. Mildred fell against the door and it opened and I saw it, just as she died."

"Mr. Thorne said that you heard Miss Wilkinson on the terrace, too."

"Yes. That is, I heard her whisper. I couldn't hear much of what she said. I waited awhile and then I came down."

And stopped on her way and looked in the newel post for the gun!

She thought of it then, for the first time. And for the first time wondered what Mildred had done with the gun, and had to decide in a split second whether or not to tell them what she knew of the gun.

Richard's gun.

It seemed to her that already there was a faint premonitory stir and question in the air, as she hesitated. She went on swiftly. "Mildred and Mrs. Thorne were in the room across the hall. The door was closed and I could only hear their voices. Then the door swung open and . . . It's all just as Mrs. Thorne said. I ran to them. Mrs. Thorne was trying to stop her, but it was too late."

"Was Miss Wilkinson unconscious then?"

"No, she put her hands up to her throat. And then she was dead."

"Did she say anything?"

"No. There wasn't time."

"Thank you, Miss Lane." He turned to Richard. "As you told me, Miss Wilkinson knew that your wife was pardoned and that a new investigation was to be opened. I don't think there's any question of the motive. Probably all this time she'd been brooding over it, and her own conscience made her collapse. It's not unusual. You'd be surprised how often this kind of thing happens. Well," he turned to one of the other men, "the doctor says definitely it was cyanide. We'll have to check the source of supply. I think that's all now."

"You mean," said Richard, "that it's all over. The inquiry and investigation?"

"Well, yes. I think so," said the lieutenant briskly. "There'll be an inquest, of course. We'll have to get some samples of her handwriting, but there's no doubt of that. You and Mrs. Thorne and Lady Carmichael have all assured me it is her handwriting and, besides, your wife saw her write it.

It's only a question of dotting the i's—checking everything. We'll take a look through her house. She may have saved letters from Manders or some such thing. We'll talk to Webb Manders too, in case he knew anything of it. But all that is mere form. Yes," he looked around the room and nodded cheerfully at Alice, "I think the case will be closed. No question of it, really. Now, then," he glanced at the stenographer, "if you'll just read all the statements again. Begin with Mr. Thorne's. . . ."

Barton brought in coffee and sandwiches. The boy leafed through his fat, ringed notebook and read briskly and exactly all the statements it contained—Richard's, Sam's, Alice's, her own, the doctor's, who had said definitely that Mildred had taken cyanide. "This poison acts very quickly," read the boy in his brisk and exact tones. "I don't know where she procured it, but I imagine she simply went to the village drugstore and bought it."

Nobody mentioned the gun. Hadn't they found it then? What had Mildred done with it?

The boy finished, the lieutenant asked briefly if there was anything anybody wanted to change, or add.

There was another small, waiting silence. Suppose somebody spoke; suppose, thought Myra suddenly and queerly, somebody said, Yes. Yes, there was something to change, yes, there was something to add. Well, what then? Mildred was a suicide; Mildred shot Jack; Mildred confessed and died. What else was there to add?

Nobody spoke.

And all at once it was over, the police and the boy with the notebook and the plainclothesmen were all leaving.

Richard went with them to the door. Tim strayed after them like a restless, inquiring colt. Aunt Cornelia, wrapped in a long white wool negligee with cherry-colored ribbons, leaned back in her chair and sighed. And Alice, only then, seemed to lose hold of the composure and courage that had sustained her and put her face in her hands and sobbed.

"Now, now," said Sam, "it's all over." He went to her and stood looking down at her helplessly. "Don't go to pieces now, Alice. It's all over. As a matter of fact, it's a good thing it happened. Terrible and tragic and all that—but it's over."

"I know," said Alice, sobbing, "I know . . ." She lifted her face and wiped tears from her cheeks.

The heavy front door closed with a jar. "That," said Sam,

"is the last of them," and went to open the French door and let the night breeze sweep through the library. "Some fresh air won't hurt us."

It was not far from dawn, although still dark. Something in the air that swept into the library was an invisible harbinger of day. And the weather was changing. The breeze was damp and cold, with a hint of chill spring rain in it.

"Poor Mildred," said Alice unsteadily.

Aunt Cornelia sighed again. "Poor Mildred," she echoed. "But whatever guilt and terror she suffered it is over, as Sam says. I am sorry for her. Yet she brought a terrible thing upon you, Alice, and upon Richard. It would be foolish to deny Mildred's cowardice and—and wickedness," said the old woman in a voice that suddenly trembled. "It would be equally foolish and hypocritical to deny our own relief now that she confessed. They might have arrested Richard. They might have done anything."

"They would have arrested Dick," said Sam. "No doubt about that."

Aunt Cornelia looked at Sam. "Is the district attorney coming here?"

"He's on his way to the village. He said it might be a couple of hours before he could get to the police station. But I don't know whether or not he'll come here to the house. In any case he'll not want to question any of us. Alice won't have to go through that again!"

"But he is coming," said Aunt Cornelia. "Why?"

"Only because of the wide publicity of this case. He said he wanted to be on the spot. I imagine the Governor asked him to come, so he'd be in a position to make a full statement to the press at the first possible moment. It's nothing to worry about."

The chill breeze from the terrace sifted across the room. Alice shivered. "Shut the door, Sam, will you?" she said. "It's very cold."

Sam's face softened as he looked at her. "Of course, Alice." He closed the door and came back to pull up a big footstool beside her. He took her hand. "Do you realize that it's all over? The Governor said he had expected a break but not so soon. . . ."

Aunt Cornelia interrupted sharply. "Did *he* think Mildred did it?"

"Oh, no, no!" said Sam. "But when we talked to him over

the phone, he seemed not a bit surprised—satisfied but not surprised. I think that's part of the reason he brought Alice home as he did, and started things moving. He was going on the principle of stirring up mud."

"Mud!" said Aunt Cornelia with distaste. "The word is not applicable now, thank God."

"I never dreamed that Mildred killed him," said Alice. Her brown eyes fixed, staring into space. "She always liked me. She must have suffered. . . ."

Sam said angrily, "She liked her own neck better. She'd have let you go to the chair."

Richard came in from the hall and Tim followed. "Well, they've gone," said Richard. He looked tired and white. All of them looked like that, thought Myra. Drawn and shocked and pale—anyone looking in at them from the terrace, not knowing what the night had held, would have thought they were ghosts, each with his private burden still tying him to earth.

Tim sat down, sprawling his legs out lengthily in front of him. "What do you suppose has happened to Webb?"

"Nothing," said Sam promptly. "He's asleep and doesn't hear the phone, that's all."

"The police will get hold of him," said Richard quietly.

"Oh, sure," said Tim. "The only thing he won't like about it is that it clears Alice."

Aunt Cornelia said slowly, "But if he knew about Mildred and—and Jack, surely he'd have told it at the trial."

"Not Webb," said Sam. "He was all out to make Alice take the rap. Dick, when is the inquest, did they say?"

Richard shook his head. "They said definitely it was cyanide but they'll have to do a post mortem just the same, and find out how and where she got the poison. They took all her things—the letter, her pen, her bag—everything . . ."

Alice said faintly, "Don't talk about it, Richard, please. I can't bear it. I never dreamed that she loved him like that!"

"Listen Alice," said Sam vigorously, taking her hand again. "You're not to feel sorry for Mildred. It's tragic, sure. She was a lonely, unattractive woman and Manders made love to her. Probably he wanted her money and then decided that money or no money he didn't want Mildred, too. Or maybe she discovered that he only wanted her money. She'd take it hard; sure she would. She's exactly the type that would go right out of her mind for a little while. She was an immensely proud woman, and spoiled, because she'd had, always, all that money. I can see how she could get worked up to shoot him rather than let him leave her. He was a bully and a brute. I've always thought so. He got what was coming to him. But don't waste sympathy for Mildred, Alice. It was bad for her, yes. We're all sorry. But she let you go to trial and she'd have let you go to the chair. Don't forget that."

Tim said, "I can see the whole thing. She knew this house as well as her own. Some time she got hold of Richard's gun. She'd planned it. That's clear. She shot Manders from the terrace door or the hall door, and then got away without Webb seeing her, without me seeing her. She took the gun with her and got rid of it. And then came here the next day, sympathizing with Alice! Don't waste time grieving about Mildred, Alice!"

"But didn't they find the gun?" asked Myra.

It interrupted someone—Sam—who stopped abruptly to look at her. Everyone indeed, looked at her quickly and with surprise. Richard said "No" giving her a rather questioning look.

Tim said, "Good God, no! She got rid of that long ago."

Sam, with decision, said, "I wish they had found the gun. It may of course turn up somewhere around the Wilkinson place, but I doubt it."

"But surely," began Myra . . . (And nearly said, "But it was here; it was in the newel post; Mildred took it out." "Why didn't you tell us," they would say. "Why?" Again there was no time to consider.) "I only thought that she might have brought it here with her."

Sam's sallow face was sharp, his dark eyes alert. He said directly, "Did you see it near her? Was it in the room?"

The phrasing of his question invited an easy reply. "No," said Myra, subscribing to the letter of the truth and denying the spirit. She'd tell Richard, she decided swiftly, but nobody else. And now it didn't matter. Richard was safe, Tim was safe. The case was closed.

Alice leaned back and sighed. Aunt Cornelia said, "It's nearly morning. I'm going back to bed."

Tim went to help her to the stairway. Barton, hovering in the hall somewhere, came waddling promptly into sight and the two men lifted her gently from her chair and disappeared on the stairs. The little clock struck briskly and suddenly. The rosy cupid smiled from beyond Alice. Sam yawned and said, "I don't think the district attorney will get here before morning—if he comes at all. I'm for bed, too. That is," he glanced at Richard, "unless you want to stay up to meet him, in case he does come."

"I'll stay up," said Richard. "I'll call you if he comes."

Alice said suddenly, "Please don't go yet, Sam. There's something I want to tell you."

Richard gave her a surprised and instantly alert and guarded glance. Sam, with a look of surprise too, said quickly, "Why, of course, Alice! Anything I can do for you . . ."

Alice leaned her fair head back and looked at Sam. "You can advise me, Sam. You see, Richard wants a divorce."

Sam's thin hatchet face, his narrow dark eyes, even his body seemed to tighten. He said nothing; he did not look at Richard or at Myra. Richard made a move forward and then stopped, with the effect of a shrug. Alice continued in her high, sweet voice, steadily, "He says that he wants a divorce in order to marry Myra. I . . ." Her voice shook a little, she leaned forward then, her small exquisite hands stretched out toward Sam. "I told them I would agree. . . ."

"Alice . . ." began Sam, going to her and taking her hands. She went on, "I told them that I wouldn't stand in their way. But I didn't know then, I didn't realize what it meant to me."

Richard did not move. Again Sam tried to speak, but Alice went on, her brown eyes large and soft and determined. "You see, in spite of the pardon, Sam, in spite of everything, I was still under a—a cloud. It didn't seem fair to Richard to let him share that cloud with me. If he wanted a divorce, I wanted him to have it. But now—now the cloud has gone. I have a right to the thing I want most in life, my husband and my home." She held tightly, like a child, to Sam's hand and said, "There is no cause for him to divorce me. And I can't divorce him, Sam. I can't. Not now," said Alice and stopped.

There was a small tense silence. Then the telephone in the hall rang sharply and demandingly.

CHAPTER 17 ■

Richard went to answer it. They could hear his replies. "Yes, this is Thorne. No, that's all right; we hadn't gone to bed." There was a rather long pause. Then he said, "I see. Right. Then that is cleared up. Thank you for letting me know."

He put down the telephone and came back, and said, lighting a cigarette, "Well, that was simple."

"What was it?" asked Sam.

"She bought the cyanide herself."

Alice cried, "Mildred bought it! How do they know?"

Richard put out the match and took a long breath of smoke. "She got it at Babcock's. . . ." He glanced at Myra. "That's the village druggist. Told them she wanted it for rats and signed the poison book. They have her signature and young Babcock, the son, he's the pharmacy man, knows her well. Nobody questioned it, naturally. Cyanide, arsenic, strychnine, any of that stuff is available."

"When did she get it?" asked Sam.

"The twenty-first of June, two years ago this summer."

Alice's eyes widened. She whispered, "The twenty-first —nine days after she killed Jack."

"Yes."

"She's had it all this time!"

"Obviously she always intended to kill herself if she was discovered," said Sam, "or if she had to confess."

"She must have suffered terribly every minute of the time that I was in prison," said Alice. "What a horrible punishment!"

Richard looked at his cigarette. His face was without expression, but he said very gravely and honestly, "It was a very terrible injustice to you, Alice. I wish I could remove the memory of it. I wish . . ."

"You can," she said. "You can . . ." Her voice was as soft as a night wind, a little smile, tender and half-coaxing touched her lovely mouth.

How could Richard resist her beauty and her feminine sweetness? How could any man? Myra turned abruptly toward the door. Richard said, "I wish I could, Alice. I'm afraid nobody ever can make it up to you. Wait, Myra, don't go . . ."

The smile froze on Alice's mouth. Myra said stiffly, "Richard, it's so late. It would be better for us to talk another time. When we've all had a chance to think and—and plan . . ." And by then she determined, inwardly, she'd be gone.

Alice said, "Richard, let me finish now, about you and me and—Myra. You see, when you came down just after I had had that frighful shock—those terrible minutes with Mildred—your only thought was Myra. Not me. Even then it hurt me."

"I'm sorry, Alice." Richard's mouth was suddenly hard and white.

"No, no, don't misunderstand me. I am not reproaching you. I am asking you to forgive me for the thing I said to you and to Myra. I said that you were threatening me. I said you were trying to force me to divorce you. I didn't mean that, Richard."

"I know . . ."

"You see, oh, it's no excuse, but I trusted everybody one time. Always, all my life, I had trusted the people I knew and loved. And then all at once, overnight, like a—a nightmare, everything was against me. I was the center of horror. The newspapers, the accusations—then the trial!"

"That's past," said Sam. He gave Richard an indignant glance. "Alice needs peace and love and care."

Alice swept on with soft vehemence. "Tonight I learned all in a minute that Mildred, my oldest friend, actually had let me go to prison, convicted of murder. And then you came and thought first of Myra. My only feeling then was despair! But now—now, I've had time to realize what divorce would mean. . . ." Suddenly she leaned forward and cried imploringly, "Richard, let me stay! Only to live in my own home again, only to see the roses bloom and to walk freely in the garden paths . . ."

Alice rose. Again it was as if she were drawn by the flowers. She went to the lilies and touched them with her fingers, she looked around the room. "My home," she said. "I used to dream that I was here again. The books, the lamps, the pictures—everything would be clear, as if I could touch it." She went to a bookshelf and ran her forefinger lightly along a row of leather-bound books. She went to the secretary and opened it, quickly and impulsively, and took the cupid again in her hand and smiled. "Do you remember, Richard, the Tanagra figure you bought for me one beautiful sunny day in Paris? So long ago . . ."

"Yes," said Richard. He turned and bent over the fire. He took tongs and adjusted the logs. "I bought a kitten for you that day, too."

"Yes. I remember. The kitten broke the little figure." Alice put the cupid gently upon the open leaf of the secretary. "I remember. I had time in prison to remember everything. But my dreams were not as sad as my thoughts. Except when I'd wake. I'd know before I opened my eyes that it had been a dream. I'd pretend it wasn't." She turned to Richard. "It was a bitter lesson—those two years. But I cannot believe that so much pain can bring no good. Perhaps I was selfish one day, Richard, childish, wrong about many things. I'll never be again." She came back to the red chair and said earnestly, "Let me stay for Myra's sake as well as mine. We've suffered so terribly already from the notoriety, the talk. If you leave me now, Richard, if we are divorced, what will they say of Myra?"

Richard dropped the log and turned around. "Myra?"

"Everyone knows that she has been living here. Everyone knows that there was no move made for a divorce while I was in prison."

"Myra came because Aunt Cornelia came. . . ."

"But she remained because of you, I think," said Alice softly. "Perhaps you didn't realize that. You weren't thinking of Myra's motive in remaining here with you so long. Oh, I'm not saying that there was anything wrong. And in any case I wouldn't blame either of you. It was bound to happen, no matter what woman was here, Myra or anyone. . . ."

How precisely Alice cut the ground from Myra's feet! How neatly and deftly Alice's words must shake Richard's faith in his own love. Myra moved stiffly to put down the cup of coffee she had in her hand so its tiny tinkle against the saucer would not betray her shaking hand. Fight for him, Aunt Cornelia had said.

As Alice was fighting, for Richard and for her home. But Alice had a firm ground, a solid fortress of truth. It was her right to fight.

Richard said, "It would be better to talk of this another time, Alice. But if you insist we can have it out now."

Rain spattered against the French door which suddenly flung itself open. A surge of wind and rain swept through the room, blowing the crimson curtains inward. Smoke billowed out from the fireplace.

Sam sprang to close the door. He turned, in the sudden silence, and said abruptly, "I'm on Alice's side, you know, Dick."

Alice said gently, "You knew, Sam. There was no surprise in your eyes. You knew that Richard and Myra . . ."

"I was afraid of it," said Sam. He glanced at Myra with a tinge of compunction but remained firmly, like a bulwark, beside Alice. "I was afraid that they would grow fond of each other. And as things were before today, I wanted them to marry. Forgive me, Alice . . ."

"I know," she said. "I understand. If he had asked me for a divorce while I was in prison—for life, Sam, for life . . ." Her voice broke but she finished. "If he'd asked me then, I'd have agreed. Oh, I thought about it. I knew it would come some time. Yet I dreaded it too—my husband and my home, the bare fact of their existence, even if I could never come here again, was like a rock for me to cling to."

"Well, that's in the past," said Sam firmly.

Richard said, "Sam will see to it that the divorce is arranged simply and quickly. You'll have, of course, any money settlement that you want. . . ."

"Richard," cried Alice brokenly.

Sam said, "Now, look here, Dick. Things are very different now."

"They will never be any different between Alice and me," said Richard quietly.

"Listen, Dick." Sam released Alice's hand and went to Richard. "Just think for a minute. I know Myra and I think she's swell. She knows that and . . ." He turned directly to Myra. "My dear, I hope you'll forgive me for what I've got to say. I've got to say it for everybody's happiness. Yours and Dick's and Alice's. Believe me, marriage is marriage and this is a happy marriage. I'm in a devil of a position," burst out Sam suddenly. "I hate to say this. But—you and Dick have been thrown together a lot. Don't you honestly think, Myra, that if you leave, if you withdraw, Dick and Alice will eventually resume the really happy marriage that they had?"

It was Alice's argument, in almost the same words. Myra tried to speak and Richard would not let her. He said definitely, "There's no use in talking, Sam. It's all settled. Alice agreed once to a divorce . . ."

Sam did not appear to hear. Alice sat in silence; only her eyes moved, watching. Sam said to Myra, gently, "It's tough. But you are too nice a person to want to break up a marriage. Nobody blames you or Dick for what happened before Alice was pardoned. You had every right then, both of you, to let yourselves"—he hesitated and said—"to let yourself believe that you were falling in love."

"We do love each other," said Myra suddenly and, to her own ears, unexpectedly.

Richard turned then and looked at her and, across the room, across the lilies Mildred had brought, through the warring, subtle elements of strife in the room, their eyes met. Richard smiled a little. His look said, It's all right, I'm in control, I love you.

Sam started to speak, saw their look and stopped.

Alice got up with a soft swish of motion. She walked quickly across the room, between Myra and Richard, her face white again as a piece of stone. Sam said, "Wait, Alice! They'll understand . . ."

But Alice turned in the doorway. She looked at Myra and she looked at Richard, and said, "You can't divorce me, Richard. And I won't divorce you. That is final."

She stood for an instant, a small, childish figure in the demure, pale-blue dress, her hand on the door casing, her fair head lifted. Then she moved again, and, without another glance at any of them, up the stairs and out of sight.

Sam said, "She's right, Dick. In time, only a little time, you'll see that she was right. You couldn't put her out of the house right away, anyhow. You can't treat her so cruelly." He paused and thought for a moment, rubbing his hand nervously over his bald spot. He said then, brightening, "That's it, of course. Take time. Give yourself time. Give Myra time to think. Give Alice time . . ."

Time. That of course was what Alice wanted; time to win Richard back.

Richard said slowly, "I'll not put her out of the house. You know better than that, Sam. I'll give her all the time she wants."

Sam's worried face lightened further. "Fine," he said. "That's the thing to do. Wait a bit. Give yourselves time to think and . . ."

Richard whirled around. "It will make no difference, Sam. I won't change—neither will Myra."

"Okay," said Sam agreeably—too agreeably, since he had won his point. "Okay. But don't be in a hurry. Alice has had a hellish break. She's got to have time to get over it, time to get her bearings again . . ."

Time, thought Myra again; time to win Richard back again, to entrench herself again in her own house. Time . . .

Obviously Sam was thinking the same thing. With time, everything would settle itself. He came to Myra and his very solicitude betrayed his certainty. He said, with real compunction and real sympathy, "I'm sorry, Myra. But after you've had a chance to think, you'll see that there's only one thing to do that's fair to Dick and Alice and to yourself . . ."

He was on Alice's side, as he had frankly said.

Richard said again, quickly, "Believe me, Sam, I love Myra and she loves me and nothing will change that."

"But you'll wait? You'll not do anything in a hurry?"

"We'll wait," said Richard. "Naturally. That's reasonable."

Sam's face brightened again. His look almost said that he—and Alice—had won. He put his hand on Myra's arm. "Everybody, Myra, some time, has a spot of rough weather. I'm sorry about all this. But I think Alice is in the right. And I think that you think so, too." He turned abruptly to Richard. "I'll go up now. If the D. A. does come around, call me."

"All right." Sam went away quickly, and up the stairs. Richard said, with a queer, half smile, "He's too good a lawyer to stay when he thinks he's won. But he hasn't won, Myra."

Richard didn't know. Alice's and Sam's plea for time seemed to him only reasonable. And it was reasonable. Fatally reasonable.

Richard said thoughtfully, "Alice will agree. I can't force her to divorce me, but she'll see that it's the only thing to do.

I'll give her time. . . ." As if time to him had a very different and specific meaning, he looked quickly then at the clock and came to Myra and put his arms around her.

"The district attorney is on his way here—that is, to the police station. He's driving. There's something I want to see about before he gets here. Wait here for me," he said. "I'll be back. . . ." And suddenly he was gone, running along the hall, stopping to snatch his coat. The front door closed again.

The room seemed very empty after he had gone, and yet, in a curious, indefinable way, inhabited. The rosy cupid smiled at her complacently—and rather slyly. Everything about her suddenly seemed sentient, aware of her—the intruder, in Alice's house, and inimical, arrayed stealthily against her.

She went to Richard's deep lounge chair and sat down and stared into the dying fire. Rain dripped unevenly on the terrace like recurrent whispered steps.

Where had Richard gone? What was it he had to do before the district attorney arrived? But it didn't matter, she thought again. Nothing connected with Jack Manders' murder mattered now, except that Richard was no longer in danger. Even if they found Richard's gun, it didn't matter.

But they hadn't found the gun!

Why not?

The house was very quiet. Nothing moved or breathed except the whisper of the rain, the hushed sigh of the fire. Yet it was as if the rain, the fire—the motionless red curtains, the walls themselves repeated it: Why not?

Murder had walked in that house and the house remembered it. Almost at her feet a man had died.

But Mildred had shot him—and Mildred had died. So the house should, now, forget. The walls, the silence, the air itself should no longer send out danger warnings.

Danger? But that was absurd; that was fancy.

Nevertheless, she sat up abruptly. She listened almost in spite of herself. She looked around the room, trying to search out an invisible enemy, to identify and conquer an inaudible voice. There was nothing there, of course.

But all at once the intangible sense of danger became tangible for it focused sharply upon the gun.

A gun was dangerous.

A gun had fired five bullets into the man who had died in that room.

Suddenly it seemed to Myra that murder itself, once summoned into being, still dwelt with stubborn furtive purpose, within that house. She rose and went to the room where Mildred had died and looked for the gun.

CHAPTER 18

She argued to herself. She told herself there was no danger. She went into the hall and the door to the ivory-and-gold drawing room was open and lights were still on, reflecting themselves brilliantly in the long mirror. Aside from a certain disorder, a mute and indefinable atmosphere of recent disturbance, there was nothing to testify to the horror and the dreadful disorder that had obtained in that dignified and gracious room. She walked past the place where Mildred had died and into the room. She closed the door into the hall and began her search.

Chairs were pushed a little awry. Someone had spilled cigarette ashes on the thin, garlanded old Aubusson carpet. Alice's portrait looked down upon it all, her brown eyes soft, her luminous and tender beauty untouched by the thing that had happened there.

The gun was not there and it had to be there. Only Mildred could have taken it from the newel post. Only Mildred could have hidden it, probably not on that terrible June night, nearly two years ago, for there wasn't enough time, but later. After Alice was charged with murder, in the hope the police would find it? In the hope that it would seal the case against Alice? So that, if any question ever arose, there was the gun, hidden in the house, mutely testifying against Alice?

Or against Richard.

But not (if she were suspected) against Mildred. The police would believe (obviously Mildred had reasoned) that Mildred herself would have had a chance to get rid of the gun forever and would have done so. But that Alice, in prison, could not have removed it. And that Richard, living in the house, able to dispose of it at a moment's notice, believed it safe. Perhaps Mildred had reasoned all of that and more; perhaps she had not reasoned at all but had acted merely at the erratic biddings of an erratic, terrified mind.

Myra looked everywhere—in the cushioned sofas, in the drawers of the small desk where Mildred had written her last words. She searched the elaborate tortoise-shell and Buhl commode against the further wall. She went to the long windows at either side of the fireplace and searched behind the stiff draperies. One window was still open and rain had blown in so there was a damp, dark patch upon the silk. Rain on the terrace murmured; the glass glittered as if eyes beyond it, in the night, watched her. She closed the window. She searched in places where she'd looked before, almost feverishly, driven by a kind of nervous tension within her, as if merely physical exertion could prevent her from thinking of herself—and Richard and Alice. She looked again among the ivory velvet cushions of a delicate French sofa and there was no gun. She looked for a third time within the depths of the same arm chair and stopped.

The gun was gone. And she didn't know and could not imagine what Mildred had done with it. She might, of course, have hidden it outside. There was probably time for her to do so before Alice came downstairs (since Mildred had entered the house either by the long window Myra had just closed, or by the unlocked French door in the library), or she might even have removed the gun earlier, before she roused Alice. In that case it could be anywhere.

Or, and in spite of Richard's and Tim's belief, the police might have it and have taken it away without telling any of them—intentionally, perhaps to test it secretly.

She went to the door and turned out the lights as she went into the hall. Richard had not returned. No one was in the library. She returned to it slowly. The night was really over —or would soon be. The clock struck a brisk half hour. It was still dark; morning would be stormy and late and dreary. She thought vaguely of turning the lock in the French

door. It was not a custom of the house but she started toward
it. And then saw that while no one was now in the room,
someone had been there.

The small Capo di Monte cupid lay smashed and shattered
as if flung by wanton, evil hands against the hearth. The
cupid Alice loved.

Small rosy pieces, a blue sash, the tiny slivered fingers of a
hand, picked themselves out rather horribly upon the hearth-
stone at her feet.

She took a step or two toward it and stopped.

The room, otherwise, was exactly the same.

But the shattered pieces at her feet seemed to confirm her
obstinate sense of danger, as if murder chose deliberately to
leave a token of its presence.

Murder.

She wanted to hurry from the room—from the drone of
the rain on the flagstones outside, the wavering curtains, the
cupid. She made herself sit down again in Richard's chair.
She would think and reason out—and then dismiss this intrusive, stubborn uneasiness which nudged at her as if it had
hands, pointing, a voice saying in a breathless whisper, look,
look, here I am: Murder.

She caught herself sharply. She made herself take a cigarette and light it. She made herself try to analyze. Jack had
been murdered, yes. But Mildred had shot him, and now,
nearly two years later, had confessed and taken poison and
died. Therefore murder as a presence, as a continuing force
did not exist. It had begun with Mildred's hatred; it had
ended with Mildred's death.

So put that on one side, jot it down on the ledger; that was
fact.

On the other side, the debit side, the danger side, were two
things where there had been one—the gun, the shattered
cupid.

And the shattered cupid carried with it another implica-
tion, another and perhaps more significant focal point of danger than the gun, and that was a hatred of Alice. And not
only a hatred of Alice but a blind, insensate rage which had
its outlet in sheer wanton destruction.

She forced herself, methodically, to consider how it could
have been done. Obviously while she was in the gold-and-
ivory drawing room, someone had entered the library and
broken the cupid. She had heard no one on the stairs or along

the hall. The French door was unlocked. Someone could have entered from the terrace. Who?

Methodically, too, she went over the too-short list of people in the house—Sam, Tim, Aunt Cornelia, the servants. None of them would have smashed the cupid and it was not an accident. She was tempted to call it accident, to dismiss it as accident, and she could not, as she could not dismiss the insidious sense of danger, pointing out its own existence.

If she accepted its existence, then what? Suppose she accepted it, only hypothetically, only for a moment. Jack's murder, of course, was fact. But could Mildred have been murdered?

It was, even as a hypothesis, untenable. Myra had seen her die. Alice had seen her die. And Alice had been with Mildred for at least ten minutes or more before Mildred's death and no one else had been there. Consequently, if Mildred had been murdered (how?), only Alice could have murdered her.

Those were facts, too. Well, then, examine them. Were they facts that allowed no loophole for the present existence of other facts? For the existence of murder?

Certainly Mildred had died of poison. The doctor, everyone, had said so; therefore it had to be self-administered. Besides, if Mildred had not been a suicide (in spite of the letter of confession she had written, in spite of the poison which Mildred herself had purchased with terrible and significant appropriateness a few days after Jack's murder), if, in spite of all this, Mildred, by any conceivable means *had* been murdered, there had to be a motive.

That was the keynote, the center, the whole basis for any hypothetical structure which included murder.

What then could that motive have been? Why would anybody desire to murder Mildred? More importantly, why would anybody have to murder Mildred? For murder has a dread and obstinate twin and that is urgency. Why, then, should anyone have been forced to murder Mildred?

Myra put out her cigarette, got up, walked the length of the room and back again, and still that hypothetical line of thought persisted, and would not, yet, be dismissed. Well, then, go on. Suppose Mildred threatened somebody.

How?

That question at last brought her in a full circle back to murder—a known murder, a proved murder. Jack Manders had been murdered, and Alice's pardon had re-opened the investigation into his death. If the manner of Mildred's death could be questioned for a moment, the basis for inquiry would have to concern itself with the recent, immediate events: Jack Manders' murder; Alice's pardon and return home; the opening of a new investigation. Could Mildred have known anything at all about Jack's murder which now became dangerous? So dangerous that somebody had been forced by that danger to kill Mildred and thus silence her?

Suppose Mildred had not murdered him (this denied the confession which no one could have induced her to write if it had not been true), but suppose, thought Myra rather desperately, Mildred had not killed Jack. What happened if one removed the fact of the letter?

But it was a full circle of thought in more ways than one, for it brought her up against impossibility again. Only Alice was present when Mildred died and Alice had no motive.

Alice indeed, of all people in the house, could have had no fear of anything that led to Jack Manders' murder, for Alice could not again be charged with Jack's murder. Alice was safe.

And besides, even if she had wanted to, even if there had been some terrible, mysterious need, she would not have murdered Mildred. She would not have risked a murder only a few hours after her pardon and release from prison, in her own house, and in circumstances which, if the word murder ever was uttered in the case of Mildred's suicide, would instantly and inevitably point to her as the murderer.

Alice would not have murdered Mildred or anybody—and only Alice was with Mildred when she took poison.

She went back to Richard's chair.

The intrusive sense of danger, as if the walls of the room, the bricks of the house knew and subtly, mutely, endeavored to reveal that warning and that secret, was wrong. Murder had once existed, but it had stopped.

Suppose Alice had not told everything! Suddenly Myra remembered the opened window, the stained wet patch on the curtain. Suppose someone else had been there, too! Someone who had, say, threatened Mildred. Suppose there had been some trickery about the poison, suppose Mildred had not intended the thing she took actually to be poison, suppose . . .

She sank back again, realizing that her fancy had traveled

too fast. Mildred had bought the poison; Mildred had brought it there; and Mildred had written her suicide letter. So she couldn't have been murdered and thus Alice could not—either knowingly or unknowingly—protect anyone else.

And who, besides Richard, would she protect? Richard could not possibly have escaped the gold-and-ivory room by the French window, run along the terrace, to enter the house and go up the back stairs in time to come running down the front stairs at the time when he came.

There was no murder. She told herself that again, and again a nagging little voice persisted, trying to refute it: who gained by Mildred's death?

What did it accomplish, if you viewed it from that angle?

Well, in the first place, it stopped the new investigation. So, therefore, it might, for the purposes of argument, be said to benefit Richard, Tim and Webb. And possibly Sam.

And more remotely herself, because of Richard, and because of Tim.

Could Alice so strongly wish to protect any of those people that she would refuse to give evidence against him, even though she knew it to be murder and knew who had murdered Mildred?

Richard?—yes. Tim?—yes. Sam?—yes.

Webb?—no.

Alice had every reason to hate Webb. If Webb had been in that room, if Webb had had anything to do with Mildred's death (yet how could anyone have murdered her?), Alice would have told it at once.

Unless she were afraid of Webb.

Yet the only fear she could hold of Webb would have had to do with Jack's murder and Alice could never again, in any circumstance, be charged with Jack's murder.

Again, methodically, Myra went over the whole circle of conjecture, and again reached the only conclusion—none of her surmises had even attempted to explain away the sheer, bald facts of Mildred's death. And all those simple clear facts still stood out in bold black letters on the safe side of the ledger and could not be erased.

For an instant, with a surrendering flare, the other side suggested some sort of chicanery (unknown by Alice, or its perpetrator protected by Alice) some sleight-of-hand trickery which had tricked and fooled Mildred—but it was

a dim sort of suggestion, obviously blocked by facts. It had
to be dismissed. It belonged to a realm of quicksand fancy,
where there was no stratum of rock anywhere for a foot-
hold.

With a feeling that a long time had elapsed, she looked at
the clock and discovered that her whole expedition into the
tortuous maze of speculation had taken exactly five minutes.
It seemed much longer and she wished that Richard would
return.

And her gaze went to the cupid. Nothing in all her journey
through the dark and twisting jungle which included murder, had explained the gun or the cupid.

Yet neither the gun, nor the cupid, could have validity.
And the warning of murder (Murder here, murder there:
Look for me, I am near; I am within touch of your hand!)—
all that was her own fancy, the trickery of her own nerves.

Someone knocked lightly at the French door.

Myra got to her feet. She backed around behind the chair.
The terror her own thoughts had conjured up caught her so
she could not speak. The knock was not repeated. The red
curtains quivered and moved as the door opened. Webb Manders said, "Don't scream . . ." and came in.

She couldn't have screamed. He shut the door. His hat and
coat were dripping. He said again, quickly, "Don't scream. I
am not going to hurt you."

He did not take off his hat. Its wet sodden brim shaded
his pale face. He shoved his hands in his pockets and eyed
her for a moment from the shadow and, as she made some
move toward the door, he said quickly again, "Stay there. I
tell you I'm not going to hurt you."

Miraculously, still in the grip of her self-induced terror,
she achieved uneven, rapid words: "They've been trying to
reach you by phone. Mildred Wilkinson confessed to having
murdered your brother. She took poison and died. The police were here. They've gone now. . . ."

He did not move. His tall figure, his half-shadowed face,
even his eyes did not seem to change, and all at once some
quality in that changelessness seemed wrong. It was too still,
too unmoved.

She cried with swift and utter conviction, "*You already
knew!*"

He said coolly, "I was out walking along the road. I saw
the police cars and followed them here."

"Where have you been . . . ?"

"I did not know what had happened. I didn't wish to be questioned. I thought it wiser to"—he shrugged—"to keep out of sight until they had gone."

So Webb had been there all the time—hiding in the shadows of the hedges? Skulking behind the glossy, concealing banks of laurels? Watching? Waiting? For what?

He said coolly again, "Don't look at me like that. I didn't kill her! She committed suicide."

"You knew that, too."

"The terrace window was open. And then I saw them take her away." He waited an instant and said, "She did commit suicide, didn't she?"

"Y-yes." Yes, certainly. But all those dim and vague and stubbornly persistent intimations of disaster, intimations of murder, came flooding back upon her. He said, "How?"

"She took poison."

"I mean, how did she confess?"

"She wrote a letter. The police have it."

"A letter saying she had killed my brother?"

"Yes."

"Why did she kill him?"

"She said he was tired of her. She had been in love with him. . . ."

Again for a long moment Webb Manders stood, immovable in his long, black mackintosh, which glittered with rain, watching her with that cold, half-hidden look. Finally he said, "Why do the police want me?"

"To tell you what had happened. And to ask you what you knew of it."

"Of Mildred's affair with Jack?" He seemed to consider for a moment and then said, almost casually, as if it had no importance just then, "I expect it was true enough. She had a lot of money. Jack was younger than I, ten years younger. He had his faults, but he kept his affairs to himself. Of course old Wilkinson wouldn't have wanted Mildred to marry Jack. He'd have stopped any plan of theirs to marry if he had known about it. Probably Jack and Mildred both preferred to keep it a secret. And then—well, I don't blame Jack if he decided that the money was all right, but he didn't want Mildred. You can't blame a man for changing his mind. I expect she killed him, all right. Probably he was the only man that ever had been interested in her and she was sore as hell. She was spoiled, too, with all that money. It's a case of a 'woman scorned,'" said Webb, and gave a dry whisper of a laugh.

"You didn't see her!" cried Myra with a sharp stab of remembered pity. "Poor Mildred . . ."

"Poor Mildred!" The derisive, half-smile on his mouth changed to something like a snarl. "She shot my brother."

How ready he was to accuse, thought Myra irresistibly. Too ready . . . He had accused Alice, and now Mildred.

In this case he was right. Yet she said angrily, all her vague dislike of the man suddenly crystallized, "You accused Alice, too."

He was still very cool, casual, as if it was an idle conversation, none of it with significance. Actually it was as if some deep preoccupation held him so engrossed that he gave the things they were saying only a fraction of his attention. "Of course I accused Alice. I thought she shot him. I thought there was some sort of affair between Alice and Jack. That's why I came here that night. I'd got home and Jack was gone and I came straight over here. I knew he'd been seeing a lot of her and if there was anything of the sort, I intended to find out and put a stop to it. She'd never have left Dick and his money for Jack. It only meant trouble for everybody. Jack was nobody's saint but he met his match in Alice. At least that's what I thought then. I never thought of Mildred." He spoke abstractedly, looking all around the room. His cold, seeking eyes found the cupid, fixed themselves upon it for an instant and went on. He said, "The case is closed then?"

"Sam thinks so. The district attorney is on his way. He's driving."

His eyes jerked back to her. "The district attorney! Oh. Well. I just thought I'd ask you what, exactly, had happened. . . ."

A sudden, rather queer question came out of his words. She glanced at the curtain, drawn securely over the French window. He could not have seen her, sitting there by the fire, engaged in her own private struggle with fear. She said, "How did you know that I was here?"

"How . . ." He too glanced at the curtain. And then again, suddenly and mirthlessly grinned. "Oh, I took a chance."

She said slowly, "You were on the terrace. You were watching. You saw me in the room where Mildred died. . . ."

"Yes," said Webb. "I saw you searching the room."

And all at once, imperceptibly yet certainly, his abstraction, his air of impersonal, almost uninterested conversation was gone. She knew it. And she knew that now, in the lifting of an eyelid, he had come to the heart of his intention.

She waited, her heart suddenly hammering in her ears. He moved toward the door, the mackintosh rattling and catching glittering highlights. He put his hand on the latch.

Surely he would hear the pounding of her heart; surely he would sense her waiting, as an animal senses a trap.

He didn't. At the door he turned and said the thing she knew he had come to say. "What about the gun?"

The gun. The center of his purpose in coming into the house. The core of his indirect questioning. He had been, she saw suddenly, trying to pump her for knowledge—not of Mildred's suicide, not of the investigation, not of anything but the gun.

She said quickly, half-whispering, "What do you know of the gun?"

And he knew something; knowledge was in the surprised, deep flash in his eyes. It was in the air between them. Then he opened the door, and wind and rain swept in. He said, "I don't know anything about the gun," and left. One instant his tall figure in the glittering, wet, black mackintosh was there, the next instant it had gone and the door closed.

The rain muffled any sound of his departing footsteps.

Again the tick of the clock seemed to grow louder.

Mildred's death automatically cleared Tim and Richard—and Webb. There was no question of that.

And if Webb had actually and secretly had some quarrel with Jack, *if he had shot Jack* and then accused Alice to clear himself—then *he might have repeated a once-successful pattern*, choosing Mildred this time instead of Alice for a scapegoat.

Except, this time, there was no chance of its going wrong. This time the victim could not return, exonerated and free.

Again the see-saw of fact and conjecture caught her. Mildred's death could not be murder. But Webb's whole intention had been to find out, from her, whether or not they were searching for the gun. And he had known something about it.

The danger that had focused like a sinister light upon the gun suddenly returned. It was so clear and strong that she was astounded at what amounted to her own disregard of that latent yet inextinguishable danger. It seemed now a fantastic negligence, an incredible procrastination.

Where was Richard?

Rain droned upon the terrace again like muffled footsteps. Then she realized that there actually were footsteps, but they were definite, nearer. Someone was coming along the hall, from the far end of it. It was Richard, she thought, and went to the door quickly. It was, instead, Tim, in pajamas, with a blue blanket flapping dismally over his shoulders. He saw her and, looking surprised, quickened his steps. "Hello," he said. "You still up? I couldn't sleep, either! Hell's bells, how could anybody?"

"I didn't hear you come down!" Had he heard her talk with Webb?

He hadn't. "Oh, I came down the back stairs," he said cheerfully. "Nearer my room."

"Where is—have you seen Richard?"

He was reaching for a cigarette in the box on the table beside her. He shot a quick look at her. "No," he said rather shortly. "Are you waiting for him?"

She nodded and Tim lighted the cigarette, and went to lean against the mantel. His hair was wispy and disheveled; he smoothed it absently and said, "Listen, Sis, I want to say something. About . . ." he hesitated. "Well, it's about Dick. And—and you. You see, I don't want you to be hurt. And I don't want—well," he swallowed, "Richard or—or Alice to be hurt."

He waited a moment, his eyes were worried, his face uneasy. Suddenly he came to her and put his hand on her shoulder. She said, "Is it that easy to see?"

"No. I don't think so. Not to other people. But you're my sister."

She put her cheek over against his hand. "I love him, Tim."

"Yes." He cleared his throat. "Yes, I know. But it's no good, honey."

"He loves me."

There was a long pause. Then, in one of the quick and astonishing—and somehow sad—moments of wisdom and adulthood that were so far beyond his rightful years, Tim said, "Yes. That's what he thinks. Or, rather, it's what he thought before Alice came home."

Fight for him, Aunt Cornelia had said. "How can I give him up, Tim?" cried Myra suddenly, despairing, wanting him, too, to say fight Alice.

But Tim did not speak for a long moment. Then he said, his voice very gentle, "Alice loves him and—well, she's his wife. I'll never forget how good she was to me, a callow, half-baked kid. She never forgot anything—Christmases, Easter, birthdays. She always had time for me. She never minded it when I showed pretty plainly how crazy I was about her. She'd laugh a little and—and I always knew she was like a—well, a sort of saint. That was when I was just a kid, you see. But I thought of her that way all through the war. I knew she couldn't have shot Manders. If she did it was all right but I knew she hadn't. And I used to—well, sort of see her—you know. We'd be coming back from a mission and I'd be cramped and damned cold and nervy. And I used to pretend that she'd be there, when I got back. Maybe it sounds silly. But sometimes I could almost see her face and that sort of childish, innocent look in her eyes." He stopped and said abruptly, "I sound like a fool. I guess I was. But . . ." Again for an instant the premature age touched him, and he said slowly, "It's not so bad for a fellow to have something like that to hold on to. In war . . ."

His mood had changed. He patted her shoulder briskly. "Well, I've spilled all over. But I wanted you to know that I'm with you—understand? I mean, well, hell, Myra, you're young and pretty and you'll meet some other guy. You're licked here, honey. Come on and live with me."

A million years ago—that afternoon, about twelve hours ago in fact—she had thought of that.

"Yes. Yes, I'd like to, Tim."

He had expected her to oppose it. His face cleared instantly. "Good girl," he said. "You've got sense."

He smoked thoughtfully for a moment and said, "Now the case is closed I keep thinking about it. All sorts of things."

"Such as what?"

"Well, for one thing—you're going to think I'm out of my mind—I always thought that Sam knew something about that gun."

She sat upright. "Sam!"

"As a matter of fact, there was even a time when I thought Sam had killed Jack."

"Why?"

His look was quickly disapproving. "Now don't get all worked up. I shouldn't have told you."

"But Tim . . ."

He said hastily, "I'm going back to bed."

"Why did you say that Sam . . . ?"

"Don't get any ideas. Sam didn't kill anybody. Mildred did it. I only thought of Sam because—well, for one thing he got here so fast that night. He was staying at the club and somebody phoned and didn't talk to Sam but left a message for him. I guess he must have got it right away and driven over here like a bat out of hell. He would, of course. But he got here so darned quick! And also because he thinks a lot of Alice. I mean, well, Sam would do anything for Alice. But he didn't. I was half out of my mind then. I suspected everybody. It makes no sense now, and never did! Forget it. Go to bed. Tomorrow's another day." He glanced around. And saw the cupid. "What's that?"

"It's—Alice's cupid. Someone broke it."

"Gee," said Tim calmly, "too bad!"

This thing at least she could speak aloud. She said, "Tim, I'm frightened."

"Huh!" He gave her a sharp look. "What about?"

"I don't know. There's something—in the room. In the house . . ."

"What on earth do you mean? There's nothing in the room to be afraid of!"

It was like trying to convince him of a ghost which only she could see. She said inadequately, "There's the cupid. Alice loved the cupid. It is as if somebody who hated her did that!"

"Nobody hates Alice! You've got an attack of nerves. Forget it. That was an accident. Coming upstairs?"

How could she explain the inexplicable? "No. I'll wait for Richard."

He did not insist. He said briskly, "Well, I'm going back and get some sleep. See you later," and went away, the blanket trailing behind him.

Richard must return soon.

The gun—the cupid. Webb. After awhile she went slowly

to the stairway again. She lifted the carved pineapple top.
The space below was still empty. She had known it would be.
Mildred could not have returned the gun.

And the gun was safe. It was a swift, unexpected thought,
coming from nowhere. The gun was safe because it was not
loaded.

She came back into the library.

Suppose Webb had the gun.

The silence in the room was again charged with knowledge. The memories within it seemed to stir, as if about to
come to life again.

She would not wait for Richard, she decided swiftly.

But she lingered, nevertheless, staring at the shattered rosy
pieces of the cupid, which could never come to life again.

She kneeled. She began to pick up the little pieces.

Alice said quietly behind her, "What have you done to my
cupid?"

CHAPTER 19 ■

Myra turned swiftly, on her knees, a jagged piece of the
cupid in her hand. Alice had changed to her soft, pink-satin
negligee. Her golden hair was smooth and shining as a golden
cap, but her face was very white with that stony, pulseless
look of a small and perfect statue. She said, "You broke the
cupid."

"No."

"You broke it because it was mine."

A sharp impatience came to Myra's aid. "I did nothing of
the kind!"

"Then what are you doing?"

Myra glanced at the shattered little heap of porcelain, the

bit of blue sash, the slivered, tiny pink fingers. She got to her feet. "I was picking up the pieces."

"Why?"

"Oh, Alice, I know nothing about it or how it happened! This is absurd. . . ."

"Why are you picking up the pieces?" Alice's soft lips were touched with a light rose lipstick. Her perfect, straight little nose and chin, the lovely curves of her cheekbones were so beautiful in their heart-stopping perfection that they might have been done in marble by an inspired sculptor.

"I don't know why!" said Myra. "Somebody had to pick them up!"

Alice's eyes were gentle as she said softly, "I expect you've got into a habit of seeing to things. Taking my place, giving orders, seeing to the servants and the flowers. But it is not your house yet, Myra."

It was childish and for that very reason rather frightening. They were adults. Myra said, "I have not tried to take your place."

"You want everything that is mine! You have done everything to destroy"—she moved toward the cupid and looked down and said—"the things I love. The things that were mine until you came."

Suddenly she pushed both her hands upward over her face, thrusting back her hair. She cried almost wildly, "*Why did you come? Why don't you go?*" And turned and ran with an abandonment Myra would not have believed possible, to the ruby-red arm chair and flung herself into it, her face in her hands.

But she was not sobbing. Myra realized, with a queer kind of shock, that Alice was watching her, behind her hands— almost as if measuring the effect of her words. Almost as if Myra was an audience which Alice intended to sway.

It was a curious and a perplexing impression. It touched Alice's gesture and words with falseness. Myra said slowly, puzzled by that tinge of falseness, "I am going, Alice. I'll go now if you like. You can have Francine pack my things and send them later."

Alice's hands dropped. "The taxis don't run after midnight," she said thoughtfully after a moment. "Besides, they say the district attorney is on his way. He may want to question us again. No, you'd better not leave tonight. But you can see for yourself that it would be an impossible situation. For you to stay more than a day or two, I mean."

The lilies Mildred had brought sent up a sweet, almost sickening fragrance.

"I'm going away. I told you that."

"Where are you going?"

"I'll live with Tim. He's got a little apartment."

"Oh. That's not far away, is it? I expect Aunt Cornelia will want you back here often."

"I'll not come, if that's what you want."

"I can't stop Aunt Cornelia from asking you. Or Richard from seeing you unless you promise . . ."

"I'll not promise anything . . ." began Myra, a sudden gust of anger shaking her, and immediately thought, ashamed: We are like children, bickering. She checked her anger swiftly. She said, wishing only to end it, "You understand me. I think we understand each other. There's nothing to be gained by our talking and quarreling, like this."

Alice put her hands over her face and again it seemed theatrical, yet Alice was sincere. She had much to lose or win. She said, after a moment, her voice muffled behind her hands, "Yes, yes, you are right, of course. I'm upset and nervous! Mildred's death—everything . . ."

Again an impulse of pity touched Myra. Yet, when she spoke, her voice was tired and cold. She said, "Mildred loved you, Alice. She talked to me about you."

Alice's hands flew from her face. "What!"

"She was crying. She . . ."

"You talked to her?"

"Yes, tonight . . ."

"When?"

"After she had seen you."

Alice's face looked blank. Myra said, "After I had taken her up to your room. You remember—you were looking at jewelry. I happened to see her when she went home. She was sitting in her car, crying. She said to tell you that she'd be back."

"You didn't tell me that," said Alice slowly.

Both women heard the front door open and then close, rather quietly, as if whoever had opened it did not wish to wake a house which already was as taut and tense as if it would never know sleep again. Myra said, "I haven't told anyone," and turned. Richard had come in and was taking off his topcoat. He tossed it onto a chair and without glancing toward the library went into the dining room. Alice said, "That must be Richard," and got up.

She touched her hair, glanced once at the cupid. She looked around the room. "It's beautiful isn't it?" she said. "I chose the colors—everything." And walked quietly out of the room and disappeared along the stairway her hand sliding along the railing. Myra watched again, in spite of herself, but it did not touch the newel post.

The slight, graceful figure in the long, clinging folds of pink satin and lace had barely gone when Richard came back along the hall, with a glass in his hand. She watched him for a moment before he knew that she was there. How well she would remember the solid, square lines of his body, the way he walked, the gesture with which he lifted his head just then and looked at her. His face lightened and he came forward quickly. "Myra! I thought you'd gone to bed. Have a Scotch and soda? I'll get you one. . . ."

"Richard, Webb Manders was here and . . ."

"Webb!"

"Oh, Richard, he knows something about the gun. I'm sure he knows. It was here. I found it and . . ."

"The gun! *My gun?*"

". . . and now it's gone. It was in the newel post. It was there all the time. . . ."

"Wait a minute!" Richard set his glass down and took her hands in his own. "Take it easy. Now what exactly are you talking about?"

It was of course a brief enough story. She told him everything, even of her stealthy little expedition to bury the shell.

He went, after she'd finished, and looked at the newel post. He lifted up the top, cautiously, and put his hand in the hollow as if measuring it. After a moment he replaced it and came back.

"Well," he said. "Well . . ."

He gave her a long look, reached for his glass and said, "If I didn't need a drink before, I certainly do now. Did you think I'd hidden the gun?"

"N—no . . ."

He eyed her speculatively, but with a rather rueful twinkle.

"But you thought I might have had a brainstorm and taken a potshot—or rather five potshots—at Jack."

"No—but they were building a case against you. Sam said so. And it *was* your gun and . . ." she stopped.

He drank, put down the glass and looked at her for a moment and laughed. He came and put his arms around her. "So wild horses, or the village constabulary, wouldn't have dragged it out of you." He put his face down against her own. He was shaken with quiet laughter. He said, "You're a nice girl! Prepared to defend me whether I shot a guy or not? Don't you know that that is not done in the better circles?"

She said soberly, "Webb knows something about it."

"Did he say so?"

"No. But I knew . . . I saw . . ." Her voice died away as she saw the still half-amused skepticism in his face. Richard, like Tim, saw no ghost of murder.

He said gently, "Webb couldn't have the gun, dear. He didn't kill Jack."

"Then where is it? It was there this evening, before dinner."

"Mildred must have taken it. Perhaps she considered using the gun instead of poison and then decided poison would be easier. It will turn up somewhere. It doesn't matter now anyway. As soon as the district attorney gets here the case will be officially closed. I went to talk to the doctor about it and . . ."

"The doctor who came to see Mildred? Why?"

"I—well, I wanted him to underline facts, I suppose. Like —touching wood, I had to make absolutely certain that the —miracle had occurred and the whole horrible business really is in the past. He'll be called on to testify at the inquest. He said that cyanide works right away; that she took the poison and died and he will testify to that and in his opinion the case is as good as closed. He said, as a matter of fact, to forget it. To write it off. So—that's that. It's finished. And a new life is ahead of us."

He looked around the room and gave a kind of salute with his glass and finished his drink. "A new life in this house, for you and me." He looked at her squarely. "It'll be the kind of life I've always wanted in this house, Myra. People, and fires going, children and Christmas trees and Easter. We'll go on trips, we'll see everything we want to see all over the world, but we'll always want to come back here to peace and home and—and happiness, Myra."

For an enchanted moment it seemed within her grasp, all of it, ready to take. It was such a bewildering glimpse that she forgot everything else and went to him and he held her warm and close in his arms. "The house always lighted," he said. "Warm and welcoming, with laughter and tenderness and you." He paused and said, "I'll talk to Sam about the divorce."

Divorce. And Alice. The enchanted moment had not been a true enchantment; already its spell dissolved. She moved in his arms, away from him. He understood it. He said, "I'm sorry we'll have all that to wade through first. But it's only a little time . . ."

She said suddenly, unexpectedly, "That is what Alice wants. Time!" Her voice was strained and harsh. She heard its tone with dismay and could not change it.

There was a puzzled, troubled look in his eyes. He said, however, directly and honestly, "It *is* better that way, Myra. I don't want a day of separation from you, but—Sam was right about that. I couldn't help seeing it while he talked."

Reason suddenly no longer counted; decisions made by reason had no validity. She cried, "No, no, Richard! I am afraid. . . ." and clung to him, as if he could stand strongly against any storm that threatened.

"There's nothing to be afraid of." He held her and kissed her and touched her head gently as one would soothe a child. "I love you," he said. "Look at me, Myra. It's really going to be all right." He held her so he could look into her eyes and said quietly, "I've got to be just and fair to Alice. I can't insist on an immediate divorce."

"No, I wouldn't want that."

"She loves this place. She has no other home."

"Yes. Yes . . ." She moved out of his arms. She walked blindly toward the narrow, fateful windows above the book-shelves and stopped, looking at the rows of books without seeing them. She felt him watching her, waiting for her to say something natural and reassuring, in her own voice, not this dry, harsh voice of a stranger.

Tim had said she was licked; he was right. Alice was right. Richard and Sam and all of them were right. The end of her story and Richard's had happened actually when Alice came home. It was inevitable. She wished for the courage to face it, then, and to say what some time she would have to say. Before Richard himself wished her to say it.

And Richard said, "I love you, Myra. Nothing can ever change that."

She turned quickly to face him, wishing to grasp reassurance at any price. The telephone rang. He waited a moment, listened, said, "I suppose I'll have to answer," and went out into the hall.

She watched him go. Some time he would go, like that, and never come back. Was this the way a farewell happened? So it wasn't at the moment a farewell—not that anybody knew about, not that anybody recognized. But years later, you knew it for what it was: the dividing line between what had gone before and what was to come after. The moment when love crossed the peak of its existence and started down the other side.

For a long time Richard would not see that its course had changed. She looked slowly around the room, fixing it in her mind: the red curtains; the lamps; the scent of lilies; and the concealed, the brief and almost casual moment which might have been farewell.

Richard came back. There was an odd expression of incredulity on his face. "That was Webb!"

"About the gun?"

"No." He gave a short, dry laugh. "He wanted to apologize! For having accused Alice. Seems inadequate, somehow. He says he's very sorry that he caused Alice or me trouble, but that he acted sincerely and that now he knows he was wrong. He went to the police station; he saw Mildred's letter and the stuff in her evening bag and there was something or other that belonged to Jack and Webb recognized it. Some piece of jewelry some aunt of theirs had given Jack. So he wants to make a full apology to Alice and me. He says there is no doubt that Mildred shot him. Says he'll tell the newspapers, everybody. He'll testify at the inquest. He says he can't do anything to undo the damage he did but he'll make every possible reparation."

"He accused Alice," Myra said slowly. "Now he's accusing Mildred."

"But Mildred confessed," said Richard. He caught her hand and added, "Darling, believe me, it's over! As soon as the district attorney gets here . . ."

The telephone rang again. "Hell," he said, "now what?" And ran to the telephone.

This time she followed. And it was the police.

"They want me to come to the station," said Richard, putting down the telephone. "I don't know why." He looked puzzled and obviously tried to hide it. "Nothing at all, probably. Some formality."

She went with him to the door. "While I'm there," he said, "I'll tell them about the gun. I'll try to keep them from bothering you." He kissed her gently. "It's really all over, Myra —a few formalities, a few talks with the police. And that's all." He opened the door.

The rain had stopped, leaving a cool fresh dampness in the air. It was still cloudy and dark, although a faintly brighter rim along the horizon suggested a late and laggard dawn. It was a cold hour. The shapes of shrubbery and trees loomed black beyond the area of light from above the steps. His car still stood out in the driveway where Mildred's car had stood earlier in the night.

He ran down the steps and toward the waiting car. The door banged and he turned on the lights. She had an odd sensation of repeated experience when the car backed out and turned as Mildred's had done, its lights glancing upon the glossy banks of the laurels. Then it vanished.

She closed the door and the house seemed emptier, colder, very silent. What would he tell them about the gun? Probably the simple truth—that she had found it and had been afraid to tell of it for fear it might be construed as evidence against Richard himself.

Another fool woman, they would say, cluttering up a clean-cut case. Another fool woman. She walked slowly back along the hall, scarcely aware of her own footsteps, to the door into the room where Mildred died, the stairway stretching up into dusk, the newel post.

When she reached the newel post she saw that Alice had come down again. She was in the library, sitting in the ruby-red chair with her hands clasped again around the arms, her fair head up. The woman in possession. Every line of her figure, and her attitude, her lifted, beautiful face, proclaimed it. "Come in, Myra," she said, "I was waiting for you."

Myra stopped beside Richard's lounge chair. "I didn't know you were here."

"You were at the door with Richard. I'd better tell you that I overheard your talk with Richard. Here, I mean, before the phone rang. I was on the stairway and I listened. I couldn't help it," she said quietly. "You came out into the

hall to answer the telephone and neither of you saw me. I
went back upstairs. I felt like a spying child, in my own
house. My own house," repeated Alice sadly and thoughtfully. And said then, taking a long breath, directly, "You
threatened me, Myra. What exactly did you mean?"

"*Threatened?*"

In spite of Alice's apparent composure she was nervous.
She picked up the cigarette lighter from the table beside her.
She toyed with it, watching Myra, her exquisite hands sliding
the lighter back and forth as if it were a piece of jewelry. As
her hands had toyed with her glittering heaps of jewelry.
But the picture of Alice and her jewelry only flickered across
Myra's mind. Actually she was in a kind of queer, blank sus-
pension of all conscious thought. Threatened?

Alice's brown eyes were soft and fixed; she snapped the
lighter open with a little sharp click.

A click. Something flickered again like a spark in Myra's
memory.

Alice could not bear the silence. She leaned forward, click-
ing the lighter nervously so it made a sharp punctuation to
her words. "You refused to make any promises; you defied
me; you said that you had talked to Mildred alone, about me.
You said that we—you and I—understood each other and
there was no need for us to talk further. You said . . ."

Myra, her lips feeling stiff and numb, whispered, "Threatened . . ."

Alice heard it. "Yes, you threatened me. You as good as
said that I killed Mildred! That you would trade your silence
for a divorce, for Richard and my house. But what you really
hope to do is send me back to prison—for killing Jack, for
killing Mildred—either charge would satisfy you. . . ."

Myra's hands went out to hold to the back of the chair.

"You did kill Mildred," she said.

CHAPTER 20 ■

Something very strange was happening in the room. An invisible change came over it which yet was almost visible, so everything in it seemed to waver and shake and then resume its place; yet nothing quite fit, everything was a little distorted, a little awry.

It was like a jig-saw puzzle that had been shaken apart and almost, but not quite, put back so the pieces do not quite fit. Or as if a swift tremor of some rock fault, thousands of miles below, had communicated itself upward, briefly, jarring, rattling, passing on, but leaving everything a little wrong and off center.

Yet nothing was changed actually except Alice's face, and Myra was only distantly aware of that change, for a deep instinctive force had taken full possession of her, excluding everything else. It made her speak, holding to the chair, very clearly, "I was near the door. I heard everything you and Mildred said to each other. I know you killed her and I know why." Her own voice seemed to throb and stop in a throbbing silence.

It was then that she perceived that a stranger sat in the ruby-red chair. Another person had come to dwell in Alice's body. The room had not changed. The little French clock, the books, the red curtains, the fire, none of that had changed. It was only Alice who had undergone that strong distortion.

And in the change her beauty had been swept away as if it had been a veil.

The white stoniness was there, but it was now alive, actuated by a fixed and terrible purpose. It sharpened her features, it flattened her head so it lifted now like a snake's head, preparing to strike. Her mouth, drained of blood so the rose

lipstick stood out, had a different, an appalling look of evil
and merciless knowledge. The obsessed and terrible woman
who now inhabited Alice's body could do anything. She had
no restraints, no inhibitions, no bonds of right or wrong.
Myra said, whispering, "You killed her. You killed Jack. You
murdered both of them."

Alice leaned forward very slowly. She put down the
lighter and stood up with an almost lethargic deliberation.
She gathered the soft, pink-satin folds of her dressing gown
around her. Myra wished to draw back, to escape, and she
would not move. She clung to Richard's chair and faced
Alice.

Alice said, "So I was right. You sneaked around and spied
and tried to blackmail me."

Her voice was different, too—curiously vulgar and coarse
in its tone, careless, too, of every possible restraint.

It was repelling. Myra's hands dug into the chair. She must
stay there, she must fight. She must not yield to an almost
overwhelming wave of physical repulsion.

But Alice was thinking. She said, "Tell me, Myra, what
did you hear?"

And she had heard nothing—a click, a laugh, fumbling motions, nothing else.

She had to answer. Alice's wide blank eyes had still somewhere in them a shrewd and seeking gleam.

But Myra knew what had happened. She knew it as clearly
as if she had seen it, as if she had overheard everything. It
was like a picture flashed upon her memory, complete in
almost every detail.

Myra braced herself against the chair and flung out those
facts which must be, *had to* be, facts.

"Mildred knew that you murdered Jack. She knew it when
she saw that locket. Jack had given it to you. She—she took
it. It was in her evening bag. Webb recognized it. You got her
to write the confession. You said—you said that you would
sign it. You had the gun. . . ."

She was winning. In the fraction of a heart-beat she was
winning. The spark left Alice's eyes; there was only blankness there. Myra held to the chair and leaned over it and
cried, ". . . You had the gun. And when she reached the
place in the confession where it could not be thought to refer
to Mildred, where it must mean you and only you, you
pointed the gun at her and tried to shoot her and—and make

it look like a suicide. But the gun clicked—it was empty—so
the poison was there and you . . ."

The picture clarified still further. It was as if a spotlight
had been turned upon it so brilliant that it was bewildering.
"You snatched the poison. You held it in her mouth. It had
only to touch the inside of her mouth for a few seconds. And
you said you were trying to stop her—when you saw
me. . . ."

She stopped because Alice was going to say something. A
kind of ripple went over that fixed and terrible regard. Then
Alice said slowly, "That damned locket."

An old-fashioned locket—black enamel and pearls. Nothing that Alice, streamlined and modern, would buy for herself but something an old woman might hand on to her
nephew. Something Webb would recognize.

Alice looked at Myra for a moment with blank wide eyes;
she moved slowly, lethargically toward the table, toward
the bookshelves. Her body had lost its grace. She looked
thicker somehow, lumpish. She looked over her shoulder at
Myra and moved aimlessly in another direction. She tossed
slurred, half-articulate words over her shoulder. "She'd never
have guessed I shot him if she hadn't seen the locket. He'd
told her about it; he'd boasted. He told her he had given it
to a woman he was trying to get rid of. In order to marry
her—Mildred! He had no intention of marrying her! But he
dared to tell me that. He stood there, on the rug. Laughing,
but angry too. All he wanted then was to end the scene. Oh,
I was making a scene—yes! He hated it. He liked his women
to give up gracefully, heartbrokenly. Not me! He met his
match in me," she said and gave a low chuckle.

She wandered in that fumbling, graceless way across the
room and back again. All her motions seemed slurred as did
her words. She said, "So I shot him. He saw the gun and
laughed. He didn't think I'd do it. He was so sure."

There was an indescribable tone of gluttony and satisfaction in it. She folded her arms across her body. "Said he preferred Mildred. He said that to me. With my beauty!"

As if the word beauty still had a power, as if it were a wire
tightening her consciousness, stirring it to the effort of
thought, she straightened. She looked directly at Myra. Her
arms dropped. Her lumpish, slurred lethargy disappeared.
She said more clearly, "Mildred laughed too, when the gun
clicked. The poison was on the table. She had bought it in

order to give it to me, if I got the death sentence. I asked her to get it for me. That's funny! She never believed that I had shot him—until she saw the locket and then she accused me. She cried. She hurried away. But I didn't think she'd really do anything about it. She hated publicity of any kind. She'd kept her little affair with Jack a secret—I suppose until she could announce an engagement. I didn't think she'd ever do a thing about it. But then she came back and made me come down to see her. I took the gun. It was here, in my sleeve—you wouldn't believe how hard it was to hold it there without her seeing it. But what a gullible fool she always was! She said I had to write the confession and then she'd let me take poison because it was more merciful; that was why she was crying. So I pretended to agree. I said I would atone." She stopped suddenly, with a kind of sullen suspicion, eyeing Myra.

For an instant Myra was afraid that her face, her eyes, some intangible thing in the air between them admitted that she had not heard the terrible talk between the two women.

And Alice said jerkily, "I'm very intelligent, you know. Everybody has always said so. I think very quickly. She wrote the confession. I slumped down in a chair and watched her, behind my hand. I said to write this and write that—but I couldn't keep it up long. I got the gun out, I intended to put her fingerprints on it. She laughed. The pill was on the table. I shoved it down her throat and held on. She struggled, we both fell against the door."

She paused and looked at Myra and said suddenly in a suffocated way, "You were there. But I knew that you would bargain, too. So I gave you your price, quickly. I told you I'd give Richard a divorce. Well, I'm not going to. And I'm not going to be sent back to prison for Jack's murder, or for Mildred's."

The momentary look of the Alice Myra had known, the momentary grace and clearness of speech were gone again, suffused and blurred. But one clear thing looked out of the stranger's eyes and that was murder.

That was the way she looked when she shot Jack.

That was the way she looked when she murdered Mildred.

"Alice," said Myra with a queer numbed gravity, "You need not have murdered Mildred."

"Mildred knew I killed him. She accused me; she saw the

locket and she said this time I'd get the death sentence . . ."

"You don't understand. It is the law. You have been tried once and pardoned. You cannot be tried ever again for Jack's murder. . . ."

There was a long silence. Then Alice whispered, "*That is the law?*"

"Yes."

Comprehension came into her blank eyes. "*You knew it?*"

"Yes."

"Who told you?"

"The Governor."

"*Not even Mildred, not anything, could have made them try me again for killing him?*"

"Nothing could have done that. No matter what Mildred said or believed or told. Nothing. You did not need to kill Mildred. You were safe until you killed her."

"Safe," said Alice consideringly. "Safe. I'm still safe!"

She was only a few feet from the door into the hall. She whirled around and charged across to the stairway like a clumsy, low-running, but very swift animal. She had the top off the newel post before Myra reached the doorway.

"It's gone. . . ." said Myra.

And Alice lifted the gun.

Standing on the steps she looked down at Myra.

That is the way she looked when she killed Jack, thought Myra. That is the way she looked when she killed Mildred.

And that is the way she'll look when she kills me.

"You'd better go back in the library," said Alice. "Out on the terrace would be better, really, away from the house."

Again a physical repulsion touched Myra. She moved backward, away from Alice, because of that really, rather than because of the gun in Alice's hand. She reached Richard's chair again, and it was again like a bulwark. The table light shone on the gun.

As it had on the shell she had removed from it!

She caught her breath and cried, "That gun is not loaded."

"Oh, yes," said Alice. "It's loaded. I loaded it."

"I don't believe you! You tried to shoot Mildred and . . ."

"You are as gullible as she was," said Alice. "All right. If you want to know: I sent you for brandy, Richard was in the coat room—the gun was in that room in there—behind the door where it fell. I took it and ran across and put it in the newel post. I had to hurry. I had to take the chance, but if Richard saw me I intended to say Mildred had brought it. The trouble was that my own fingerprints were on it, none of Mildred's. But I had to take the chance and I did."

"It was not loaded. . . ."

". . . and then I came down, after Richard had said he was determined to divorce me. Remember?" Her mouth twitched but she did not laugh. She came a step nearer. The gun looked enormous in her small hand. "I took the gun out of the post. I took it upstairs. The box of shells was in Richard's room. I loaded it. I brought it down and put it back in the post, while you were there at the door with Richard. But it doesn't matter . . ." She started toward Myra again. All the slurred effect of her motion and speech had gone. She was sharply, precisely articulate.

Talk, thought Myra, *talk!* Maybe Richard will come back. Maybe somebody will come downstairs. Maybe . . .

She said, "You'd be a fool to shoot me, Alice. Everybody will hear you. Everybody will know . . ."

"I intend to put your fingerprints on it. You have cause for suicide. You're in love with Richard and now I've come back. Oh, it's a chance," she said. "But otherwise I have no chance at all. You'll tell them . . ."

"You'd have been safe if you hadn't killed Mildred. Nobody can try you for killing Jack. All that you told me, all that I know, can't make them try you again . . ."

Alice's quiet, precise advance stopped. She looked at Myra. She looked at the gun.

And the creature of fury that possessed her, the blind and lethal obsession of rage, disappeared, vanished, dropped back like a primeval beast into its native slime.

Alice herself looked up brightly. Her beauty was back, her loveliness, her grace—if memory had not stamped another visage there.

She said in her normal, high and musical voice, "Why, I'm still safe!" She laughed. She turned the gun and looked at it. "I'm still safe! Nobody can touch me. You least of all."

She gave a kind of shrug. She straightened up again, slim and graceful. She touched her hair, put the gun down beside her on the table and adjusted the belt of her dressing gown.

"Mildred," she said, "is a suicide. There's absolute proof of it—the letter, the poison, your own first and original corroboration of what I told them. You can tell them anything you want to, now, but they'll never believe it. You see, I had no motive for killing Mildred."

"You had a motive. You didn't know that you could not be tried again for Jack's murder. . . ."

"So you say," said Alice lightly and pleasantly. "But look at the thing reasonably, Myra. Who will believe you? They will only say that you want Richard, that you are trying to discredit me, that you are accusing me as Webb once accused me. . . . Why, Myra, you haven't got a thing against me that anybody in the world will believe!"

She smoothed her golden hair and pulled up her lovely slender body so its graceful lines were firm and triumphant.

Myra said slowly, "Alice, if you think for a second that I'll not tell them the truth . . ."

"You can't do a thing to me. If you accuse me, you will only turn Richard against you. Richard, Sam, Tim—everybody. Not one of them will believe you."

"Do you really think I'll let you go? You . . . Why, you're like a snake! You're horrible. You've killed two people . . . !"

"Go ahead. Accuse me. You'll only lose Richard! And you'll lose him anyway. I'll see to that. Look at me . . ." said Alice and preened.

Myra said, "I've got to tell him. How would I dare not to tell him? It would be like letting a tiger loose to prey . . ."

"Tell him, if you like. I'm safe." She glanced at the gun and said, "I'm not going to hurt you, Myra. Because you can't hurt me."

As if to prove the truth of her words she walked across the room, still preening, still conscious of her body and its beauty. Myra thought, I'll take the gun. I'll tell her she must confess.

But Alice was watchful of the gun, too, surreptitiously, pretending not to be aware of it. Myra could not have reached it before Alice.

Alice said airily, "Why don't you threaten me with the gun, Myra? Haven't you got the courage? You'd shoot a snake, couldn't you? You'd shoot a tiger—that's what you called me! They'd say you shot me from jealousy. You'd be tried for murder."

"No, I'm not going to do that," said Myra, "but there's law, there's . . ." She stopped as she remembered someone who was there, someone who knew the law, someone who was

Richard's friend. "I'm going to call Sam. He'll know what to do."

For an instant a small spark of anxiety came into Alice's eyes, then it cleared. "I'm safe. Nobody can do anything to me. Call him. Tell him!"

"Yes," said Myra, "I'm going to."

She moved from the chair which had been like a brace and a shield and walked across the room. Alice moved nearer to the table. She watched half incredulously. But she did not touch the gun.

Myra turned; the slight motionless figure in pink did not seem to move. Another step and another and there was still no sound of motion from the library. And suddenly she reached the hall above. She followed it around the turn; she stopped at Sam's door. But there a protecting sese of unreality left her; her voice was like a sob, her hands flung the door wide.

Sam was awake. The light in the hall outlined her. He cried softly, "Myra! What is it? Has the district attorney come?"

"Sam, come downstairs. Hurry . . ."

"What . . . ?"

"Alice killed Mildred. She killed Jack."

"*What are you saying?*"

"It is the truth, Sam. She told me."

He was out of bed, a dim, thin figure in pajamas. He caught her wrist. "Where is she? Where is Alice?"

"In the library. Sam, she killed them both. She'll hurt Richard. She's different, she's terrible . . . Sam, help me . . ." Her voice was shaking; she was incoherent. Sam released her wrist. He snatched up a coat and flung it around him. He took her by the arm and they were in the hall. They were hurrying, running. Her breath stung her throat.

He went down the stairs first. He ran into the library and then brought up short.

Alice was sitting again in the ruby-red chair. She was composed and quiet.

There was no faint resemblance to the woman Myra had seen in her. She looked up quietly at Sam.

He leaned suddenly against the table. He wiped his forehead with the back of his hand. He gave a shaky laugh. "Thank God, you're all right, Alice," he said. "I didn't know what had happened!"

Alice said, "I'm so glad you are here, Sam. Myra is hysterical. She's saying terrible things. I'm sorry for her. For her own sake, Sam, please try to quiet her."

Sam wiped his forehead again. "I'm sorry for Myra too," he said. "But I'm not going to let her hurt you."

CHAPTER 21 ■

And there was not one scrap of proof.

Not one written word, not one shred of evidence. No one besides herself had heard Alice's words and Alice would not have uttered those words if she had not already believed that Myra knew the truth; if Alice had not thought at once, when she discovered Myra so near in the very moment when Mildred died. Danger! Danger from Myra; Myra has heard; Myra knows the truth! And if, with swift and ugly shrewdness, Alice had not put herself in Myra's place and reasoned what she would have done with a weapon so conveniently placed in her hands.

She had offered instantly the price she would have exacted had she been Myra. She had broken into Myra's own brief story of the few things she had really heard and seen, to offer that price, to say quickly, instantly, almost in so many words, I'll give you a divorce—only keep quiet. Don't tell. It's easier that way, quicker that way, less likely to turn Richard against you than to accuse his wife of two murders. Much less trouble all the way around! It seemed incredible to Myra now that she had not recognized that offer. Instead, she had only thought, bewildered, how out of place and wrong such a talk was at that moment.

And then later, when the police had gone, with an almost equally outré insistence upon discussion of a divorce, Alice had flatly and finally retracted her offer because she felt safe. Because she began to believe that Myra, really, knew nothing.

And then the account of the brief little meeting Myra had had with Mildred (Mildred who was heartbroken by the discovery of Alice's imperfection, distraught at the realization that the woman she loved best in the world had killed the man she loved), the brief account of that meeting had frightened Alice again, had shaken her out of her assuredness. "You didn't tell me," she'd said, and Myra, unaware of the significance that Alice might read into her words, distracted by Richard's return and the sound of his entrance, had answered, "I've not told anyone."

So, later: "You threatened me," said Alice.

It was a clearly marked path. So clear that Sam must recognize it, must see the truth as truth. She would tell him. She would show him. She would need no other proof, thought Myra swiftly.

He had wrapped his coat around him and was sitting on the arm of a chair, lighting a cigarette, his face still angry and intent.

But Alice had observed the growing confidence in Myra's face. It was as if she had followed Myra's thought and waited for the exact instant of attack. She took a quick breath and said, "Sam, Myra says that I killed Jack. She says that she's going to tell everyone that she listened to everything Mildred said to me. She's going to say that I made Mildred write that letter and then I made her take the poison." She lifted her shoulders in a kind of helpless shrug and said, "I know how it sounds. Nobody could have made Mildred do that. But— I've suffered so from the terrible accusation that Webb made . . ."

"That's what made Myra think of it," said Sam and turned toward Myra. "Listen, Myra. You're only hurting yourself . . ."

"It is the truth," cried Myra. "Alice admitted it. She told everything . . ."

"You're having a brainstorm! If you'll just forget this and . . ."

"You've got to believe me. She's dangerous. She has murdered two people . . ."

"Myra!" He got up and came toward her. "Stop that!"

"Alice was in love with Jack. He was going to leave her. She dictated Mildred's confession. Mildred brought the poison for Alice to take and Alice put it in her mouth. . . ."

"Mildred took the poison herself," said Alice.

Sam cried, "This is fantastic! Alice couldn't have made Mildred take poison. . . ."

"Mildred knew Alice had killed Jack. Oh, you *must* listen, Sam! She told Alice she had to atone, she had to take poison, or go to trial. Alice believed her. She didn't know that she couldn't be tried! She promised to sign a confession if Mildred would write it."

Sam seized her hands and she wrenched them away from him. And knew with a kind of sickening quake that of the two, it was she who seemed hysterical and irresponsible, wild and erratic in her look and her words, and that Alice was composed and quiet and utterly convincing in that composure.

And safe.

Sam said sternly, "You've got to stop that, Myra."

"But she admitted it. She told me everything. . . ."

"Myra, be reasonable." Alice's high lovely voice was sad but unperturbed. "If I had done such terrible things would I have told you? Would I have told anybody? Myra, try to pull yourself together. Everybody loses some time. I know it sounds trite, I know that just now you think you'll never forget Richard, but try to be a good loser. Try to be game. Sam and I won't tell Richard any of this. Let him remember you as he knew you. Not . . ."

"I haven't lost," said Myra, suddenly cool. For there was the gun on the table, gleaming in the light.

Sam had not yet seen it. It lay behind the lilies Mildred had brought. Myra avoided Sam, who would have stopped her as if she intended to do Alice some physical injury, and went to the table. "There's the gun. Alice hid it in the newel post. She hid it the night she shot Jack."

Sam had come to her side. He stared at the gun, his face a white, sharp mask of concentration. "It is the gun! At least it looks like it!" he cried.

A flicker of something like credulity touched his face. Myra said swiftly, "She put it in the newel post. The top is loose. She—she must have hidden it, held it so Webb did not see it. Yes, yes, that's what you did." She turned to Alice. "You had on a long, full white skirt. You knew the top was loose; you held the gun so Webb could not see it. You ran into the hall when he told you to phone for the police. He went to the curtains at the other end of the room. He could not see you. You lifted the top of the post, dropped the gun there then ran to the phone. And nobody ever knew until . . ."

Alice said, "Myra, where did you get the gun? Did Mildred leave it in that room? Did you take it and hide it, so as to accuse me? Even then—in the very moment when a woman was dying—did you think of that?" The faint, half-dawning credulity in Sam's face flickered out. He picked up the gun.

"It's loaded," said Myra quickly. "Alice loaded it . . ." She looked at Alice and saw by the unperturbed and calm look in her brown eyes that it was not loaded. What had she done with the shells? Thrown them out, across the terrace, into the rain and darkness while Myra went to summon Sam?

Sam said, "Where did this gun come from, Myra?"

"It was in the post. I found it. I . . ."

Alice said, "First you accuse me, now you say that you found it. Oh, Myra, Myra—you've lost! But lose with dignity, my dear. Lose with courage. Don't make it impossible for us ever to want to see you again. Don't destroy the friendship and the memory Richard and—and I too, would want to hold for you. Sam, make her go to bed. Give her a sedative. Keep this from Richard. . . ."

Myra turned desperately to Sam. "You must listen. Even if you think I'm hysterical and wild, listen to me. Listen to the whole story. . . ."

"You've lost your head," said Sam. "I'll take care of this gun and . . ."

"Her fingerprints are on it. They must be on it," cried Myra suddenly.

He held the gun in his hand, nevertheless. He said, "You must not talk like this, Myra. It is a criminal act. You are making a completely baseless and very terrible accusation."

"But it is true . . ."

He turned to Alice. "I'm sorry you've had this to go through, Alice. But don't let it worry you. Nobody for a moment will believe Myra. The facts of Manders' murder are now too well established. She'll see that when she's had time to think . . ."

Richard opened the front door and came quickly and happily along the hall. He was whistling, and the gay, clear sound seemed to belong to another world. With a surge of returning confidence, Myra started toward him. And this time Sam caught her wrist and held it as if his own hand were made of steel. He cried: "You're a fool if you try this with Dick. For God's sake, Myra, *think!* For your own pride, don't let him see you like this."

Richard came to the door. "Has the district attorney got here?" he asked.

"No . . ." said Sam and tightened his hold on Myra. Richard, too full of his own news to sense immediately anything strange in their attitudes, anything wrong in the room, went on hurriedly, "Everything's over! The district attorney got to the police station just as I did. He's coming here to take a look but the case is closed. All they wanted me for was to ask me about the gun." He looked at Myra and explained, "Webb did know something of it. You were right. He found the shell that you buried. Willie apparently followed you and dug it up and Webb happened upon it in the path. He said his foot struck it and he looked at it and knew it had no business there, and that somebody had very recently buried it. So he leaped to the right conclusion that somebody *had* had that gun and . . ." He glanced around and said, "Golly, it's cold in here. Why don't you build up the fire?"

He went to the fireplace and stooped over to take the tongs.

Alice said softly, "The gun is here. Myra had it . . ."

Sam said, holding her, "Myra, for your own sake . . ."

Richard had heard neither of them. Richard had not reached for the tongs. Richard, in fact, was suddenly and curiously immobile, as if frozen, staring downward.

All of them perhaps were aware of that sudden fixed stillness.

And then he straightened.

He turned around and faced them.

His face was as changed as if a different man stood before them, an older man, at once saddened and fearful. He looked swiftly around the room. There was a terrible apprehension in his eyes. He looked at Alice and said, "*What have you done now?*"

He came to her and cried in white, grim anger and fear, "*What have you done? Tell me.*"

She moved back in the chair as if it were a lair. Her eyes were blank and sullen.

"I haven't done anything."

"Don't lie! When did you smash the cupid? Before"—
he stopped and seemed to brace himself against the impact
of his own words and said—"before Mildred's death? Or
after . . . ?"

"No, no! Afterward—I didn't hurt her—I didn't touch
her. . . ."

"Alice, tell me the truth. I *know* you when you are like
this. . . ."

She moved her head slowly, sluggishly, from side to side.
He turned to Sam. His face was drawn and white with the
fear he had not spoken until then. His eyes had still that look
of horror, of grim and terrible apprehension. "Has she hurt
anybody, Sam? She'll do anything when she's like this. She's
like a woman possessed. But I thought she'd learned to control it. I thought . . . Did she kill Mildred? Tell me the
truth."

Sam did not reply. His hand on Myra's wrist relaxed. It
became completely slack and nerveless and dropped away.
Myra looked at him, and he was looking at Alice with utter,
stunned revulsion in his face.

She saw that and knew.

She knew what she would see when she looked at Alice.
She knew that Alice was powerless then to check or conceal
her own devouring fury.

Richard saw it too. He said, "For God's sake, Alice . . ."

Myra looked at Alice then and that other creature had
come into possession again.

There was a strange, deep pause as if the room held its
breath.

And Sam said in a numb and icy voice, "I always wondered
about that. The five slugs. Five slugs into him where one
would have been enough. I wondered who could have been
capable of such rage, such a passion of vindictive fury." He
paused and said as gravely as a judge pronouncing a death
sentence, "You killed Manders. You shot him. You looked
like that when you did it."

There was complete conviction in his voice. There was
the full power and recognition of truth.

Alice got up clumsily, humped and sluggish. She cried in
that slurred and coarsened voice, "I'm glad I killed him!"
She whirled upon Richard, "You did this to me! You made

them see the truth! I'll kill you, too!" she cried in blind and obsessed anger and flung herself upon him. He caught her. Sam ran toward them and she twisted out of Richard's grasp and clawed at Sam.

"Hold her hands," cried Richard. "Catch her hands . . ."

Someone had entered the hall, had come along it toward the library, had stopped in the doorway. Myra was distinctly aware of it, but she could not look, could not take her sickened gaze from that terrible searing instant of struggle.

It suddenly stopped. Alice, panting, stood quite still in Sam's grasp.

She drew herself up. She lifted a piteous, beautiful face toward Sam. She said in her own high and musical voice, "Sam, you are my friend."

Sam's hand dropped. He stepped back, staring at her. Richard said warningly, "Look out . . ."

And Alice, with heartbreak in her beautiful face and in her voice said, "They are both against me, Sam. My husband and Myra—they want to get rid of me. They've planned and plotted . . . Oh, Sam . . ." Richard caught her arms and with a sudden twist she escaped Richard's hold and ran to Sam and put her arms up toward him. "Sam, you've always loved me. Haven't you, Sam? I've seen it in your face, in yours eyes. I need you now. I need you."

Her arms went up around his neck and he pulled them down and held her rigidly away from him. Slowly, with sad and desolate conviction in his voice, he said, "I don't love you. Nobody could love you. Not as you really are . . ."

The figure in the doorway was utterly still. Myra realized in some remote awareness that it had stood immobile for some time, listening. Alice cried piteously, "Don't desert me, Sam, don't . . ."

Her blank brown eyes sought his and found, perhaps, adamant judgment. She looked around and saw the gun where Sam had left it on the table. Her eyes fastened for an instant upon it.

Her hair had become disheveled. She put up her hand to smooth back the golden flying strands. Her pink, lacy dressing gown was in disorder. She pulled it about her, adjusted the belt. She was beautiful in that instant. Sam started forward. Richard cried, *"Alice, don't!"*

Alice said in that sad and broken voice, "If Richard does

not love me, if you, Sam, have no faith in me, I cannot live
—there's nothing left in life for me. . . ."

She pointed the gun at her heart, and Myra thought
swiftly, she's too cool, too sure. She knows exactly what she's
doing. There's some motive.

Then she knew it for what it was, an appeal for Sam's sympathy, a frantic and clumsy pretense with an empty gun,
designed to frighten Sam and Richard.

Sam swayed forward and stopped. The figure in the doorway dashed into the room and a strange voice shouted, "For
God's sake, take it away from her . . . !" And Alice pulled
the trigger.

But the gun was not empty. A crash of sound broke over
them like a wave. It filled the air with chaos, with a choking
smell of powder.

For a second Alice did not move. A look of dazed bewil-
derment, of disbelief, was on her face. Then she lowered her
hand very slowly. She said, "But I unloaded it—I took out
the shells—I put them in the red chair. . . ."

Still with that stunned, sleepwalking look she turned. She
dropped the gun which fell, hard and heavy, upon the floor.
She moved past the man, the strange man, the newcomer in
overcoat and hat who had stood there watching. She went
into the hall very slowly, tentatively, somehow, one step
after the other. She reached the room where Mildred died
and where her own portrait hung.

Richard and Sam ran after her. The tall man, the stranger,
said, "But she killed Manders. She must have killed that
woman tonight. She murdered them both. . . ."

He too, ran, into the hall.

Something of the spell of horror held Myra. She could not
breathe; the air choked her. She went to the French door.
She opened it with awkward, fumbling hands. The fresh
cold air of dawn swept into the room and carried away the
smell of smoke fumes. Myra leaned against the casing of the
door and let the chill, clean air touch her face.

After a long time Richard came back into the room. He
stood in silence for a moment, an older Richard, white and
drawn. Then he went to the ruby-red chair and lifted the
cushion. She watched him draw out the shells that lay there.

"Three," he said, counting, "four, five." His hand sought
all around the chair again. He replaced the cushion. "Only

five . . . She didn't mean to kill herself. She used to threaten it; she never meant it. I thought tonight it was only another pretense. I thought the gun was empty. So did she. But she left one shell."

Sam came to the door. "The district attorney heard almost the whole thing, Dick. He'll do everything that's necessary. And I—so will I . . ."

He came to Richard and put his hand for a moment on his shoulder. Silently, Richard showed him the shells. Sam said, "Five—she thought the gun wasn't loaded. She thought she'd got them all out."

The strange man came into the doorway again. He had taken off his hat. He said heavily, "Putnam, I'll have to have some statements—the whole story."

"All right," said Sam. "We'll tell you everything. But can you give us a few minutes?"

The district attorney's eyes were understanding. "Certainly, certainly . . . I heard her confess, you know. I'd have had to get a death sentence. Believe me, it is better this way. Better for her . . ."

"Yes," said Sam. "Yes . . ."

The district attorney went back into the hall. Someone was running down the stairs. Tim swung around the newel post and ran across the hall. "I head *a shot*! what . . . ?" His voice stopped.

Sam said, "I'll tell him. . . ."

Richard said, "I was afraid she'd killed him. I was afraid she had killed Mildred. But I went to see the doctor. I asked him if it could be murder. He convinced me—against my instinct."

"Perhaps you wanted to believe she didn't do it. God knows, I didn't want to believe. . . ." Sam took the shells from Richard's hand and went slowly away, solemnly, his head bent, thinking perhaps of the sentence he, himself, had pronounced.

Low voices in the ivory-and-gold room seemed very remote, far away, in another world.

Richard stood for a moment quite still, then he came slowly toward Myra and stopped beside her in the doorway, looking out across the terrace.

The rain had gone, the sky was lightening, a lemon-colored rim upon the horizon promised coming dawn. The Sound was like a silver ribbon, very still, very tranquil below them, but a morning breeze drifted gently upward across rain-wet lawns. It, too, was clean, washed and fresh. It, too, held a promise.

They stood without speaking, while the day began.